GUNNER

SATAN'S FURY MC- MEMPHIS

L. WILDER

Gunner
Satan's Fury MC Memphis
Copyright 2019
L. Wilder All rights reserved.

L. Wilder

Cover Design: Mayhem Cover Creations
www.facebook.com/MayhemCoverCreations

Editor: Lisa Cullinan

Proofreader- Rose Holub @ReadbyRose

Teasers & Banners: Gel Ytayz at Tempting Illustrations

Personal Assistant: Natalie Weston PA

Catch up with the entire Satan's Fury MC Series today!
All books are FREE with Kindle Unlimited!

My Temptation (The Happy Endings Collection #1)

Bring the Heat (The Happy Endings Collection #2)

His Promise (The Happy Endings Collection #3)

❀ Created with Vellum

HER GOODBYE

August 19, 1994

Gus,

I've been lying here watching you sleep for hours, just thinking about the time we've shared together. This summer has been the best few months of my life. I can honestly say I've never been happier, and that's all because of you. I love you, Gus. I love you with every fiber of my being. You mean so much to me, more than I thought possible. With you, I've learned how it feels to truly love and to be loved. That's why this letter is so hard to write.

I've done a lot of thinking over the past few weeks, and I've come to realize that it doesn't matter how much I love you or you love me. It just isn't enough. We're from two different worlds, headed down two completely different paths, and if we stay together, we're only going to end up destroying one another. I can't bear for that to happen. I love you too much. It breaks my heart to say this to you, but I'm leaving Memphis. I am asking you to please respect my decision. Don't try to find me.

Don't call me. Let me find a way to move on, and I will do the same for you. It's the only way either of us will ever make it through this.

This wasn't an easy decision for me. In fact, it's killing me to walk away from you, but deep down I know it's the right thing to do. Please remember—I love you today, I loved you yesterday, and I will love you tomorrow and always. That will never change.

Love,
* Samantha*

PROLOGUE

When I joined the Marines, I didn't have any preconceived notions about being in the military and going to war. I'd seen and heard enough to know it wasn't going to be easy—far from it. It was one of the hardest, but greatest, things I'd ever done. I worked my ass off, fought for my country, and learned just how far I could be pushed without breaking. But it came at a price. Every waking moment I'd wondered if my time was about to run out, if I'd seen my last sunset or had lain my head down on my pack for the very last time. Even if I'd managed to survive long enough to see the sunrise the next morning, there'd been little consolation in knowing I'd just have to go through that same hell all over again.

I thought I'd find peace once I was finally back in the States with my family and friends and able to sleep in my own bed or walk down the street without feeling like I was under a constant threat—but I'd been wrong. I never realized just how wrong until a shotgun wound forced me to go home.

* * *

WHEN I GOT off the plane, I found my mother waiting for me at the gate. As expected, she was alone and still wearing her green Food and More grocery smock. Her tired eyes filled with tears the second she spotted me walking in her direction. "Cade!" she called, rushing towards me with her arms opened wide.

She was just about to reach for me when she suddenly stopped and looked down at my arm. After getting shot in the shoulder, I had to have reconstructive surgery, which meant wearing a sling for the next couple of months. "I'm okay, Mom."

She eased up on her tiptoes and carefully wrapped her arms around my neck, giving me one of her famous mom hugs. Damn. I was a grown man, and her hugs still got to me the same way they did when I was a kid. "I can't tell you how good it is to see you, sweetheart."

"Good to see you too."

"I've been worried sick about you. Your father has too."

"I know." I gave her a quick squeeze, then said, "I'm sorry I worried you."

"I'm just glad you're home where we can take care of you." She gave me a little pat as she stepped back and smiled. "Have to fatten you up a bit."

I was six-four and weighed about two hundred and forty pounds. Before I was shot, I worked out every day and knew what condition I was in. I glanced down at myself and told her, "I'm not exactly skin and bones here, Mom."

"Well, you look like you've lost weight to me ... and you're a little peeked."

"Yeah, well … you'd look a little peeked too if you'd just spent the last sixteen hours on an airplane." Before she could respond, I added, "Let me grab my bag, and then we can get out of here."

As she followed me over to the baggage claim area, she explained, "Your father wanted to come tonight, but you know how he is around crowds. We both figured it would be easier if he just waited at the house for us."

My father was a brilliant man. There wasn't a mathematical problem he couldn't figure out, which made him one of the best accountants in town. But he'd always been a little *different*. He wasn't a fan of crowds or loud noises. He'd fixate on things from historical facts to the changes in weather, obsessing on every detail, and he wasn't exactly big on showing affection—except for when he was with my mother. He'd always been different with her— touching her, holding her hand, and even hugging her. I'd always hoped that some of that would rub off on me, but it never did. "It's fine, Mom. I wasn't expecting him to be here."

"Well, he's really looking forward to seeing you."

Even though I knew that wasn't true, I replied, "I'm looking forward to seeing him too."

"Oh, and Brooklyn is planning to come by the house tomorrow."

As I lifted my duffle-bag off the conveyer belt, I asked, "She been making it okay?"

"You know your sister … she's always on the go." Mom shrugged. "But I guess that's a good thing. It keeps her out of trouble."

We headed outside to the parking garage, and once we got to Mom's car, she popped the trunk and I tossed my bag inside. I slammed it shut and then we both got in the car and started home. We hadn't been driving long when I heard her let out a deep sigh. I glanced over at her, and even in the dark, I could see the dark circles under her eyes. "Have you been working double shifts again?"

"No ... it's just been a long week."

"Why's that?"

"Let's not talk about that right now," she interrupted, then quickly changed the subject. "I've got your room all ready for you and got your rehab appointments all lined up. CJ and Dalton are planning to come by and see you once you get settled."

"That'd be cool."

It had been years since I'd seen my best friends from high school. We'd all gone our separate ways, so I was surprised when she said, "Did you know that CJ and his girlfriend, Adeline, are expecting?"

"Hadn't heard that."

"I don't think it was something they were planning, but ... you know how those things go."

Mom continued to ramble on about all the latest gossip in town until we pulled up in the driveway. As soon as she'd parked, I got out, grabbed my bag, and followed her up to the front door. She motioned for me to go inside as she said, "You get settled, and I'll go start dinner. I'm making pork chops and mashed potatoes."

"Okay, sounds good." When I walked into the living room, I found Dad sitting in his recliner with his TV tray in front of him. He was studying one of his patches through a magnifying glass, something I'd seen him do a thousand times before. It was a hobby that started when he was a kid. In hopes of helping him make friends, his folks had signed him up for the Boy Scouts. While their plan for him to make friends didn't pan out, he did gain an interest in patches. That interest turned into an obsession—an obsession that carried over into his adulthood. He didn't even look up when I walked over to him. "Hey, Pop. How's it going?"

"Good."

I swallowed back the feeling of rejection that was creeping up inside of me and tried once again to get his attention. "You get some new patches?"

"Um-hmm." Without turning to look at me, he held up the long, narrow patch and said, "It's an Unteroffizier-vorschule cuff title."

"I got no idea what that is, Pop."

Like he was reading straight from the encyclopedia, he spouted off, "*Unteroffiziervorschule* is German for NCO Preparatory School. The German military created the school to train lower ranks in leadership and initiative. Their students eventually became commissioned officers."

"Wow, that's really something."

"Also found a set of World War II German rural police collar tabs."

"Oh, really?" There was a time when it bothered me that my father showed me little to no attention, but as I grew older, I realized that it wasn't his fault. My father had Asperger's Syndrome. I had no choice but to accept the fact that he'd never be the kind of father I hoped he would be. "Are those good ones?"

Like a child, he brought it close to his body, protecting it as he answered, "Yes. Very good."

"That's great, Pop." As I started towards my room, I told him, "I'm gonna go get settled in." Without replying, he turned his attention back to his magnifying glass, and just like always, it was like I'd never been in the room.

I went upstairs to my room and lay across the bed. As I stared up at my old Bon Jovi poster, I was surprised by how different it felt to be here. Everything was exactly the way I'd left it, but for some reason, everything in the whole fucking house seemed different. What had once felt like home was now completely foreign to me.

Over the next few days that feeling had only grown stronger. When my buddies from high school had come by to see me, it was like they were complete strangers. After the first few minutes, the conversations became forced and awkward. I couldn't even talk to my mother and sister. It was like I was stuck inside my head and couldn't find the right words to say to anyone. I'd told myself it would pass, that things would get back to normal eventually, but they didn't. With each new day, things only seemed to get be getting worse. Hell, even the shit with my father was fucking with my head. He'd never talked to me or showed that he gave a damn about me, and I'd adapted to that. I'd stopped hoping that things would change, but I could feel the resentment building inside of me, making me feel like I was going to explode at any minute. I just couldn't take it. I needed to get the fuck out of that house and out of my head, or I was going to lose my mind. I grabbed my keys and headed downstairs. Just as I was about to walk out the front door, Mom called out to me, "Cade? Wait! Where are you going?"

"I'm going out."

"Again?" Confusion crossed her face. "Is something wrong?"

"No, Mom. I'm just—"

She gave me one of her looks as she interrupted, "You're just *what*, Cade?"

"I can't do this anymore. It's just too much."

"What are you talking about? What's too much?"

"*Everything.* This house. This town." I let out an aggravated breath as I grumbled, "*Dad.*"

"I know it's not easy coming home after all you've been through, but we love you, sweetheart. We like having you here with us."

"Why do you keep saying *we*?" I huffed. "Dad could care less if I'm alive or dead."

"That's not true, Cade. Your father loves you."

I shook my head as I argued, "Yeah, right. He's never once given me a second thought, and you damn well know it."

"Come with me. I want to show you something." She walked into my dad's office and over to the glass case where he kept his prized patches. As she opened the top latch, she explained, "A few days after you left for training, your father started a new collection."

I glanced down at the case and my chest tightened as soon as I saw it was lined with various Marine Corp patches, from the seal and crest to old veteran patches. "There's so many of them."

"I know, honey. He might not be good at showing it, but you've been on his mind every day."

I could feel the emotion building inside of me as I muttered, "I didn't know."

"I know." Mom had always understood my father in a way I never could. As far as I could tell, my father had never given me a second thought, but as she stood there staring down at those patches, she seemed to think otherwise. She slipped her arm around my back, doing her best to reassure me as she said, "That's why I wanted you to see this."

It meant a lot to me to see those patches, to know that I'd crossed my father's mind. That realization made me feel like the walls were closing in on me. I couldn't breathe. I needed to get some air before I totally lost it. I leaned over and kissed her cheek. "I'll be back in a couple of hours."

I rushed out of the house, got in my truck, and cranked the engine. There was only one place for me to escape the thoughts that were rushing through my head —Danvers Pub. When I walked in, it looked exactly how it did five years ago. They were even playing the same damn songs on the jukebox, but I didn't give a rat's ass about the music or the décor. I needed a fucking drink. Hell, I needed a slew of them. I went over to the counter, placed my order for three shots of chilled vodka, and downed them one right after the other. I ordered three more, immediately knocking them down, and was about to order three more when a man came over and sat down next to me. I took a quick glance at him and an uneasy feeling washed over me when I saw that he was wearing a Satan's Fury cut. Their MC was known for being a group of badasses who didn't take shit from anyone, and from the looks of the patch he was sporting, this guy next to me was the biggest badass of them all. He was a big guy, maybe in his late forties, but he was fit and looked like he could hold his own and then some. He called the bartender over and said, "Bring us another round."

The bartender nodded, then placed six shot glasses on

the counter, quickly filling them to the brim. "Anything else?"

"For now ... just keep my tab running." He lifted one of the shot glasses and asked, "You got a name, kid?"

"Cade."

"Couldn't help but notice the military cut. You in the service?"

"I was." I ran my hand over the top of my head as I replied, "I just got back a few days ago."

"Well, here's to you, Cade. Thanks for your service." He motioned his hand towards my round of shots and waited for me to lift mine, and then we both threw them back. "So, you got plans to go back?"

"Nah. Pretty sure that chapter of my life has closed. My shoulder guaranteed that."

"What's up with your shoulder?"

"Bullet fucked up my rotator cuff."

"Damn." He shook his head as he reached for another shot. "That's a tough one, but you're young, you'll be back like new before you know it."

"You sound pretty sure of yourself."

"That's because I am," he said, then he pulled back the sleeve of his t-shirt, revealing a wound similar to mine. "Hurt like a bitch, but eventually healed and so will yours."

"Good to know." I took another shot, then immediately reached for the next. "Thanks for the round."

"Least I can do. After all, you seem pretty damn determined to get tanked tonight, so I thought I'd help you out."

"Needed to clear my head."

"Vodka isn't gonna help you with that."

"Maybe not, but after the day I've had, it's worth a try."

"Been one of those days, huh?"

"Yeah," I muttered. "You could say that."

"Life has a way of throwing some pretty hard punches … some harder than others." He looked me dead in the eye. "You've just gotta take the hit and find a way to get back up."

"I've had one too many hits, man. Not sure I see the point in getting back up anymore."

"Put your hand on your heart." He waited silently as I did as he requested. "You feel that? As long as your heart's beating, then you've got a purpose. You've just gotta figure out what it is."

"I'm trying, but it's just so damn hard." I ran my hand down my face and sighed. "Every fucking thing is exactly the same as it was when I left … my folks, my house, this whole damn city, but it feels so different. How is that possible?"

"Because you've changed. You can't expect things to be the same when you're not the same man you were when you left."

"I'm still me, though."

"Yeah, but now you're a different version of yourself." His eyes narrowed as he asked, "You ever ridden before?"

"A motorcycle?"

"Not talking about a fucking moped, son," he scoffed.

I shrugged. "Ridden a couple of times when I was younger but never actually had one of my own."

"Might be time to try again."

"Maybe so."

"*Maybe* isn't an answer, son." Then he leaned towards me and said, "If I've learned anything in this life, it's that we only regret the chances we didn't take. It's time for you to take that chance."

"I hear ya." I reached for my last shot and added, "But I don't own a motorcycle, and even if I did, I couldn't ride with this shoulder."

"That's two problems, son." He chuckled. "Both can be solved with time."

He reached into his pocket, pulled out a card, and offered it to me. "The name's Gus. When you get back on your feet, come by the clubhouse. We'll take that ride together."

"Sounds good. I'll do that."

"I'll be looking forward to it." After finishing off his last shot, he stood up and started to walk away. "Drink to your heart's content. Just be sure to get a ride home, son."

"Will do."

There was something about the way he'd called me *son* that got to me. As odd as it seemed, it felt like he actually meant it. Until that moment, I hadn't realized how much I needed to hear it. That one word had me looking down at the card Gus had given me, and I knew at that moment I would be taking that ride with him. What I didn't know was how that decision would change my life forever.

GUNNER

"Give me a second," I called out to Blaze. "I'll be right back."

"Whoa … Where are you going?" His eyes narrowed as he watched me start across the parking lot. "We're going to be late."

I was following Blaze, Shadow, Murphy, and their ol' ladies into the gas station when a gorgeous brunette in the parking lot caught my attention. She was pacing back and forth in front of her car. I couldn't tell for sure, but it looked like she was crying as she talked to someone on her cell phone. When we came back out and she was still there, I figured something must be wrong. There was something about a woman in need that got to me, especially when she was smoking hot with curves made for sin. As I continued walking towards her, I glanced back at Blaze and said, "No, we won't. I'll just be a minute."

"Um-hmm. I've heard that shit before," he complained. Murphy, the club's sergeant-at-arms, was a good guy, always played by the rules and never let a brother down, so I wasn't surprised when he said, "We still gotta drop the girls off, and if we're late for church, Gus is gonna be pissed."

"I already told ya ... We won't be late."

As I made my way closer to the woman, I heard her say, "Are you sure about this?" A gust of wind whipped passed us, and I quickly became mesmerized by the way her long, dark hair fluttered around her face. Damn. It was like I'd been pulled into some romantic, chick flick where everything was moving in slow motion. I needed to shake it off before I made a fucking fool of myself. She tucked her hair behind her ears as she continued, "I'm not certain. I think I'm close, but I took the wrong exit. Don't worry, I'll figure it out." After another brief pause, she said, "I'll let you know."

When she ended the call, I put on my best smile and asked, "You lost, darlin'?"

The gorgeous brunette glanced up at me for a moment, and her dark eyes quickly drifted over me. Clearly unaffected by my dashing good looks, she looked down at her phone and replied, "No."

"You sure about that ... 'cause you're a long way from heaven."

I cocked my head to the side and smiled, hoping she'd find the humor in my corny pickup line. Sadly, she was totally unfazed. Instead, my words just hung in the air, completely disregarded as she stared down at her phone. "I'm sure you're a nice enough guy and all, but I really don't have time for this right now."

"Okay, then. Tell me how I can help." I wasn't sure what to make of her. I knew she wasn't from around here, otherwise she'd know how dangerous it was for her to be standing out in the parking lot with every thug around checking her out. I couldn't blame them. Hell, she looked like a knockout in those hip-hugging jeans and low-cut t-shirt. I could only imagine what she'd look like wearing nothing at all. Just the thought made it difficult not to readjust myself. Unfortunately, I didn't have the same effect on her. In fact, she seemed unimpressed by my southern charm and was doing her best to disregard me completely. I could've just walked away, kept what was left of my ego intact, but that would have been too easy. "Seriously ... you got any idea where you are?"

"Actually, I do. I'm in Memphis and"—she glanced up at the store front sign— "at the Citgo gas station on Frayser Road."

"So, you know you're in Frayser?"

"Umm ... Yeah." Her eyebrows furrowed as she asked, "Why?"

"Not exactly safe around here, darlin'." I lifted my chin, motioning my head towards the hood-rats smoking dope at the side of the building. "There are some real bad folks around these parts."

Her gazed drifted downward as she took a moment to study my torn jeans, leather cut, and tattoos. She shook her head, then clipped, "And what about you? Are you one of them?"

"Depends on who you ask."

"Um-hmm. If had to guess, I would say you and your friends are just as dangerous, *if not more so*, as those men over there." With a cocked brow and a half-smile, she sassed, "Regardless, I'd already be gone if you weren't here ... *you know*, distracting me."

"Well, that's as much your fault as it is mine." I let my

eyes slowly drift over her, taking my time to study every gorgeous inch of her, as I said, "If you weren't so damn beautiful, I wouldn't be over here talking to you. Besides, I had to at least try and see if there was something I could do to help. Wouldn't want anything to happen to you while you were out here all alone."

"You're good. I'll give you that." She shook her head and scoffed, "A regular knight in shining armor, but you're wasting your time with me. I'm fine."

"I don't know about that." A smirk crossed my face as I added, "This is no place for someone like you, so if you're lost, I'll be glad to help you find wherever it is you're trying to go."

"Thanks, but I think I've got it figured out." She got in her car, and just before she closed her door, she looked over to me and said, "Maybe you'll have better luck with your next damsel in distress."

Before I had a chance to respond, she started her car and drove out of the parking lot. I watched as she pulled out onto the main road, and moments later, her tail lights disappeared into the traffic. When I turned around, I found the guys sitting on their Harleys with their ol' ladies, watching me with goofy grins plastered across their faces. Doing my best to ignore them, I walked over, got on my bike and started up my engine, revving it several times. My brothers never moved. They just sat there staring at me like three jackasses. "What?"

"Is your bike burning oil?" Blaze poked with a shit-eating grin. "Oh, no. That's just *you.*"

"What are you talking about?"

"Your ass just got smoked."

"What the fuck are you talking about? I didn't get smoked," I argued.

Shaking his head, Shadow asked, "You get her number … or even her fucking name?"

"No."

Shadow was the club's enforcer. He was usually pretty quiet, keeping to himself and remaining eerily intense. He wasn't normally one to fuck around, but that didn't keep him from joining in. "Then, *your ass just got smoked*."

"Fuck y'all."

Rider shrugged. "We're just calling 'em like we see 'em."

"Well, you saw this one wrong. I wasn't trying to pick that chick up," I argued. "I was being a Good Samaritan."

"Um-hmm … You know, we aren't buying that shit for one minute, brother," Shadow taunted. "Just admit it. You've lost your edge. Hell, it's gotten so bad you can't even pick up a chick in the fucking hood."

"Give the guy a break, guys," Alex fussed. She was Shadow's ol' lady and a real sweetheart of a chick. I'd always thought a lot of her, especially now. "At least he tried."

"Tried and failed," Blaze joked.

Kenadee leaned forward as she looked over to me and said, "Don't let them get to you, Gunner. You can't win them all."

"Thanks, Kenadee." Before the guys had a chance to respond, I started to back out and said, "I thought we had to get to the girls home."

Blaze looked over to Shadow and Murphy as he said, "He's right. We better get going."

With a quick nod, they each started up their engines, and one by one, we backed out of the gas station. As we pulled out of the lot, I thought back to the beautiful brunette and cursed myself for not trying harder to get her number. I could tell just by looking at her that she was one of those once-in-a-lifetime kind of women. I hated that I'd let her slip through my fingers, but in truth, I knew it was all for the best. I didn't need the distraction, especially with a run coming up. Since the day Gus became president of the Memphis chapter, he'd worked his ass off to make it what it is today—one of the most notorious clubs in the South. It hadn't been easy. Shit, it took one hell of a fight to take claim to such a dangerous territory, but he'd done it. More than that, he'd managed to do it without compromising his beliefs. He always remained loyal to his brothers, always putting us above all else—even if that meant putting his needs second. It was no wonder that we all respected him and followed him without question.

I tagged along as Murphy and the others dropped their ol' ladies off, then we all headed over to the clubhouse. By the time we arrived, the others had already started to gather in the conference room. Gus had called us all in to go over the final details of the run, ensuring that we all knew exactly what was expected before, during, and afterward. This particular run meant a great deal to us all. Gus had worked with Cotton, the president of the Washington chapter, to create a pipeline among several of the other chapters, enabling us to distribute twice the product in half the time. Since its creation, our shipments had almost doubled in size, making this one of our biggest deliveries to date. It was important for us to make sure that everything went exactly as planned.

Once everyone was seated, Gus stood up and said, "I want to make something clear with you boys. This isn't the first time we've done this particular run, so by now, you should be feeling pretty comfortable with the way things are run. I don't want you letting that get in your head. This is no time for any of you to be getting comfortable. You gotta keep your head in the fucking game. Stay alert. Be looking for problems before they arise. Watch your back. Always assume that someone's watching, 'cause if we don't stay vigilant with this thing, we're gonna lose everything we've worked for. You got me?"

"Understood. We won't let you down, Prez," Riggs assured him.

"I know you won't, son. None of you will." His expression softened as he added, "We all had different reasons for joining Fury. The way of life. The freedom. The ride. Whatever brought us here, we all stayed for the same reason ... Family. There's not a one of us in this club who wouldn't take a bullet for the other, and that alone is what keeps us going. Even when shit gets hard ... so hard you think it'll break ya, you always know you've got a brother who has your back. So, remember that as you get ready for this run. I want every one of you doing your part to make sure this goes off without a hitch."

"You got it, Prez," Blaze answered.

"You, T-Bone, and Riggs will be with Murphy, Rider, and Dane." Gus looked over to Shadow as he said, "I want you with Gunner and Rip."

Rip and Dane were two of our newest prospects. Both were good guys but green as shit. They were still learning how things worked, so it wasn't a surprise that Gus had

19

split them up. Shadow nodded, then asked, "When do we head out?"

"Tomorrow morning … 8:00 a.m. sharp." He looked down at his watch and directed, "Get me a final count on stock before you start to load up. We need to make sure everything is accounted for. As of right now, you have just under twenty-four hours to get things in order."

"We'll be ready."

"Moose and I will be here if anything comes up, otherwise I'll see you all in the morning."

While the brothers started to disperse, I remained seated, and as I watched them file out of the room, I thought back over what Gus had said about the club. I was twenty-four years old when I first met Gus at Danvers Pub. It took a few months for my shoulder to heal, but as soon as it did, I took him up on that offer for a ride. It was on that very day, just over eight years ago, that I decided to prospect for the club. Not because of the way of life, the freedom, or the ride. Hell, it wasn't even about family—that came later. I'd made my decision to join the club because of Gus. I saw how he looked after his brothers, making sure they had everything they needed. He led them with pride and determination, and his loyalty to them never wavered. In him, I saw the father figure I'd longed for my entire life, so when he offered me a chance to become a member of his family, I didn't hesitate. Even though I'd almost lost my life twice and had a body full of scars, it was the best decision I'd ever made.

I was still sitting there, lost in my thoughts, when Gus came over and put his hand on my shoulder.

"You all right, son?"

"Yeah, Prez. I'm good."

"You sure about that?" he asked with concern. "Looks like you've got something on your mind."

"Nah. Just doing a little reflecting. Everything's good."

"How's that niece of yours?"

My sister, Brooklyn, had been married for almost three years, and they'd just had their second child—a little girl named Chloe. Her brother, Thomas, wasn't much over three. He was the reason why my sister had gotten married at such a young age, but things seemed to be going okay for her and Gary. I was glad to see that she was happy. It meant a lot to me that Gus asked about her. It always amazed me how he managed to keep up with our lives outside of the club. "She's doing good. Up to twelve pounds now."

"That's great. Glad to hear it." He patted me on the back, and as he started for the door, he said, "Come on. I smell fresh-cooked bacon. Let's head to the kitchen for some breakfast."

I nodded as I stood up and followed him towards the door. We were just starting down the hall when T-Bone called out to Gus, "Hey, Prez. There's someone out front who wants to see you."

"Who?"

"Got no idea." He shrugged. "Rider just said that there's a chick at the gate who's asking to see you."

"And you don't got any idea who it is?"

"Nope." While his smile might lead you to think otherwise, T-Bone was not the kind of man you'd want to come across in a dark alley. He was a monster of a dude with thick biceps the size of tree trunks, and he knew how to use them. One hard blow from him, and you're done. He shrugged as he replied, "Rider said she wouldn't tell him anything. Just that she seems pretty freaked out and she's adamant about seeing you."

"Damn." He let out an irritated sigh. "Tell him to bring her to the bar. I'll meet with her there."

"You got it."

As soon as T-Bone radioed over to Rider and relayed the message, Gus continued down the hall. Over the years, Gus had had countless visitors, but never once had a chick, especially a chick none of us knew, ever come to see him at the clubhouse. I was beyond curious as to who was knocking at his door, so I followed him to the bar. When we walked in, I quickly realized I wasn't the only one. Blaze, and several of the others must've gotten wind of the girl's arrival and were sitting at the counter. They were pretending to talk amongst themselves, but it was clear they were there to eavesdrop. Even though I was there to do the same thing, I couldn't stop myself from calling them out. I looked over at their full beers and said, "You boys are at it pretty early this morning."

"Just taking a break before we head out for the day," Blaze lied.

"Yeah." I shook my head as I sat down next to them. "Figured I'd do the same."

Riggs looked over to me. "What do you have going today?"

"Gonna head down to the garage and see if I can get that carburetor finished up."

"Good," Blaze interjected. "Eddy was hoping to have it back by tomorrow."

"I'll have it ready this afternoon."

I'd barely gotten the words out of my mouth, when the front door opened and Rider stepped inside. The sun was shining bright, making it difficult to see who was standing behind him. The second the door closed, a knot formed in the back of my throat. It was the girl from the convenience store. As I sat there staring at her, I couldn't help but think that fate had brought me a second chance. Blaze nudged me in the ribs as he said, "Holy shit. Isn't that the chick from the gas station?"

"Yeah, that's definitely her."

"What the hell is she doing here?"

"Hell if I know."

We all watched intently as Gus walked over to her, and the room fell quiet the second she asked, "Are you Gus?"

"I am." He studied her for a moment, then asked, "What can I do for you?"

"I'm August ... *August James*." She clenched her fists tightly, until her nails dug into the palms of her hands, but she didn't seem to notice. The only thing she was really aware of was Gus. I totally understood her reaction. Our president was a fierce man, inside and out, and with a simple cock of his brow, he could make the toughest of men shake in their boots. It was clear from the way August's shoulders dropped into a slight cower that he was having the same effect on her. "My mother sent me here from Nashville. She said if anyone could help me, it would be you."

"And why would she say that?"

"I have no idea. I was hoping you could answer that."

"All right, well ... let's start with her." He crossed his arms then asked, "Who's your mother?"

"Samantha Rayburn."

"Samantha Rayburn?"

She paused for a moment, then said, "I think you knew

23

her by her maiden name ... Samantha Travers. She married my father, Denis Rayburn."

At the sound of her mother's name, Gus was rendered completely speechless. His face was growing whiter by the second as he stood there staring at her. It was like he'd seen a fucking ghost. In all my years of knowing him, I'd never seen him so spooked, and I hated that I had no idea why.

AUGUST

*W*hen he didn't respond, I asked, "Do you remember her?"

"Yeah, I remember her."

Gus's voice was harsh, almost angry, as he answered, making me regret my decision to go there even more. His dark eyes seemed to pierce straight through me, and not in a good way. I didn't understand why he was so angry. My mother told me that he was a good man, that he was kind and caring, and once I explained who I was, he'd help me. She'd failed to mention the fact that he was a large, scary biker who was as big as an ox, muscled up with tattoos and had a long, burly beard. The guy seriously looked like he could snap my neck like a twig without even trying. The mere sight of him made me wonder if I should have come to the clubhouse.

I thought back to my mother—the person I trusted most in this world—and remembered how she'd always given me such sound advice. Through thick and thin, she'd had an idea on how to fix things when they went wrong, and she was usually right. I tried my best to hold onto that thought as I told him, "I'm sorry to come unannounced like this, but I had no other way of reaching you. Mom tried to find it, but she didn't have your number."

"Yeah. I'm guessing she lost it a long time ago," he grumbled. "You're a long way from home, August James. I'm just curious ... how old are you?"

"I'm twenty-four."

"Hmm." There was something about his posture and the way that he was studying me, like I had just kicked his dog, that made me uneasy. His brows furrowed as he asked, "When were you born?"

"April of '95." His question seemed odd, so I asked, "Why?"

Instead of answering, he roared, "She wouldn't ... Damn it!"

Completely thrown by his reaction, I asked, "Am I missing something here? Did I say something wrong?"

"You don't know?"

With all the questions and his agitated tone, I was starting to worry that he might turn me away and refuse to help. "I have no idea what you're talking about, so apparently not."

"Of course, she didn't," he scoffed with a shake of his head. "Damn it all to hell."

With that, he walked out the door, leaving me to fend for myself. I turned to the one who'd brought me into the bar and asked, "What just happened here?"

He shrugged. "I got no idea."

"Should I go?"

"No." He glanced over at the door as he told her, "Just give him a minute."

I was trying my best to keep it together, but I was struggling. I was breathing hard, my palms were sweating, and my pulse was racing out of control. I tried to calm myself by looking around the bar. I'd never been in a motorcycle clubhouse. I'd tried to envision the place, but the Fury clubhouse was nothing like what I had imagined. For some reason, I'd thought it would be a run-down hole in the wall, but I was completely wrong. It was actually a nice place. Much like the exterior, it had a rustic feel to it with old light fixtures and exposed brick walls. I was looking around at all the different memorabilia, old motorcycle parts and vintage signs, and pictures of roughneck bikers hanging on the walls, when one of the men sitting at the end of the counter caught my attention. Unlike the others, he was facing me, and not only that, he was looking directly at me. It took me a moment, but then I realized he was the guy who'd come up to me at the gas station.

At the time, I was panicking over being lost, otherwise I might've noticed how handsome he really was. He was tall and muscular with messy blonde hair that seemed to be in perfect disarray. His eyes were fierce, but there was a kindness behind them that I found oddly appealing. Had I'd noticed how hot he was, I might've thought his cheesy pickup lines were kind of cute, but like now, I was too wound up to give him a second thought. I turned back towards the door and sighed when I saw no sign of Gus. With every second he remained outside, I was becoming more and more anxious. I'd almost convinced myself to just give it up and leave when he finally came charging into the room.

With a look of determination, his eyes locked on mine as he walked back over to me. I swallowed hard, trying to brace myself for whatever he was about to say. He took in a deep breath and tried to remain calm as he said, "I need you to tell me ... Why did Samantha send you here?"

"I'm really sorry if I said something to upset you. I didn't mean to say the wrong thing or ..."

"No. It's not anything you did, August," he interrupted. "Now, I need you to answer the question."

"Because there is no one else who can help me." He stood there waiting for me to explain, but I was having a hard time forming the words. The past few days had been the worst of my life, and just thinking about what had happened brought tears to my eyes. "My daughter is missing. She disappeared three days ago."

"Have you notified the police?"

"Yes, but they haven't been able to find her."

"That's not surprising," he scoffed. "What are they saying?"

"Nothing. Instead of searching for her, they keep asking me the same questions over and over again. It's like they think I did something to her, but I didn't. I have no idea where she is."

"The cops always focus on the parents first. After they figure out it wasn't you, they'll move on to another suspect."

"But there's no time for that!"

Tears started streaming down my face as I thought about the possibility that I may never see my precious daughter again. I was terrified that someone might hurt her, and I wouldn't be there to stop them. Just thinking about her out there alone, crying for her momma to save her ripped my heart out. I was overcome with guilt and couldn't seem to pull myself together. Gus took me by the arm and led me over to one of the tables. Once he helped me into a seat, he sat down next to me and said, "Look, I don't know if there's anything I can do to help you, August. I really don't. I won't know that until I find out exactly what's going on. You falling apart on me isn't going to make that any easier."

"You're right. I'm just so scared." Trying my best to collect myself, I inhaled a deep breath and wiped the tears from my eyes. "My daughter means everything to me."

"I get that and if there's something I can do, I will … but first, I need you to tell me everything you know about what happened to her."

"I don't even know where to begin."

"Let's just start with her name … and maybe a picture."

I pulled out my phone, and after I found a recent picture, I handed it over to him. "Her name is Harper. She'll be three years old this Christmas."

A strange look crossed his face as he studied the photograph. After several long moments, he handed my phone back to me and asked, "Where was the last place you saw her?"

"I dropped her off at Bowties and Butterflies, um … her daycare, Monday morning on my way to work," I stammered nervously. "Ah … That was around eight in the morning. I got a call about two o'clock saying that she was missing."

"And where is this daycare?"

"It's just a few miles from our house in Hillsboro Village."

"They got any idea what happened?"

"No, not really. They think she squeezed through a broken part of the fence and wandered off, but Harper would never go off on her own. I tried explaining that to them, but no one would listen to me. They sent out search parties, sent out an Amber Alert, but there's been no sign of her anywhere."

"Have you or your husband gotten any notes or phone calls about a ransom?"

"*Ex-husband*, and no. At least, I haven't. I have no idea about David." Just the thought of him made my stomach turn. Remembering our last conversation, I told Gus, "My ex-husband has been putting on a good front, talking to the media and pretending to be distraught over his daughter's disappearance, but honestly, I think it's just for show."

"What makes you say that?"

"Because I know David. He'd just as soon tell a lie than tell the truth, and he's pretty damn good at it too. That's why he's always made such a great politician," I grumbled as I thought about the countless lies he'd told me when we were together, including the times he said he was working late but was actually having an affair with his assistant.

Gus leaned forward as he asked, "Wait ... David James, as in David James the mayor of Nashville? That's your ex-husband?"

"That would be him."

"Damn." He pondered a moment, then asked, "He's a good bit older than you, right?"

"Yes. Seventeen years older to be exact."

I was twenty-one and naive when I started working as an intern on David's campaign. I'd thought his plans to renovate areas of downtown and improve our city's educational programs were incredible. I also thought he was extremely handsome and was excited to be working on his team. I'd only been working there a few weeks when I caught his eye. We started dating, fell in love, and after a few months, I found out I was pregnant. David wasn't happy about the news. In fact, he wasn't happy at all. Thinking the scandal might affect his campaign, he asked me to marry him. When he won the election, I thought he would be happy, but six months after Harper was born, I caught him in our bed with his office assistant.

We had an awful fight, and he finally told me the truth about why he'd gotten involved with me—my family. Even though he'd died years earlier, my grandfather had served as governor in Tennessee for eight years, and my father, Denis Rayburn, was his lawyer and became his right-hand man. Together, they'd made connections that would last a lifetime, and David hoped he'd could use those connections to further his career. I was heartbroken to hear how he'd used me and I left him. Once the dust settled, he tried to take back what he'd said, but the damage was done. I filed for divorce and never looked back. "It took some time, but I've learned all his tells. I know when he is lying or keeping something from me, and this time is no different. He's definitely hiding something. It's written all over his face."

"You think he's the one who took her?"

"No, but I think he might know who did." I thought back to the afternoon when I'd rushed into David's office to tell him that Harper was missing. He didn't even freak out. In fact, he didn't react at all. It was like he already knew she was missing. "Maybe I'm wrong ... God, I hope I am, but something in my gut tells me that something bad is going on with him. It's a feeling I've had for a while now, even before Harper came up missing. I tried telling the detective that I thought something was up with David, but he refused to listen."

"So, they didn't find any reason to believe that he was involved?"

"I'm not sure what they're thinking." I shrugged. "Even if they believed David was guilty, there's not much they would or could do about it. I guess you could say that's one of the perks of being mayor. He has too many people in his pocket. No one's gonna take the chance of going against him ... not without taking a huge risk."

Gus reached into his front pocket and brought out his pack of cigarettes. After he lit one, he took a long drag, then looked over to me and said, "You know, this isn't a lot to go on, August, and Nashville isn't exactly close. We're talking three and half hours away here."

"I know it's a lot to ask, but I have nowhere else to turn."

"I'll make some calls, but I can't promise anything."

Feeling relieved, I reached out and placed my hand on his. "Thank you, Gus. I really appreciate this."

"It's gonna take some time ... I'll have one of the boys show you to a room. You can wait there until I find out something."

"That's okay. You don't have to go to any trouble. I can go to a hotel."

"Not any trouble." When he noticed my startled

expression, he explained, "Besides, if something comes up, you'll need to be where I can get to you."

"Okay."

He motioned his hand over to one of the men at the bar and lifted his chin. "Gunner, take her down to one of the empty rooms and help her get settled."

To my surprise, the man I'd met at the convenience store nodded, then stood up and started in our direction. Gus took another long drag off his cigarette, then smashed what remained into the ashtray. When Gunner made it over to us, Gus stood up from the table and asked, "Your mother ... She live in Nashville too?"

"Yeah. She's still in the same house where I grew up. It's about twenty minutes from me."

"Has she been doing okay?"

"I guess. For the most part anyway ... She's worried sick about Harper, but she's holding it together."

He nodded, then his eyes dropped to the ground. He stood there silent for a moment. I had no idea what was going through his mind, but I could tell from his expression that something was troubling him. Finally, he lifted his head but didn't look at me as he asked, "Is she happy?"

There was something in his voice, regret or sorrow, that made his simple question seem like there was something more—something I wish I understood. It might've actually explained those nights when my mother cried herself to sleep or would sit for hours just staring off in space, but only she could answer that.

"When I was a kid, I thought she was happy ... but now, looking back, I'm not so sure. She's had to face some hard times, more than her fair share, but she always tried to focus on the positive side of things and encouraged me to do the same."

"Yeah, I remember that about her." He started to walk away, but suddenly stopped and turned back to me. "Hey ... You ever wonder where you got the name August?"

Another odd question.

"It's not exactly a common name, is it?" I shrugged. "I just figured Mom was trying to come up with something unique ... I figured it was the month she got pregnant with me or something like that?"

"Yeah, I guess that could be a possibility."

With that, he turned and left, leaving me more confused than ever. Once he was gone, his biker friend motioned me forward. "Come on. I'll get you to your room."

As we headed down the long, narrow hall, I expected him to say something about our previous encounter, but he didn't say a word. He wouldn't even look at me. I was already unnerved, and his silence wasn't helping matters. I was trying to think of something I might be able to say to him, something that might help smooth things over, when he stopped in front of a door. He opened it and waited as I stepped inside. To my surprise, the room looked like your typical hotel room. There was a full-sized bed with a desk in the corner and a flat-screen TV mounted on the wall. It even had its own bathroom with a shower. His tone was short as he pointed to the bedside table and said, "There's a remote to the TV in the drawer, and I'll have one of the girls bring you a bite to eat."

"Thanks, but you don't have to do that." I gave him a half-smile, wishing he'd go back to behaving like the playful guy I'd met at the convenience store, but his expression didn't change—not even a little. "I couldn't eat right now even if I wanted to."

"Okay." He took a piece of paper and pen off the table and started writing. Once he was done, he handed the paper to me. "You need anything, just call or text this number."

"Okay, thank you."

Before I could say anything else, he walked out of the room and closed the door. As I sat down on the bed, my mind drifted back to the moment I entered the clubhouse and how scared I was. It was like I'd entered a different world—a world filled with secrets and danger. I found myself wondering if my mother had felt the same way when she'd first come to the clubhouse all those years ago. I was even more curious about her relationship with Gus. Hoping to find some answers, I reached into my purse and took out my phone. I dialed my mom's number and as soon as she answered, she asked, "Did you find the clubhouse?"

"Yeah, I'm here now."

"Did you talk to Gus? Is he going to help you find Harper?" she asked frantically.

"He's going to try."

"Oh, thank god," she replied, sounding relieved. "Did you tell him about the daycare and—"

"I told him everything, Mom."

"Good. Then, he'll find her."

"You really think so?" My throat started to tighten. "'Cause I'm not going to be able to survive it if something happens to Harper."

"We're going to find her, sweetheart, and I really do

think Gus will help us get some answers. That's more than anyone has been able to do."

"I hope you're right."

"I am. You'll see."

I couldn't shake the feeling that she was keeping things from me, so I asked, "What's the deal with you and this Gus guy?"

"I've already told you. He's an old friend of mine."

"I know that's what you told me, Mom, but I've got a feeling there's a lot you aren't telling me about him ... *and his club.*" Thinking about how prim and proper she'd always been with her little pant suits and refined etiquette, I told her, "I wouldn't think that these are the kind of people you would've run around with ... at least not with Gran around."

"I met Gus when I was still living in Memphis. He helped me when some guy tried to steal my purse. We spent some time together, but that ended when I accepted a job in Nashville. I started seeing your father shortly after, so I lost ties with Gus. Simple as that," she answered nonchalantly.

"So, you guys dated?"

"Yes." She exhaled a deep breath before saying, "It's hard to explain, sweetheart. Just remember ... you can't always judge a book by its cover."

"Maybe not, but some things are hard to overlook."

"It's not as hard as you might think." She paused for a moment, then asked, "By the way, how is he?"

"Gus?" I thought for a moment, then replied, "Umm ... fine, I guess. He kind of freaked out when I told him I was your daughter."

"Did he seem angry?"

"It's hard to say what he was feeling. He stormed out of the clubhouse for a few minutes, but when he came back, he seemed okay. That's when I told him all about Harper. After I finished telling him everything, he asked about you."

"He did?"

"Yeah. He wanted to know how you were doing and if you were happy."

"Oh. That kind of surprises me."

"Why wouldn't he, especially if you two dated?"

"It's complicated." I could tell she was ready to change the subject when she asked, "Have you heard anything from David or the police?"

"I got a call from Detective Haralson earlier, but I wasn't able to take it." I looked down at my watch and was surprised to see that it was after ten. "I should call him back."

"Okay. Keep me posted."

"You know I will."

When I ended the call with my mother, I had every intention of dialing Detective Haralson's number, but instead, I opened my pictures on my phone. I started scrolling through all the different photographs of Harper, and my heart literally ached with grief. I missed her terribly. I'd never been away from her this long, and it was killing me. I thought back to the day I found out I was pregnant. At first, I was nervous, but that changed when I started to feel her growing inside me. Early on, I knew that she was going to be special. I could just feel it, and when she was born and I held her in my arms for the first time, she took my breath away. I'd never seen a more beautiful creature. She was so absolutely precious with dark, soulful eyes, full rosy cheeks, and tiny fingers and toes. As she grew older, her little personality started to blossom, and anyone could see that she was kind and so very smart. I've always been so proud that she was mine and that I was her mother—and as her mother, I would do whatever it took to protect her—even if that meant putting my own life in danger to do it.

GUNNER

hen I got back to the bar, I was relieved to see that the guys were still sitting at the counter. They were talking amongst themselves, and from the looks on their faces, they still had no idea what was going on. As I sat back down next to Blaze, I asked, "Where is he?"

"The last I saw, he was headed to his office," Riggs answered.

"He didn't say anything to any of you?"

"Nope. Not a word."

Concern crossed Blaze's face as he asked, "Did you see the look on Gus's face when she said her mother's name?"

"Yeah. It was hard to miss."

"So, it's not just me?" Blaze had always been good at reading people, especially his brothers. Whenever something was going on, he was one of the first to pick up on it. This time was no different. I could see the wheels turning in his head as he looked over at us. "You guys think there's more going on with this chick than just her missing daughter?"

"Definitely. Just not sure what," Murphy answered.

"You boys can stop trying to figure it out," Moose told us as he walked into the bar. He was the club's VP and knew Gus better than anyone. Moose was there when he started the Memphis chapter and has stood by him ever since, making him one of Gus's closest friends. "Gus will talk to you when he gets good and ready. Until then, this conversation ends here."

"Understood. We wanted to make sure everything was okay with him."

"Everything will be fine as soon as we find August's daughter." He walked over to Riggs and said, "I'm gonna need you to find out everything you can on David James, and not just the basic stuff. If he's dealing with any under-the-table bullshit, I want to know about it."

Riggs was our club's computer hacker, and he was amazing at his job. There wasn't anything he couldn't do on that fucking computer, including gathering intel on folks that no one else could find. He stood up to leave and told Moose, "I'll see what I can dig up."

Once he was gone, Moose looked over to me and said, "Gus wants you keeping an eye on August."

"Whatever he needs me to do."

"Just make sure she isn't left alone. If you aren't around, have a prospect on her."

"He thinks she's in danger too?"

"No way to know for sure. This thing with the kid could be a random kidnapping or it could be something more. We just don't know yet. Until we do, Gus doesn't want to take any chances. All of you need to stay alert.

You see anything out the norm, you be sure to let Gus know about it."

Before he walked out, T-Bone asked, "What about the run?"

"We're still on for the morning. We'll have to make some changes, but it's too important to postpone." He shook his head as he headed out of the bar. "Timing isn't on our side, but we'll just make the best of it."

Everyone had things that needed to be done so we all left the bar, and without saying a word, went our separate ways. Following Gus's orders, I started down the hall towards August's room. I'd almost made it to her door when Rider called out to me. "Yo, Gunner."

"Yeah?"

"Gus wants to see you in his office."

"Okay, I'll be right there."

I figured I still needed to check in on August, so I knocked on her door. When she answered, I could tell she'd been crying, and it tugged at me in a way I didn't expect. I wanted to console her in some way, but there was little I could do. Her eyes were red and puffy, and she was still sniffling as she asked, "Did he find out anything?"

"Not yet. I just wanted to make sure you're okay." She looked at me—not with a quick glance, but really looked at me. Sadly, her eyes were masked with heartache and pain, making it impossible to know exactly what was going through her mind. "Do you need anything?"

"No." She shook her head as she wiped the last of the tears from her eyes. "I'm okay."

"I need you to stay put. No going outside or even down the hall without me at your side."

"Why? Is something wrong?"

"Just taking all the necessary precautions to make sure you're safe," I tried to assure her. "If you need me, you've got my number."

"I do."

"Try to get some rest. I'll be back when I can."

"Okay. Thank you ... umm ... What was your name again?"

"Gunner."

"Right. Thank you, Gunner."

As soon as she closed the door, I went down to Gus's office to see what he needed. After I knocked, I stepped inside and found Gus sitting at his desk with Riggs and Murphy seated in front of him. While Gus didn't look as on edge as he had earlier, it was clear from his demeanor that something was weighing on his mind. "Rider said you wanted to see me."

"Have a seat, son." Having no idea why he'd called us all in, I sat down next to Murphy and watched as Gus leaned back in his over-sized leather office chair. He crossed his arms and looked over to us with a fierce expression. "I've got something to discuss with you boys, but I'm trusting you to keep this conversation between us. What's said in this room, stays in this room. Is that understood?"

"Understood," we each replied.

"I wouldn't even be telling you any of this, but you need to know how important this all is to me." We nodded, then waited for him to continue. "I'm sure you've noticed that over the years I've never taken on an ol' lady."

"We have," Murphy answered.

Gus had been known to take advantage of the club's hang-arounds from time to time. They were always eager to please the president of the club in hopes that he might take them on as something more serious, but that never happened. Gus never got attached to any female, only using them for the task at hand, and then he'd move on, leaving a trail of broken hearts in his wake. I never thought much about it. Figured he just didn't want the distraction or the hassle of taking on an ol' lady. I never realized that there was more to it than that until he said, "I've had my reasons for that."

We each settled back in our chairs as we waited for him to continue.

"You weren't around when this charter started, but you've heard the stories. You know how we built this club from scratch."

"Yeah, I've heard 'em," I confessed. "I've also heard the club would've never been as successful if you weren't the man running the show."

"I don't know about that, but I'll admit, it wasn't easy. There was a lot of shit that had to be done with getting the clubhouse together and opening the diner and garage … but that was only a small part of it. We fought tooth and nail to stake our claim over the territory, but I was damn-well determined to make it happen. We were just getting our start when I met Samantha Travers." His expression changed the moment he spoke her name. "I'm pretty sure I fell for her the minute I saw her. *Damn.* She was a beautiful thing. Way out of my fucking league, but we ended up hitting it off. Spent the whole damn summer together. I loved her like crazy."

Anguish crossed his face as he continued, "I don't know how to explain it … I knew from the start she was the one. Knew even then there'd never be another. I was gonna put a ring on her finger and a property patch on her back, but she left before I got the chance."

"Wait. So, she just up and left out of the blue?" Riggs asked.

"Yep. I had no idea she was even thinking about it. Went to bed with her in my arms and woke up alone the next morning with a fucking Dear John letter resting on the pillow." I could hear the pain in his voice as he said, "Nearly broke my fucking heart."

Sounding surprised, Murphy questioned, "You didn't try to go after her?"

"Not at first. I kept thinking that she'd find her way back, but she never did. When a year passed and I still hadn't heard anything from her, I went to find her. That's when I learned she was married. Found her a fella that fit into her world perfectly—a way I never could have. I knew then why she hadn't come back. Couldn't say I blamed her." He brought out his cigarettes and lit one. After taking a long hit, he let out a breath of smoke and said, "That was over twenty-five years ago. I haven't heard a word from her in all those years, and then today her daughter shows up ... a daughter named *August* who was born eight months after Samantha left Memphis."

"Oh, shit." I leaned forward as I asked him, "You think August is your daughter?"

"Can't say for certain, but sure as hell looks like it," he grumbled.

"You didn't know Samantha was pregnant?"

"Didn't have a clue. She never told me, and if I had to guess, I'd say that August doesn't have a clue about any of this either." He slammed his fist against the desk, then sat there with a blank expression until he said, "If August is my daughter, then that means it's my granddaughter who's out there missing. We have to find her."

"I'm here to help you any way I can," Murphy assured him. "We all are."

"I appreciate that, brother." He looked over to me as he said, "I want you keeping an eye on August. I'm trusting you to make sure nothing happens to her."

"You can count on me, Prez."

"Always have." He ran his hand over his beard. "I put a call into the Ruthless Sinners clubhouse and spoke to their prez, Viper. He's putting feelers out to see if he can come up with anything on Harper. While I was at it, I asked him about the mayor."

"And?" Riggs pushed.

"He said he's all kinds of shady. Far from the up and up, so August might be right about him knowing more about Harper than he's letting on."

"Damn, that makes things complicated."

"Yeah, but it doesn't matter." His voice was low and full of warning when he added, "In case there's any question … I'm gonna find her, and when I do, she better be okay or I'm gonna fucking end whoever took her."

After we were done talking, Riggs and Murphy went to check in with their ol' ladies while I went to the kitchen and gathered up a couple of drinks, a sandwich, and some snacks. As I carried them down the hall to August's room, I thought back over everything Gus had said. Since I'd joined the club, I'd done everything in my power to do right by him. I'd proven to him and my brothers that I was loyal to the club, that nothing came before them, and I almost screwed it all up when I tried to pick up Gus's daughter at a fucking gas station. Granted, I had no idea who she was at the time, but I knew exactly who she was now, and there'd be no more fucking around. Like it or not, the beautiful August James was off limits. I knocked on the door, and when she answered, I was pleased to see that her eyes were no longer red from crying. She looked down at all the food I brought, and a soft smile crept over her face. "What's all this?"

"Thought you might be hungry."

"That was really sweet of you, but like I said earlier ... I'm really not hungry. There's just too much going through my head right now."

"I can totally understand that." Knowing she needed to eat something, I walked over and set everything down on the desk. "I'll leave it here in case you change your mind."

Her gorgeous dark eyes met mine as she said, "Thank you, Gunner."

I only held her gaze for just a moment, but the damage was done. I knew it was a mistake. I had a job to do, but as I stood there looking at her, I wasn't thinking about Gus or the club. I wasn't thinking of what was at stake. I was only thinking about her and the need I felt to get closer, making me realize I was in serious trouble. Fuck me. This woman was going to be harder to resist than I thought. Doing what I could to pull my head out of the fucking clouds, I cleared my throat and said, "No problem. You sure you don't need anything?"

"Just my daughter."

"We're working on that. It's just going to take some time."

"But shouldn't we be out there looking for her?"

"You've said it yourself that the cops were out there looking for her, so there are people out there working on it," I tried to assure her. "A man like Gus has the ability to look in places they can't. You did the right thing coming to him. You just have to be patient and let him do the job you've asked him to do."

"I'm trying. I don't know Gus … at least not the way my mother did, so it's hard to trust that he can really find her, you know?"

"I get it. You're just gonna have to go with your gut on this." I looked her in the eye and added, "You wouldn't have come here unless something inside you told you it was the right thing to do."

"Yeah, I guess you're right."

"I am. Now try to get some rest. I have some things to see about, but I'll be back in a couple of hours to check in on you." As I started towards the door, I told her, "If you need anything, Gash will be right outside."

"Gash?"

"He's one of our prospects." I opened the door and stepped into the hall. "Like I said earlier, we're taking every precaution to make sure you're safe."

She nodded, and I closed the door. After I made sure Gash was posted outside of August's door, I headed down to the garage to finish working on that carburetor I'd promised Blaze I'd have done by the end of the day. I only needed a couple of hours to get it up and going and knew I could trust Gash to keep an eye on August until I returned.

Back at the garage, Blaze and the others were busy working on their own projects and didn't even notice when I walked over to my station. Relieved that I didn't have any distractions, I got straight to work. The entire time I was putting that damn carburetor back together, I was thinking about August. Gus knew I had to come by the garage, but I couldn't shake the gnawing feeling that it should be me who was there with her, watching over her and keeping her safe. Thankfully, I managed to get the carburetor completed quicker than I'd thought. Once I got things cleaned up, I took it over to Blaze and said, "Got her done."

"Thanks, brother." As he took it from my hand, he asked, "You headed back to the clubhouse?"

"Yeah. Need to get back and relieve Gash. He's keeping an eye on August while I'm here."

"Any word on her kid?" Blaze asked with concern.

"Not that I'm aware of, but figure Riggs will have something soon."

"I'm sure he will. Heard neither of you will be going on the run with us tomorrow. Guessing you both will be helping out with finding the kid."

I didn't want to say too much, so I just nodded and said, "Doing what we can, but I'll be around in the morning to help y'all get loaded."

"Good deal." When I started to leave, he said, "See ya then."

"Count on it."

I went out to the parking lot and got on my bike. The clubhouse was only a few miles away, but the ride back did wonders to clear my head. By the time I pulled up, I was feeling more like myself, but that feeling quickly diminished when Rider rushed up to me and said, "Gus wants you and August to meet him in the conference room. *Now.*"

AUGUST

"*I* made a few calls, and it turns out you might be right about your ex."

I was sitting in a conference room surrounded by Gus, Gunner, and two other men Gus had introduced to me as Riggs and Moose. They sat quietly, listening intently as I asked, "What makes you say that?"

"One of my contacts said he's in bed with the mafia, and they might have something to do with Harper's disappearance."

Shocked, I replied, "The mafia? David? That can't be right. I've always believed that he was up to something, but the mafia? That's a little extreme."

"Do you know anything about Sal Carbone?"

"No, not that I can recall. Why? Who is he?"

"He's the front man for Anthony Polito, the head of the Italian mafia in Tennessee," Gus answered flatly.

"Okay. So, what does this guy have to do with David?"

"He funded over half of your ex-husband's campaign and helped raise money for his new renovation project downtown." He slid two pieces of paper over to me and I was surprised to see that they were deposits made by Sal Carbone into David's account. "You weren't aware of their connection?"

"No. I had no idea David even knew him." I stared down at the papers in total disbelief. When I'd interned for David, I'd spent hours upon hours trying to come up with different fund raisers to help raise money for his campaign. We all did. I didn't want to believe that they were used to accept bribes, but the proof was right in front of me. "There's no way someone would pay eighteen thousand for a weekend trip to Kiawah Island, and I never knew anything about a three million dollar donation?"

"We didn't think you did."

I placed the papers on the table as I asked, "But, I don't get it. Why would some Italian mafia guy contribute all this money into David's campaign?"

"From what I'm hearing, his crew has recently moved into the area. They were rooted out west but have been working to move their network closer to the center of the state. From what we've heard, they're working primarily out of Nashville now," Gus explained.

"Okay. I've heard stories about the mafia and the cartel. These are really powerful people who do some really awful stuff like sex- and drug trafficking, and god knows what else. But why in the world would the Italian mafia ever want to have anything to do with a place like Tennessee?"

"No way to tell. Maybe it's because no one would suspect them to be here, or it's a midpoint between Florida and New York." Gus ran his hand over his salt and pepper beard. "The real question is, what is their connection to David?"

"I have no idea. Only he can answer that."

"Then, I think it's time we ask him a few questions."

"Why? It's not like he'll answer."

"Oh, he'll answer. I guarantee you that," Gus grumbled.

"Wait ... why are you so concerned about this mafia guy?" He didn't answer right away, which I could only take as a bad sign. I'd heard the horror stories of what those men could do, and just the thought of them having Harper made my heart beat so hard I could hear it pounding in my chest. With each second that passed it got louder and faster, to the point where I couldn't breathe. Just as I was about to hit a full-blown panic attack, I felt Gunner's hand on the small of my back. It was a simple gesture, but it was enough for me to collect myself. "Please. I need to know. Do you think they might've taken Harper?"

"We won't know for sure until we talk to David."

Riggs looked over to me. "You know him better than any of us. Do you have any idea where we'd be able to meet up with him without drawing any attention?"

"When?"

"The sooner the better. Three and half hours from now."

"He works out at one of the local gyms after work. He's usually done around seven thirty or eight. You might be able to catch up with him there."

Gus looked over to me and said, "We'll need the name of the gym and a recent photo."

"Fitness for All, on Dupont." I took out my phone and pulled up a picture of David. "This is the most recent picture I have. You might find a better one online. The media is always taking pictures of him, especially when he's out with his new girlfriend, Melanie."

"This should do it."

I looked back over to Gus and asked, "So, what happens if this Polito guy has Harper?"

"We'll figure that out when we get there. Right now, we just need to focus on finding out if there's any connection between her disappearance and your ex-husband."

"Okay."

"Are you comfortable in your room? Is there anything we can get you?" Moose asked with concern.

"The room is great. I just need to get my bag out of my car."

"I'll grab it for you," Gunner replied. "Anything else?"

"No, that should do it."

When they all started to stand, I did the same and followed them towards the door. Before we left, Gus turned to me and said, "Treat the clubhouse as your own. The kitchen is fully stocked, and you're welcome to anything in the bar."

"Thank you for all of this, Gus. I can't tell you how much I appreciate it."

"You don't have to keep thanking me, August." Then he placed his hand on my arm. "I wouldn't be doing any of this if I didn't want to."

Before I had a chance to reply, he turned and started down the hall with Riggs and Moose following close behind. Gunner silently motioned me forward, and I followed him back down to my room. He opened the door and once I'd stepped inside, he said, "I'll go grab your bag. Just need your keys."

"Let me get them." I grabbed them off the desk, and as I handed them over to Gunner, I told him, "It's in the trunk."

"Got it. I'll be right back."

Once he was gone, I reached into my purse and took out my phone. When I checked my messages, I was surprised to see that I had another message from Detective Haralson. Hopeful that he might have some news about Harper, I quickly replayed the message but was immediately let down when he gave me the same old song and dance he'd been giving me from the start. He still had no idea where Harper was or who might've taken her. In fact, he seemed more confused than ever about her disappearance. Before he ended the call, he told me to be patient and that he would be in touch soon. I was so upset with his lack of information, I decided to call and check in with the private investigator I'd hired. "Hi, Pete. It's August James. I was checking in to see if you had any news about Harper."

His voice sounded utterly defeated as he replied, "I'm sorry, Ms. James, but right now I keep coming up with dead-ends."

"Have you looked into David like I asked?"

"I have, but I'm not finding anything that looks suspicious. He seems equally concerned about your daughter's disappearance."

"Pfft." I silently cursed myself for hiring someone out of the yellow pages. This guy clearly had no idea what he was doing. I should've known by his greased back silver hair, twenty-year old suit, and lopsided grin that he was just looking to make a buck. Hoping that he'd managed to find out something we could use, I pushed, "What about the daycare? Has anyone come up with—"

"No," he interrupted. "There's nothing new from anyone. I'm sorry, August. I promise I'm doing everything I can to find your daughter."

"Okay. Just please call the minute you hear anything."

"I will."

I hung up the phone and was returning it to my purse when Gunner returned. He tapped on the door as he stepped inside.

"I got your luggage."

"Thank you for doing that."

"No problem." He walked over and placed the bag on the floor. When he noticed that I hadn't touched the food he'd brought, he looked over to me and asked, "You want something else?"

"I'm good."

"You sure? When I went out to get your bag, I saw that the girls are making up fried chicken and mashed potatoes. Smelled good ... really good."

"The girls?"

"Yeah. We have a few hang-arounds that help out in the kitchen and with other things."

There was something about his tone that told me that there was something he wasn't telling me. Curious, I asked, "What kind of other things?"

"I think that's best left for another day." He motioned his hand forward and waited for me as he said, "Come on. Let's grab a bite to eat."

"Okay."

I followed him down the hall, and as soon as I smelled

the food cooking, my stomach started to growl. We stepped into the kitchen, and just like he'd mentioned, there were several young, scantily dressed women hovering over the stove and sink. Each of them seemed to have their own part in preparing dinner as they chatted amongst themselves. As soon as they noticed that we'd walked in, one of the women looked over and gave Gunner a flirtatious smile. "Hey there, handsome. You want me to fix you a plate?"

"Yeah, Candace, that'd be great." He nodded his head over in my direction as he told her, "Fix one up for August while you're at it."

"Sure thing. What can I get you two to drink?"

Gunner looked over to me and asked, "Iced tea good with you?"

"Yes, that's just fine."

"Iced tea if you've got it."

"Sure thing."

As we sat down at the long wooden kitchen table, I took a moment to look around. It was a big room, much bigger than my kitchen at home, with all new appliances and very few decorations—just a checkered curtain over the window and a large mural of a motorcycle on the back wall. While it was definitely masculine, it felt warm and comfortable. I was still looking around when Candace brought over our glasses of tea and placed them on the table. She gave me an odd look as she said, "I haven't seen you around here before."

Before I could respond, Gunner gave her a sharp look. "She's a friend of Gus's."

"Oh." A big, fake smile crossed her face as she feigned her sweetest possible voice, "Well, a friend of Gus's is a friend of mine. It's great to have you here, darlin'. Let me grab those plates for ya."

She rushed over and grabbed two plates filled to the brim with food, then rested them on the table. "Thank you, Candace."

"No problem at all." As she started back towards the others, she let her fingers trail over the back of Gunner's neck. "You two let me know if you need anything else."

I'd never been one of those people who could hide how I was feeling. Mad, happy, or sad, it was always written all over my face, so I wasn't surprised when Gunner asked, "What?"

"Nothing," I answered, trying to play it off.

"Oh, no. There's definitely something. Whatcha thinking?"

"Nothing really. I'm just taking it all in," I lied.

I glanced over at Candace in her short miniskirt and halter top, and for reasons I couldn't begin to explain, I was overcome with an urge to thump her right in the head. I was imagining doing just that when I heard Gunner say, "She isn't all bad."

"Who?"

"Candace." He took a bite of mashed potatoes, then said, "Just like most of the girls who hang around here, she's had some hard times. Parents are both cracked out. Don't seem to care if she's coming or going, so she spends a lot of time here. We do what we can to look out for her and the others."

He'd barely gotten the words out of his mouth when a tall, brute-of-a-biker with a bald head and tattoos covering his enormous biceps walked in. I watched as one of the girls sashayed over to him, only stopping when her boobs were pressed seductively against his chest. I cringed as I watched the blonde place her hand on his shoulder and whispered something in his ear. As I continued to watch her little display, I leaned towards Gunner and whispered, "I'm guessing these girls don't just do the cooking and cleaning around here."

"Yeah. Some go above and beyond." He chuckled as he looked over his shoulder at the girl then shrugged. "But, what can I say? They're eager to please."

My words dripped with sarcasm as I replied, "From the looks of it, they are very eager to please."

I was taking a drink of my tea when I noticed the bald man walking in our direction. He patted Gunner on the back as he sat down next to him and said, "Missed you at the garage today."

"I wasn't there long."

"Blaze said you got that piece-of-shit carburetor up and going."

"I did." Gunner cocked his eyebrow as he asked, "What about that manifold? You manage to get that finished?"

I totally missed his response. I was too busy watching the commotion over at the stove. The blonde from earlier had started cooking another batch of fried chicken when some of the oil spilled out, causing fire to rise up from beneath the frying pan. Without realizing what she was doing, she took her glass of water and tossed it on the flame, doing little to put it out. Frazzled, she reached for the frying pan and yelped when it singed her hand. The other girls stood there frozen, completely clueless as to what to do. Knowing the fire could quickly get out of hand, I rushed over, grabbed the flour off the counter, and quickly dumped it on the fire, snuffing the flame completely.

The room fell silent as I moved from the stove over to the girl. I calmly reached for her hand and led her over to the sink. "We need to get some cold water on that burn before it gets any worse."

Sniffling, she nodded and slipped her hand under the cold water. Looking completely amazed, she turned to me and she asked, "How did you know to do that?"

"Do what?"

"Put that fire out like that."

"It's something my mother taught me." I smiled as I said, "I've had to use that little trick more than once myself, and I'm sorry to say, it makes a bit of a mess."

"It's okay," one of the girls called out as she grabbed some paper towels. "We'll get it cleaned up."

"Thank you."

I was still holding her hand under the water when Gunner and the big, bald-headed guy came up behind me. "Looks like you saved the day with your quick thinking, little lady."

"I don't know about that."

"Well, I do," he argued. "In a couple more minutes, this whole kitchen could've been up in flames."

"I'm sure someone would've gotten it out before that happened." As I lifted the girl's hand, I told them, "I think she's gonna need to get something for this burn."

Gunner looked over to the young girl and said, "Go down and let Mack take a look at it."

"Okay." I turned off the water, then wrapped her hand in a clean, wet rag. Once I was done, she reached out and hugged me. With a sweet, sincere tone, she whispered, "Thank you for your help. I really appreciate it."

"No problem. Glad I could help."

Once she'd turned to leave, the man turned his attention to Gunner as he asked, "You gonna introduce me to our guest?"

"August, this is T-Bone."

"Hi, T-Bone. It's nice to meet you."

"Right back at ya." He gave me a wink and a friendly smile. "Good to have you here."

"Thank you." As I stood there looking at them both, a strange feeling of anxiousness washed over me. I had no idea why, but I needed to get out there. I turned to Gunner as I said, "If it's okay, I think I'm just going to go back to the room."

"Sure, it's okay. I'll go with you, if you want."

"No. I'm fine," I assured him. "I just need a minute."

"Okay. I'll come down and check on you when I'm done."

I nodded with a feigned smile, then rushed out of the kitchen and down the hall. When I got to my room, I walked in and collapsed onto the bed. I stared up at the ceiling as I thought about what the detective had told me. The first forty-eight hours are critical when it comes to finding missing children. Those forty-eight hours had already come and gone for Harper. Dread washed over me as I listened to the clock ticking on the wall—a reminder of the time that was quickly slipping away from me. Just like the beating of my own heart, I couldn't stop it or even slow it down. It just kept pounding away, and with each tick, it was another second I'd lost with my precious daughter—another second she was out there alone and in danger. The all-consuming fear and dread of what may come weighed on me like an invisible beast, looming over me as it reveled in my torment. I tried to push it back, but those dreadful thoughts kept circling around my mind until there was no room for anything else. My chest continued to tighten and my hands started to tremble, and I knew it wouldn't be long before I'd have a full-blown panic attack.

I'd laid there for almost an hour, trying to pull myself together, but nothing was working. I couldn't take it a minute longer, so I got up and headed down the hall. When I got to the bar, I was thankful that the place was completely empty. While I felt a little awkward just helping myself to their alcohol, my need for an escape was stronger. I took a shot glass from beneath the counter and a bottle of vodka from the freezer, then went over to one of the tables in the back of the room. Once I'd sat down, I poured myself a shot and quickly drank it. The cold liquor burned as it slipped down my throat, causing me to wince as I swallowed. Ignoring the sensation, I poured myself another and another. By the third shot, I was starting to feel the effects of the alcohol, and the tension I was carrying in my muscles started to ease. I leaned back in the chair and listened to the upbeat lyrics of the song playing on the jukebox. When the song was over, I started to pour myself another round but stopped when I noticed Gunner walking in my direction. "I went by your room and got worried when you weren't there."

"Sorry." I shrugged. "I needed to get out of there for a little while."

"How many of those have you had?"

"Not many. I just needed a little liquid strength." With

his eyebrow cocked high, he looked at me like he wasn't buying a word I said. Ignoring his look of displeasure, I motioned my hand towards the bottle of Vodka and asked, "You want one?"

"Liquid strength?"

"I need something to numb the ache." I hated the weakness I heard in my own voice. It made me feel so inadequate and needy. "I'm just not strong enough to handle all of this. It's too much."

"You're kidding me, right?" he argued. "You've gotta be one of the bravest, strongest chicks I've ever met."

"How can you say that? All I've done is cry for the past three days."

"No. You've done everything you could to find your daughter, more than most would ever be able to do on their own. Hell, you even came here ... to a clubhouse filled with guys you don't know—some scary guys at that." He chuckled. "But you didn't let that stop ya. You just kept at it, and if I had to guess, you'll find your daughter. I'd bet my life on it."

"I hope you're right." I inhaled a deep breath as I poured myself another and drank it. "Have one with me?"

He nodded, then got up and grabbed himself a shot glass. When he returned, I filled his glass three-fourths full and then filled mine to the brim. With a smirk, he took his shot, then watched as I picked up mine and drank the entire glass. I was about to pour us another round when he reached for the bottle. As he took it from my hand, he smiled and said, "Easy there, killer. You haven't had much to eat. This will hit you a lot quicker than you think."

"Good. That's the point. I want it to hit me. The

quicker the better." I pointed to the bottle of vodka as I ordered, "Now, do me a favor and pour me another."

He filled my glass as he warned, "You know, drinking like this is gonna make you sick as a dying dawg."

"Maybe, but it can't be any worse than the way I'm feeling now." I downed the shot, then leaned back in my seat with a huff. "I'm tired of worrying. Tired of not knowing where she is and if she's okay. I just want my baby back."

"I know you do, but I don't think getting sauced is going to make you feel any better."

"Maybe. Maybe not." As I took my next shot, the fog started to hit and I found myself saying things I would normally never say. "Why do you care anyway? It's not like you know me, and I wasn't exactly nice to you at that gas station. And I'm sorry about that, by the way. If it was any other day, I would've been flattered that a guy as good-looking as you would even try to talk to me."

"Flattered? Why the hell would you be flattered?"

I shrugged. "I guess I have that whole 'mom' vibe going on. It's like instant repellant for guys. I'm surprised it didn't do the same thing to you."

"I hate to break it to you, but there ain't nothing about you that would ever be considered a repellant to *any man*, including me." His eyes roamed over me as he said, "You are all kinds of smoking hot, and the fact that you have a kid doesn't change that. In fact, knowing that you are actually a good mother who loves her kid only makes you that much more attractive, so get that thought out of your pretty head."

"Aww," I slurred. "That was so sweet of you to say."

"Not trying to be sweet here, August. I'm just telling it like it is."

"Pfft. Okay. Whatever," I scoffed. Feeling slightly embarrassed by his compliments, I turned away from his heated gaze and found myself looking up at all the different motorcycle parts they'd hung along the walls. When I looked closer, I realized that all the pieces were damaged in some way. The headlight was crackled, an old MC vest was ripped, a fender was crumpled, and those were just a few of the various beaten-up motorcycle pieces. Curious why they'd chosen to hang them in their bar, I asked, "What's with all the busted motorcycle parts?"

"That was Gus's idea. He has a thing for broken stuff." I looked up at the ripped vest as he continued, "He says they help remind us of lessons learned, lives lost, or second chances. He's right. Every time I look at that busted headlight, I remember the night I got on my bike after one too many beers and almost lost my life because of it."

"I like that idea. Maybe I should start my own wall of broken things. I have plenty I could add to it."

"We all do, but that's what makes life so interesting."

Maybe it was the effects of the alcohol or maybe the stress I was under, but Gunner, the hot biker with an adorable smile and sexy dimples, was starting to grow on me.

GUNNER

I just didn't get how a woman as gorgeous as August James could ever doubt for one second that she was smoking hot. Hell, I'd never seen a more beautiful woman, and she was quick on her feet, too. She'd put that fire out without breaking a sweat and tended to the burn on Halley's hand like it was second nature to her. If I had to guess, I'd say there wasn't anything she couldn't do. I don't know why she doubted herself like she did, but I sure didn't. Damn. I was completely captivated by her. It took every ounce of my willpower to resist leaning in towards her just so I could get a little closer, especially with the way she was looking at me. I knew it was just the alcohol getting to her, but damn, it was hard not to let myself wonder if she was really in to me or if it was just my fucking imagination. Not that it mattered anyway. It wasn't like I could do a fucking thing about it. I had a job to do, and I wasn't going to let Gus down. It was time to redirect our conversation before things got out of hand. "So, what do you do for a living?"

"I was working in politics ... helped run my ex-husband's campaign, then started working for Senator Adams, but I quit. I just couldn't take it anymore." She reached for the bottle of vodka and poured herself another shot. "Right now, I'm working as a pharmaceuticals rep at a place where my mother used to work. The money's good, and I can work my own hours. What about you?"

"I do a little of this and that, but mainly work in the club's garage. We renovate classic cars." Following her lead, I poured myself another shot. "You like living in Nashville?"

"Yeah, for the most part." She shrugged as she lifted her drink. I watched as she brought the shot glass up to her full lips, letting the cool liquid slip into her mouth. Damn. I knew I was struggling, but I didn't know how much until I found myself feeling jealous of a fucking shot glass. Totally unaware of what was going on in my head, she lowered the glass to the table and said, "I'd always felt safe there, but now ... not so much."

Her words were starting to slur, and her eyelids were getting heavy. If I didn't do something soon, she was going to end up totally wasted. "Hey, you want to go outside and get some fresh air?"

"Yeah, that's probly a good idea," she mumbled as she poured herself a shot. Once she drank it, she stood up with a stumble and said, "I'm fahh-lowing you."

I stood up and took a hold of her elbow as I led her away from the vodka bottle and out the back door. She was a little wobbly, so I guided her over to one of the picnic tables. We both sat on top of it with our feet resting on the bench seat below. I was relieved that it was a nice night out. Tennessee was known for its humidity in the summer, and lately it had been damn near unbearable, but tonight it wasn't so bad. The sky was clear, and there was actually a nice cool breeze. I glanced over at August, and she was looking up at the stars as I asked, "You come from a big family?"

"No, not really. I'm an only child." She was still focused on the sky above as she continued, "Pretty much just me … my mom, my uncle, and Harper."

"And your father?"

"My father was great … *when he was around*. He's long gone now. I haven't heard anything from him in years … He and my mother split a few months after my grandparents died in a car accident," she said, then looked over to me. "You know … I used to think they broke up because Mom couldn't deal with her parents' death, but lately, I've been thinking it's something more."

"Like what?"

"No idea." She lowered herself down on the table and put her hands under her head like a pillow. "We all have our skeletons in the closet. Secrets, lies, and whatever … I have a feeling that my mother's secrets are bigger than most."

"I'm sure she has a reason for those secrets."

"Hmm, maybe." I could see the wheels turning in her head before she asked, "Do you have any kids?"

"Nope. Not yet."

"A wife or girlfriend?"

"Nope. Not yet,"

"Oh, that's nice." She closed her eyes and totally missed

that Riggs and Shadow had just pulled into the parking lot. She also missed the fact that they had a guest sitting in the back seat. Knowing it wouldn't do her any fucking good to see her piece-of-shit ex-husband, I decided it was time to get her back to her room. I stood up and quickly lifted her into my arms, cradling her close to my chest. As she rested her head on my shoulder, she asked, "Where are we going now?"

"To bed."

"Hmmm … *okay*." She wound her arms around my neck and melted into me. "I … liii-ke you. You're sweet."

"Not sweet, August."

"Um-hmm. Yes, you are. The big, bad biker is toe-tally sweet. Gunner … Gunner … Gunner is *sweeeet*."

"What is it about you?" Shaking my head, I entered the clubhouse and started towards her room. "How can you get to me the way you do?"

She looked up at me with drunken eyes as she asked, "I get to you?"

"Um … yeah, *you do*." I kept moving forward then said, "You're gonna have to stop doing that."

"Okay, I'll stop." Without skipping a beat, she mumbled, "What kind of name is Gunner anyway? You got a thing for guns?"

"Uh … no, not exactly." Hoping she wouldn't remember in the morning, I admitted, "I got a thing for getting shot."

"Someone shot sweet Gunner? That's just not right." She laid her head back on my shoulder and said, "Gunner's not your real name."

"No, it's not." I continued down the hallway. "Gunner is my road name. My real name is Cade."

"Cade," she purred. "Ooohhh ... I like that even better. You look like Cade."

"If you say so."

I opened her door and carried her over to the bed, carefully lowering her down on the mattress. I was about to stand when I realized her arms were still wrapped around my neck. She had that come get me look in her eyes as she pulled me towards her and pressed her mouth against mine. I knew I should pull back, but instead, I found myself leaning in, deepening the kiss. I just couldn't help myself. Her lips were so warm, so soft, and having her body so close to mine just felt so right. I wanted to relish the sensation for just a brief moment, but that would turn out to be a mistake. Kissing August James ignited a fire inside of me, a fire that burned me to the core, and I feared I may never be able to put it out. The thought caused me to immediately pull back, breaking our embrace. Disappointment flashed through her eyes as I said, "I gotta go."

"Please don't go. I want you to stay."

"You've had too much to drink. Get some sleep, August," I ordered as I stood up and headed for the door. "I'll check on you in a bit."

"Cade," she whispered. "I'm sorry. I didn't mean ..."

"Nothing to be sorry about." I stepped into the hall and before I left, I told her once again, "Get some sleep."

After closing her door, I went down the hall to Gash's room and told him to keep an eye on August. Once he was positioned beside her door, I headed out to find Riggs and the others to see if they'd made any leeway with David. I wasn't surprised to see that they'd taken him to one of Shadow's rooms—a place no man would want to be.

Shadow was our club's enforcer, and he had a gift for extracting information from the toughest of men. We'd all seen what he could do, so I had no doubt he'd get David to talk. When I stepped inside the room, Gus and Riggs were standing in the corner watching as Shadow bound David's hands above his head. Sweat was streaming down David's face as he tried to pull away from Shadow, but his efforts were in vain. Shadow was simply too strong. Once David was restrained, Shadow secured him to the chains that were hanging from the ceiling. The chains were just a few inches short, making it impossible for David to stand with his feet flat against the floor. As he stood there on his tiptoes, he started shouting, "You assholes are going to regret this!"

"You sure about that?" Shadow slammed his fist into David's ribs, forcing the air out of his lungs. David started thrashing around, pulling at the chains as he gasped for air. Shadow stepped towards him and growled, "Hate to break it to you, Mayor, but you aren't going anywhere—not unless you start talking."

"Just tell me what you want to know!"

Remaining eerily calm, Shadow leaned towards him and growly, "I want to know where your daughter is."

"My daughter?"

"You heard me," Shadow barked. "Where is she?"

"She's been kidnapped or something," he babbled. "I have no idea where she is."

"Now, we both know that's not true, Mr. James." Shadow slipped on a pair of brass knuckles, then punched him in the ribs once again. Before David had a chance to recover, Shadow slammed his fist into his abdomen, and then the side of his face. If he'd hit him any harder, he would've broken his fucking jaw. David was groaning in agony as Shadow growled, "I'm only gonna ask you one more time. Where's your daughter?"

"I ... already ... told you ... I don't ... *know.*"

Then Gus stepped forward and asked, "What's your connection to Sal Carbone?"

"What?" David gasped. "How do you ... know about ... that?"

"That's not an answer," Gus spat.

"He's just some asshole ... he ... he donated money to my campaign."

"Tell me something I don't already know, asshole. And you better make it good or I'm gonna let my brother pull out his tools. Trust me when I say ... *you don't want that to happen.*"

"Okay ... okay. Sal is Anthony Polito's right-hand man ... Polito is some ... kind of mob boss or something. He got wind that I was in need of money, lots of money ... to finish ... my restoration project downtown, so he offered to help me out."

"And why would someone like Polito give a shit about your fucking restoration project?"

We all knew why a man like Polito would want a mayor in his pocket, so none of us were surprised when he answered, "Completing that project ... was the only way I could win the election ... so he offered to help, but he ... he expected me to do some favors in return."

"What kind of favors?" Shadow pushed.

"The kind where I'd make sure ... the cops kept their distance from him and his crew. He was looking to expand his business, and he ... wanted to do it without any hassle from the police," he answered, visibly in pain.

"Have you been making good on these favors?"

David lowered his head as he replied, "More often than I should, but this time …"

"This time *what*?"

"Nothing. I'm handling it," he lied.

Gus looked over to Shadow, giving the nod, and seconds later, Shadow was plowing into him again—this time really giving it to him. When he stepped away from him, David was barely conscious. Gus gave him a moment to recover, then sneered, "I don't like the runaround, Mr. James. When I ask a question, I expect a fucking answer."

David managed to lift his head long enough to nod.

"What did Polito want from you this time?"

"They had an exchange or … something go b-bad … really bad. Cops showed up … without any warning. One of … his top guys … got arrested. He wanted me … to … get him … out, b-but it's not that easy."

"Why's that?"

"The guy … killed a fucking cop." David was bleeding from his mouth and was struggling to maintain consciousness. His eyes fluttered shut as he continued, "I tried telling him … m-my hands are … tied and I needed more time, but he … wouldn't listen to me. He thought I was reneging on our deal … that's why he t-took her."

"Took her? You're telling me Sal is the one who took Harper?"

"Polito. He's the one who took her. He th-thought I'd make good on my promise if he held my daughter's life over my head," he huffed. "He didn't get the fact that I can't just snap my fingers and get this guy off. It took some time, but I got … it sorted."

"Why does he still have her if you got it sorted?"

71

"Because he's waiting until the bail hearing Friday." Suddenly sounding confident, he explained, "I've got it worked out where his guy will be able to get out on bail. Once that happens, Polito will return Harper and this thing will be over."

"And what happens if this guy is considered some kind of flight risk and doesn't get bail?"

"He'll get bail," he answered adamantly. "I pulled a few strings and got him on Judge Michaels' docket. He owes me a favor, and we also have a witness that will testify that the cops didn't give him his Miranda rights. That by itself is enough to get the charges dropped."

"How will he get Harper back to you?"

"As soon as the hearing is over, we'll meet up with him somewhere ... Probably at the diner where we've met before. It's not a big deal. I swear it."

"It's your daughter, asshole," Gus shouted as he slammed his fist into his gut. "It's a big fucking deal!"

Gasping for air, David muttered, "That's not ... what I meant. I know it's a big deal, and I'm telling you ... I'll get her back."

"You better hope the hell you do, because if you don't ... if so much as one hair is touched on her pretty, little head, I'll end you with my bare hands." Gus took a step towards him as he growled, "I have a half a mind to go on and do it right now after the hell you've put August through."

"August?" A look of surprise crossed his face. "Is she h-how I ended up here?"

"She came to us out of concern for her daughter," Gus barked. "If you were any kind of man at all, you'd get that."

"I should've known she had something to do with this.

Dammit! She couldn't just leave it alone," he complained. "That fucking … cunt has been a pain in my ass for two and half years now. Always on my ass … Bitching and moaning when I can't make it to Harper's goddamn birthday party. *Fuck* … It's not like she won't have another one. I should've saved m-myself the hassle and had her dealt with ages ago."

I wanted to punch him in the fucking mouth for threatening August like that, but Gus beat me to it. He reared back, using every ounce of muscle and anger he could muster, and slammed his fist into David's jaw. Before David had a chance to recover, Gus hit him again, knocking him out. "Worthless piece of shit."

When Gus took a step back, Shadow asked, "What do you want me to do with him?"

"Leave him," he ordered as he turned and walked out of the room.

We followed him into the hall and waited for him to cool off. After several minutes passed, Shadow looked over to him and said, "How do you want to play this?"

"I got no idea." He ran his hand through his hair with a frustrated sigh. "If we wait and the guy doesn't get out on bail, they could hurt Harper, but there's a chance that he's right and they'll hand her back over once the guy is released."

"We need to figure out where she is," Riggs suggested. "That way, we'll at least know where to go get her if things go south."

"Agreed. How do you suggest we do that?"

"Call in a few favors? See if we can find someone who's heard something?" Shadow recommended.

Riggs thought for a moment, then said, "I'll do some

more digging and find all the properties purchased by this Sal fella or Polito. Then, we can go to each one and check them out … see if they have her hidden in one of them."

"That might actually work." Gus turned to him and said, "You get me the list, then I'll give Viper a call over at the Ruthless Sinners' clubhouse. He already knows what's going on. I'll have him and his boys check out the locations for us and see if they can find any sign of Harper." He thought for a moment, then said, "First thing, Friday, we'll go to Nashville with David and August to make sure they get Harper back. If not, we'll figure things out from there."

"What about August?" I asked, concerned that she still needed time to sleep off the alcohol. "When you planning on telling her about all this?"

"It's late. I don't see any point in waking her up now." I could see the worry in his eyes as he said, "She's been through hell. Not sure how she's gonna feel when she finds out she was right about her ex."

"That asshole thought he had it rough when we were wailing on him," Shadow scoffed. "Something tells me he hasn't seen nothing yet."

"Whatever she says or does, it won't be enough. That douche-bag deserves to be six feet under for the shit he's pulled," I snarled.

"He'll get what's coming to him. You have my word on that," Gus spat as he turned and started down the hall. "You boys get some rest. We're gonna have a long one tomorrow."

I followed Gus and Shadow back inside, then went back to August's room to make sure she was okay. I relieved Gash, then eased her door open. Just as I expected, she was sleeping soundly. Trying my best not to wake her, I walked over and sat down on the chair, quietly propping my feet up on the desk. As I sat there watching her sleep, I thought about how happy she'd be when Harper was back in her arms. There was just one drawback. After we got her daughter back, I might never see her again. It wasn't a welcomed realization, especially after the kiss we'd shared earlier tonight. When I thought back to the feeling of her mouth on mine, how fucking incredible it felt, it pained me to think that I'd never experience that feeling again. I didn't want her to leave. I didn't want to lose her, but the more I thought about it, the more I realized it was for the best. August James would never, *could never*, be mine. End of story. But damn, it would be nice if she could. No ... It would be fucking incredible.

AUGUST

$\mathcal{I}$ was a mess, completely riddled with emotions —anger, anxiety, and heartache—and they were only growing more intense with each mile we drove. I was sitting in the backseat of the SUV with Cade and Riggs in the front, and we were following Gus, Shadow, and David as we drove towards Nashville. We were on our way to hopefully get Harper back from the men who'd taken her, and I was struggling to get a grip on the feelings I had boiling up inside of me. It was like my worst nightmare had come true. When Cade told me everything that David had shared with them, I was stunned. I'd thought of nothing else since I'd heard the news, and I still couldn't believe that he'd actually put our daughter's life in danger. I knew he was up to something, but I never dreamed it would be something like this—that he'd actually conspired with the devil himself. There was a time when I actually cared for David, loved him, but at that moment, I hated him with every fiber of my being.

I could barely make out his silhouette in the SUV in

front of us, and I couldn't stop staring at him. When Cade noticed that I was practically burning a hole through the back of David's head, he asked, "You doing okay back there?"

"I've been better," I answered as I clung to Harper's favorite stuffed animal, Floppsie. My mother had given it to her years ago, telling her that it had once been mine when I was a little girl. Since that day, Harper always carried it around with her, treasuring it like her own little security blanket. I brought it up to my nose, inhaling my daughter's scent, and I almost missed it when Cade asked, "You've got the plan straight, right?"

Pulling myself from my thoughts, I nodded and said, "Yeah. We'll wait at the convenience store across the street while David meets with whoever is in the restaurant."

He nodded. "That's right. And if something happens and they don't show up, we have a good idea where they're keeping her."

"I'm just ready for this to be over."

"I know you are. It won't be long now."

I was still staring at the back of David's head when I asked, "Do you think it's bad that I want to hurt him ... like *really, really* hurt him? Like ... I'm thinking honey and bee stings, or some crazy Chinese torture kind of thing where they drive toothpicks under his fingernails."

"I think you're being too easy on him."

"Really?"

"Definitely. This guy deserves something major. You're gonna have to get creative ... like some *Games of Thrones* or *Vikings* kind of shit. Something that will leave a lasting impression."

"You're right. He really doesn't deserve to have any

more children." Mischief flashed through her beautiful eyes as she snickered, "I'm thinking an old school castration might be in order, and that's just to start."

"There ya go." He chuckled. "Maybe some peanut butter and a basket full of rats."

"That would be perfect!"

"Damn, y'all. You're making my dick draw up just thinking about that shit," Riggs complained.

"Sorry," I scoffed. "I couldn't help myself."

"No, no. I completely understand. This guy definitely has some bad mojo coming his way. You can count on that."

"I hope so."

Our conversation had given me a brief reprieve from my anxiety, but it quickly returned when I looked out of my passenger window. As soon as I saw that we were getting closer to our destination, I felt my stomach twist into a knot. We pulled up to the convenience store and waited as Gus pulled around to the back of the restaurant and let David out of his SUV. It wasn't long before David came walking down the alley. I watched with disgust as he adjusted his suit jacket and tie before stepping into the diner.

I was biting at the bit as I sat there waiting for some sign of Harper, each moment passing more agonizing than the one before. Finally, after twenty minutes or so had passed, David came walking out of the restaurant with Harper in his arms, and for the first time in days, the tension in my body started to fade and I felt like I could actually breathe. Seeing that Harper was so close made me want to jump out of the SUV and race over to them, but that wasn't an option. I had to stick to the plan. Gus had arranged for us to meet David down the street, away from any watchful eyes, so I just had to be patient for a little longer.

As soon as David was back in the SUV with Gus, we followed them down several blocks to a hotel parking lot. Riggs barely had a chance to park before I was out of the SUV and rushing towards David and Harper. The second I made it over to them, I reached for Harper and pulled her into my arms, hugging her tightly. Tears of utter relief streamed down my face as I cried, "Oh, my sweet baby. I've missed you so much!"

As she hugged me back, she said, "My momma."

"That's right, sweetie. Momma is right here."

David ran his hand through his salt and pepper hair as he sighed and said, "I told them I'd get her back."

I was caught off guard by his black eye, busted lip, and various other bruises and scratches that were covering his entire face, but I didn't bother asking what happened to him. I honestly didn't care. As far as I was concerned, he deserved much more. In just above a whisper, I snapped, "Do not say another word, David, or I swear to god, I'll tell the whole world what you've done."

"You don't know what the hell you're talking about," he barked. "I haven't done anything except bring your daughter back to you."

"You're a real hero, David." I didn't want Harper to hear anymore, so I took her over to Cade's SUV. Once I had her settled inside with Riggs, I picked up her stuffed rabbit and offered it to her. Her little eyes lit up as she reached for it and cried, "Fwoppsie!"

"She's been missing you." Harper hugged the rabbit

close to her chest as I told her, "Momma has to talk to your daddy. I'll be right back."

Harper nodded, and once Riggs closed the door, I went back over to David.

"You're a real piece of work. You know that?" I snapped. "You took bribes from those men, and by doing so, you put our daughter's life in danger! What the hell were you thinking? I should expose you for what you've done ... let the people of Nashville know who they have elected as mayor!"

"I didn't have a choice! My campaign was going down the toilet, thanks to you. I was going to lose the election if I didn't do something!" he shouted. "I'm not going to apologize for fixing the mess you made."

"The last time I checked, it takes two to conceive a child, but if it makes you sleep better at night, *blame me*." I took a step towards him as I said, "I'll gladly take the blame for bringing Harper into this world. In fact, blame me for everything that's gone wrong in your life."

"That's it, August. Spin this into something it's not, just like you always do," he complained. "Don't you ever get tired of that holier-than-thou act you've got going on?"

"Screw you, David." I was too busy giving him the riot act to notice that Gus, Shadow, and Cade had walked over to us. "At least, I'm not in bed with the mob."

"No, you're in bed with a bunch of fucking bikers."

"Watch yourself, Mayor," Gus warned.

David's eyes skirted over them with pure revulsion. "I'm done with this. You and your friends have a nice life."

With that, he stormed off. When he got into a cab, Riggs got out of the SUV and brought Harper over to me. "She's been asking for you."

"I'm right here, sweetie," I told her as I took her into my arms. "I've got you."

I was still hugging her tightly when I heard Shadow ask, "Is it just me, or was that too fucking easy? Polito just handed her over ... no questions asked. Doesn't seem right."

"That's because it isn't. If they took her, there's nothing to keep them from doing it again, or worse," Gus grumbled. "We're going to have to find a way to make sure that shit doesn't happen."

My voice trembled as I asked, "How are you going to do that?"

"Let us worry about that. You just focus on having your daughter back." Gus turned to Harper and me, and as he looked down at her, he smiled and said, "Her pictures didn't do her justice. She's beautiful like her momma."

"Thank you, Gus." I reached up and hugged him. As I held him close, I thought back to what Mom had said about not judging a book by its cover. She couldn't have been more right. Gus might've been a tough MC president, but at the same time, he was kind and compassionate, making me wish I'd had the chance to get to know him even better.

"No need to thank me, August. It was my pleasure." He gave me a quick squeeze, then turned to Cade and said, "Gunner, I'm gonna need you to hang back and stay with them for a couple of days to keep an eye on things."

Concerned that Harper might still be ʿin danger, I asked, "Do you really think that's necessary?"

"Don't want to take any chances." Gus looked over to

Gunner as he said, "You good with staying? Need anything?"

"I'm good. Got a change of clothes in the truck."

With Gus and Shadow following close behind, we walked over to the SUV. I was about to get inside when I heard Gus call out to me. "August?"

"Yeah."

I turned and found him standing behind me with a strange expression on his face.

"I got something I need to discuss with you." He didn't sound like himself—self-assured and confident. Instead, his voice was filled with uncertainty as he continued, "Now isn't the time, but I would like to get in touch with you soon. You okay with that?"

"Yeah. Absolutely. I'm definitely okay with that." The anguish I saw in his eyes made me ask, "Is something wrong?"

"Nothing for you to worry about. Just some unfinished business." His eyes grew even more intense as he ran his hand over Harper's head. He studied her for a minute, then turned his attention to me. We both stood there quietly for several moments and it was clear that he was struggling with something, but I had no idea what. Finally, he broke his silence and said, "I'll be in touch soon."

"Okay." I was beyond curious about this unfinished business but decided not to push it. "I'll be looking forward to it."

He helped me and Harper inside the SUV, and once we were settled, he closed the door. After talking to Cade for a few seconds, he followed Riggs and Shadow back over to the other SUV. Before pulling out of the parking lot,

Cade turned to me and asked, "You said you lived in Hillsboro Village, right?"

"Yes. My address is 802 Cabin's Creek Road."

"Got it."

As soon as he had the address plugged in, he drove out of the parking lot and started towards the house. Knowing my mom was waiting to hear from me, I reached into my purse for my phone and dialed her number. As soon as she answered, I told her, "We got Harper back."

"What? When?"

"Just now. It's a long story, but she's fine. All safe and sound, sitting here next to me."

"Oh, that's wonderful, sweetheart. The best news I've heard in ... forever." I could hear the excitement in her voice as she asked, "When can I come see her? I've missed her so much!"

"Give me an hour or so. I'm going to run her by the doctor's office just to make sure she's okay. You can meet us over at the house when we're done."

"I'll be there. I can't wait."

"Okay, I'll see you then."

When we hung up the phone, I turned to look at Harper. She was sitting quietly as she stared out the window—which I found odd. Normally, she would be talking ninety to nothing, asking questions and trying to tell me something that she thought was cute or funny. I had no idea what she'd been through during the past few days, but it had clearly taken its toll on her. I placed my hand on her little head and asked her, "Are you okay, sweetie?"

"Um-hmm."

She didn't look at me, letting me know she was far from okay. "Can you tell Momma about where you've been? Did they hurt you?"

Without turning to look at me, she shook her head. "No."

"I'm so sorry I wasn't there to get you, baby. I didn't know where you were." When she didn't respond, I leaned over and gave her a kiss on the forehead. "It's okay, Harper. You're with me now. You don't have anything to be afraid of."

My heart literally broke when she turned and looked at me with those dark, sad puppy-dog eyes and said, "I no want to, Momma."

Before I could respond, Cade looked over his shoulder and said, "It's not my business, but you might wanna give her a little time. She has to be a little shaken up by everything that's happened."

"I just want to know if they hurt her."

"I know you do, and she'll tell you when she's ready," he assured me.

"You're right." I looked down at her as I said, "I'll stop pushing."

I'd wanted to talk to him about the night I'd had too much to drink, but with everything that had been going on, Cade and I hadn't really had time alone together. He'd spent the early morning hours helping his brothers prepare for some run they had to make, and he was quiet and anxious while they were gone. I didn't think it was the right time to broach the subject, but I'd held it in as long as I could. His mood seemed better since his brothers' return, so I figured it was time to clear the air.

While I didn't remember every word that was said, I

did remember that I'd kissed him. Even though I was mortified by my behavior, that kiss was absolutely incredible. In fact, it was the best kiss I'd ever had. A part of me thought it would be better to just pretend it never happened, but there was another part of me—a part of me that wondered if that kiss had been just as incredible for him as it had been for me. There was always that possibility that he was completely unaffected and had already forgotten about the brief moment we'd shared. Either way, I felt the need to clear the air. "By the way, I'm sorry about … kissing you like I did. I drank too much and got carried away."

"It's understandable. You were worried about Harper."

"I know, but that doesn't excuse my actions." Suddenly feeling awkward, I looked down as I said, "You were being sweet, listening to me and being there for me, and I had to go and …"

When my words trailed off, he glanced back at me for a moment, then said, "As far as I can remember, you weren't the only one in that room last night … I think it's best if we just put it all behind us and forget it ever happened."

GUNNER

'd always prided myself on being a man who was honest and upfront, no matter the situation. I'd never backed down when things got difficult and had always faced whatever I was dealt with head on, but with August, I found myself not only lying to her, but to myself. It was the only way I could get through this. I decided I'd do the job Gus asked me to do. Nothing more. Nothing less. I kept that mindset as I walked the perimeter of August's house, checking for any security issues that might arise. She lived in a nice middle-class subdivision with average-sized homes that were closed in with their own personal wooden fences. There were people out mowing their yards and walking their dogs, each of them seemed friendly enough, but none of them actually spoke. They just gave a quick wave or a nod which suited me just fine.

As I made my way around to the backyard, I could see August standing in the kitchen with her mother. Samantha was a beautiful woman, just like her daughter, and she had a warm smile. I watched as she and August doted on Harper, hugging and kissing her as they chatted back and forth. Samantha was not only stunning but loving, which made it easy to see why Gus had been so fond of her. I continued forward, and when I made it to the back fence, I noticed that several of the boards were coming loose. I was looking to see how I could fix it when my burner cell started to ring. I pulled it out of my back pocket, and as soon as I answered, Gus asked, "How's Harper?"

"She's good. August ran her by the doctor, and everything checked out fine."

"Good. Glad to hear that. You make it back to her place okay?"

"Yeah. We're here now. Everything's good ... August contacted the detective that was handling Harper's case and let him know she'd been found. He didn't seem surprised."

"He didn't have a lot of questions?"

"Not like he should have. Hell, he didn't even send someone over to corroborate her story."

"That's fucking insane."

"I thought so too. Only person who's even been by here is August's mother, and she was just here to see Harper." Assuming he'd want to know, I told him, "Samantha seems good. Looks just like her daughter."

"Um-hmm ... and her husband? He there, too?"

"No. He's not here." With the run and everything else we had going on the day before, I hadn't had a chance to tell him what August had told me about the husband or Samantha's parents. "I meant to tell ya ... that dude's long gone, Gus. He ran out on Samantha a few months after her parents died. It's just Samantha now."

"Wait ... Samantha's parents died? How the hell did I miss that?"

"No idea. They were killed in some car accident or something several years ago, and the husband left not long after. Don't know much more than that."

"Damn."

"Yeah. I think it took a toll on both of them."

"Fuck. I wish I would've known. It would've been nice to know a lot of things." He paused for a moment, then said, "So, no sign of trouble?"

"No. Everything looks good here."

"Hopefully, it'll stay that way. Just let me know if anything comes up," Gus ordered.

"You know I will."

After Gus hung up, I continued checking the backyard for any other possible issues that would need tending. Once I was finished, I made note to come back and fix the fence, then headed back inside. Harper was in the living room coloring while August was still in the kitchen talking to her mother. It looked like Samantha was about to leave, so I slipped down the hall into the guest bedroom in hopes of not disturbing them. I pulled off my cut and draped it across the chair before sitting on the edge of the bed. I was just about to start taking off my boots when I felt someone staring at me. I looked over at the doorway and was surprised to see Harper standing there. After all she'd been through, I had no idea what I should say or do, so I just said, "Hey."

"Hi."

She stood there, studying me with her brows

furrowed and her head cocked to the side. Something was clearly bugging her, but I had no idea what it was. After a couple of minutes, I asked, "You got something on your mind?"

"You bad man?"

"No, sweet-pea. I'm not a bad man." I tried to keep my voice calm and steady as I told her, "I came here to keep you and your momma safe."

Her chubby, little cheeks were rosy red, and her hazel eyes were wide and full of hope as she asked, "Fwom bad man?"

"Yeah, from the bad man."

She took a step closer, then whispered, "I no wike bad man."

"I don't like the bad man either." I didn't want to push her, but I had to ask, "Did the bad man hurt you?"

"He skeer me."

"He did?"

"Um-hmm." She nodded. "He mean and skeerwie"

Her little eyes filled with tears, and it nearly gutted me. "How was he mean and scary?"

"He welded bad wods at me and Gab-we-ella."

"Who's Gabriella?"

"I dunno?" She shrugged. "A gorwl."

"Was she a little girl like you or a big girl?"

"Big wike Bar-bee. See pweddy … see was nice to me." She took another step closer as she said, "Da bad man wock-ded us in da woom. I no wike it. She no wike it. I wa-ned my momma, buh he no wet me see her."

"I'm sorry he did that, but I'm here now." I looked her in the eye as I promised, "I won't let him scare you like that again, Harper."

Her eyes grew wide with hope as she asked, "You pwomise?"

"Yeah, sweet-pea. I promise." Relieved, she eased over to me and wrapped her arms around my neck, hugging me tightly. I gave her a quick squeeze and patted her on the back as I told her, "Everything's going to be okay. I promise."

I was just about to release her when I noticed August standing in the doorway. When I saw that her eyes were red with tears, I knew she'd overheard our conversation. Harper took a step back, and when she looked at me, the tears were gone and she was actually smiling. "You wanna nack?"

"Yeah. A snack would be great."

She reached for my hand and gave me a quick tug. Chuckling, I stood up and followed her over to the door. When she reached August, she said, "We wanna nack, Momma."

"Okay, sweetheart. Let's go to the kitchen and see what we can find." As we stepped into the hall, August looked over to me and whispered, "Thank you."

"Nothing to thank me for. That was all her."

When we got to the kitchen, I noticed that Samantha was no longer there. "Your mom leave?"

"Yeah. She had something she needed to take care of, but she's going to stop back by tomorrow. And if I know her, she'll keep stopping by until she knows we're okay."

"Can't blame her there."

Harper started opening all the cabinets, sifting through all the different crackers and chips, and an excited look crossed her face when she came across a bag of orange fish-shaped crackers. As she took out the bag, she announced, "Gowd Fish are my fave-wit."

"What do you know? They're my favorite, too."

August grabbed a couple of bowls and filled them with crackers, then went over to the fridge to grab a couple of drinks. "Do you guys want to eat outside on the porch or in the living room?"

"I wanna watch cawtoons," Harper announced.

"You got it."

We carried the snacks into the living room and turned on the TV. Once Harper had found her favorite show, she curled up on the sofa next to August while I sat down in the recliner next to them. We sat there watching one episode after the next until it was well after dark. When August realized what time it was, she stood up and gasped. "Oh my goodness! It's almost eight, and I haven't even gotten dinner started."

"No need to go to any trouble ... at least not for me. I'd be good with a pizza or Chinese. My treat?"

"Hmm ... Chinese does sound pretty good."

"Then, Chinese it is. You got a place that delivers?"

"I sure do."

"Good deal. Order whatever you two might want, and I'll have the sesame chicken." I reached into my back pocket for my wallet. "And order a couple of extra egg rolls."

"You got it." August pulled up the restaurant's number on her phone, then called in our order. As soon as she was done, she looked over to Harper and said, "Okay, peanut. Let's go get you a bath and into your pajamas before dinner gets here."

"Kay," Harper answered as she followed her mother down the hall.

Moments later, they were both in the bathroom talking, but I couldn't make out what they were saying because the tub was running. When the water turned off, I heard August say, "Yeah, I like him too."

"Is he gonna wiv wit us?"

"No, sweetheart. He's just staying a few days to make sure everything's okay."

"Oh."

"What's wrong, baby?"

Harper's voice was low, in almost a whisper, but I could hear the fear in her voice as she answered, "I no wan da bad man to come back."

"Well, Cade's here to make sure that he doesn't," she said as the water splashed around. "Now, let's get you cleaned up before our dinner gets here."

A few minutes later, August and Harper returned to the living room. Harper was now in her pajamas, and her hair was still damp from her bath. She rushed over and asked, "Wanna watch a movie?"

"Sure. What movie do you wanna watch?"

Harper rushed over to the DVDs, she happily shouted, "*Fwozen!*"

"Harper, I doubt Cade wants to watch another cartoon," August fussed.

"Are you kidding?" I smiled. "Cartoons are my favorite."

"We can find something else."

"No, it's fine. Really."

"Okay." August looked over to Harper and said, "You can put it in."

We both watched as Harper slipped the disc into the DVD player. As soon as the movie started playing, Harper went over and crawled up on the sofa with August. The movie hadn't been playing long when the doorbell rang. I got up and got the food from the delivery man, then carried it into the kitchen. August came over to give me a hand, and once we had our plates made, we took them back in the living room with Harper. We continued watching Harper's movie as we ate, and when we were done, I brought the plates back into the kitchen and put them in the dishwasher. By the time I returned, Harper was sound asleep in her mother's arms. "She's finally played out."

"I see that. You want a hand getting her to her room?"

"Do you mind? She's got me kind of pinned in."

I leaned down and slowly slipped my hands underneath her. Careful not to wake her, I slowly lifted her into my arms. August pulled herself up off the sofa, and I followed her into Harper's room. Once she'd pulled back the covers, I lowered Harper onto the bed, then quietly took a step back so August could tuck her in. Harper looked like an angel lying in that little bed, and it was hard not to just stand there and watch her sleep. Not realizing what I was doing, I quietly muttered, "Damn, she's getting to me too."

"What?" August asked.

"Nothing." Knowing I needed to pull it together, I looked over to August and said, "I'm gonna hit the sack. Let me know if you need anything."

When I started for the door, August called out to me. "Cade?"

"Yeah?" I asked as she came up next to me.

"I had a really nice time tonight. Thank you."

"I did too." I chuckled. "I may never get that song out of my head, though."

She smiled and rolled her eyes. "Try watching it a million times a day every day for months. It'll try your patience."

"I'm sure it can." I didn't want things to become awkward, so I said, "I guess I best get to bed. Good night, August."

As I walked out of the room, she whispered, "Night, Cade."

I went to my room and closed the door, then lay down on the bed. The second I closed my eyes, the lyrics to that crazy song started going through my head, and I knew then it was going to be a long night.

I couldn't believe my eyes. I was standing at the kitchen window watching Cade push Harper on her swing. She was holding onto Floppsie and laughing as he pushed her higher and higher. It just didn't make sense to me. He was a tough-as-nails biker, and yet he was so unbelievably handsome and sweet at the same time. He'd been so protective of both of us, constantly walking the perimeter of the house, checking windows and locking doors, making sure that we were safe day in and day out. The whole thing seemed crazy to me. I'd seen bikers riding down the road or strutting through bars, but not a one of them looked like Gunner and they certainly didn't act like him. But then again, who's to say how they would act.

I'd never been around a biker and had no idea how they would behave. I was quickly learning that my mother was right— *"you can't judge a book by its cover,"* especially where the men of Satan's Fury were concerned. They'd treated me with nothing but kindness and understanding, and I would forever be indebted to them for helping me get Harper back. I owed even more to Cade. He'd been there to listen to me when I was falling apart. He didn't judge me or think poorly of me for losing it, instead he was just there, helping me get through—much like he was with Harper. I couldn't believe how well the two of them got along. It was like they were long lost buddies, and it did my heart good to see that she wasn't afraid of him, especially after what she'd been through. Hopefully, she and I both could put this horrible experience behind us, and we'd never have to see Polito or his men again. But I had a nagging feeling in my gut that we hadn't seen the last of them.

When I noticed Cade and Harper walking towards the back door, I quickly turned my attention back to the lunch I'd been making. The door flew open and Harper came barreling towards me. As she looked down at the plate, she asked, "What's dat?"

"Lunch. Are you hungry?"

"Um-hmm."

"What about you, Cade? You want a sandwich?" I asked as I looked over my shoulder.

"Sure."

Harper lifted up on her tiptoes, and her nose crinkled with displeasure when she saw I wasn't making peanut butter and jelly. "I no wan dat. It wooks icky."

"It's ham and cheese, Harper. It's not icky."

I'd barely gotten the words out of my mouth when there was a knock at the door. Seconds later, my mother stepped inside carrying a kids' meal from Harper's favorite fast-food restaurant and a handful of balloons. "Hello all."

"What's all that?"

Before she could respond, Harper rushed over to Mom, wrapping her arms around her waist as she shouted, "Gammy!"

"Hey there, sweetheart. I brought you some goodies."

"Ba-woooons!" Harper squealed as she took a hold of them and started running around the room like a wild Indian. "My ba-woons!"

"Harper, come over here and eat your lunch," I scolded. Once she was seated, I looked over to Mom and said, "Are you hungry? I have an extra sandwich."

"Sure. I could have a bite."

"Well, come on. It's ready."

Cade walked over, and as he picked up a plate, he told me, "I'm gonna take this outside."

"Don't be silly," Mom fussed. "Come sit with us."

She grabbed her plate, then motioned for him to follow us over to the table. Even though Harper was busy tugging at her balloons, she'd managed to eat half of her chicken nuggets. To my surprise, she took one of the strings and offered it to Cade. "You wan one?"

"I love balloons, but you keep 'em." He smiled. "I'll show you a trick later."

"What kind a twick-k?"

"It's a secret." He smiled. "I'll show you tonight before you go to bed."

"Pwomise?"

"Yeah, I promise."

"Harper, are you finished with your chicken?"

"Um-hmm," she nodded.

"Then, you can go play."

With that, Harper got up and carried her balloons to

her bedroom. Once she closed the door, Mom turned to Cade and asked, "How long have you been with the club?"

"Several years now." He took a bite of his sandwich, then said, "I started prospecting when I got out of the military."

"What about Cyrus and Moose? Are they still with the club?"

"Yes, ma'am. I think T-Bone might've been around back then too."

Mom smiled as she nodded. "Yes, I remember T-Bone. I had some really good times hanging out with that crew."

"They're definitely a handful, but they're really good guys, especially Gus. I've never known anyone like him."

"Yeah, he's a one of a kind." She stopped mid-sentence, and a sad look crossed her face. "You know, I can still remember the night we met ... Oh ... um ... Never mind. That was such a long time ago."

When she picked up her plate and carried it over to the sink, I asked, "Is something wrong?"

"No, nothing's wrong. I'm just going to check in on Harper for a minute." As she started towards Harper's room, she explained, "I can't stay long. I'm playing bridge at Connie's this afternoon, and I don't want to be late."

"Okay." Seconds later, she disappeared into my daughter's room, leaving me alone with Cade. I turned to him and asked, "What do you think that was about?"

He shrugged. "No idea."

"Well, something is definitely going on."

When we finished eating, I cleared off the table while Cade went out to check things around the house for the hundredth time. I'd just started putting the dishes in the sink when Mom came scurrying by. She opened the front door, and as she headed outside, she shouted, "I'm gone. I'll give you a call later!"

I was about to go after her, but stopped when I looked out the window and saw that she was already in her car. It was clear something was bothering her, but I would have to wait to see what it was. I finished putting the dishes away, and after I checked in on Harper, I went back into the living room. Cade had returned from outside and was sitting on the sofa watching the news. As I sat down next to him, I remembered something he'd said to Mom. "I didn't realize you were in the military."

"Yeah." He shrugged. "I probably would've stayed in longer, but I got shot and it blew out my shoulder."

I cocked my eyebrow and gave him a playful smile. "Is that what you were talking about when you said you had a thing for getting shot?"

"You remembered that, huh?"

"Yeah, I remember lots of things about that night." I giggled. "So, spill it. Is that why you got the nickname?"

"Let's just say it didn't help matters." He chuckled.

"What about your family? Do you still see them?"

"Not as often as I should, but it's complicated."

I could tell by the sound of his voice that it was a touchy subject, which was a feeling I knew all too well. "I understand. Mine is pretty complicated, too. The whole thing with my dad leaving and my grandparents' dying was tough, but it was complicated long before that."

"How so?"

"It's hard to explain. My mother didn't exactly get along with her parents, but she tried to pretend everything was perfectly fine, especially when other people were around." His leg brushed against mine as I spoke. It was just a simple touch, but it sent a small shiver down my spine, making me wish it would happen again. Before I realized what I was doing, I found myself leaning towards him as I continued, "It was like they were always putting on a show, and I hated it. I think my mother did too."

"Your grandfather was the governor at one time, right?"

"He was, and he reminded us of it all the time. He believed we owed it to him to be on our best behavior at all times, but my grandmother was worse about it, especially with my mom." He shifted in his seat, casually inching closer. I could smell his cologne, feel his arm against mine, and I was finding it difficult to keep my train of thought. "I'm pretty sure she's the reason why my parents got together."

"What makes you say that?"

"I overheard them talking about it. I didn't get the whole conversation, but from what I gathered, my grandmother thought their marriage would be good for my grandfather's campaign ... or something like that." I shrugged. "It was a long time ago. I was just a kid, and I probably heard it wrong."

"Sounds like your mom might've had a hard go of it."

"She did, but when it was just us ... when she was away from Dad and her parents, things were different. She could be herself with me. Those were the times I liked best."

"My mom and I were always close like that. Never had much of a relationship with my dad."

"Oh, really? Why's that?"

"He has Asperger's Syndrome. It's different for everyone, but for him, communication seems to be the hardest. He's never been all that great with people … Unfortunately, that included me." He ran his hand through his hair and sighed. "It wasn't easy having a father that I couldn't talk to. I couldn't get his input on girls or even football. He was only interested in his own stuff. Never mine."

It pained me to hear the sorrow in his voice, and I wished there was something I could say to take some of that hurt away. "I'm sorry, Cade. That had to be hard for you."

"I learned to deal with it. We all did." He chuckled, then said, "My sister tended to use his lack of interest in us to her advantage. Hell, the girl got away with murder."

"Most daughters do." Curious, I asked, "Were you two close?"

"Yeah. I guess you could say we were like most brothers and sisters. We put up with each other when we had to. She knows I'd be there for her if she needed me, and she'd do the same for me."

"That's awesome. I always wished I had a brother or sister." I sighed as I thought back to my childhood, and all those long afternoons when I was left to play alone. "My dad felt the same way, but my mother was adamant about not having any more children. So, it's always just been me."

We continued to talk for several hours, sharing stories about our childhood and later years. Cade would get up from time to time to check things outside, but we'd pick right back up with our conversation as soon as he returned. I listened intently as he told me about the day he'd met Gus in the bar, and weeks later, when he'd gone to the clubhouse for the first time. It was clear from the way he spoke that he cared a great deal for the men in the club, especially Gus. I got the feeling he'd filled a void for Cade, and that was a big draw for him when it came time to join Satan's Fury. He also told me about some of the brothers he was closest to, and how their lives had changed when they each met their significant other. I'd met Shadow and Riggs but had yet to meet Blaze, one of the other guys he'd mentioned. It was hard to believe that these men who seemed so fierce, so intense, were the same men in the funny stories he shared. I loved hearing him talk about his life with them and was looking forward to hearing more, but our conversation was cut short when my cell phone started ringing. I got up to answer it and was aggravated to see that it was David.

"What do you want, David?"

"I was calling to check on Harper. How's she doing?"

"She's fine, no thanks to you," I snapped.

"Has she said anything about ... you know ... where she was and who had her?"

"No, David. She's a very confused little girl who's just glad to finally be home."

"I'm really sorry about that. I wish—"

"Save it. I don't want to hear any of your lame apologies," I huffed. "You've gone too far this time ... There's no coming back from this."

"You're wrong, August. I just need a chance to explain."

"Explain what? How you got involved with the mob and put our precious daughter in danger? 'Cause I'd love to hear you try to explain that."

"I've already told you. I'm sorry that they brought

Harper into this. That wasn't supposed to happen. I would never intentionally put Harper in danger!" he shouted.

"I wish I could believe that, but after all that's happened, I just can't. And once I tell everyone what you've done, no one else will believe a word you say either."

"You can't do that, August," he pleaded. "I'm up for re-election. Something like this could ruin me."

"I hope so."

"August ... I know we've had our disagreements, but we have history. We were married ... we were happy once, really happy ... and I'm still Harper's father. That has to mean something."

"It did once, but now ... it means nothing." I was done listening to him carry on, so I said, "I'm done, David. I'm done with all of it, and by this time next week, you'll be done too."

"I can't talk you out of this?"

"Not a chance."

"I'm sorry to hear you say that."

Before I had a chance to respond, the line went dead, and I was left wondering what he meant by his last statement. Choosing not to let him get to me any more than he already had, I tossed my phone on the table and went into the kitchen for a bottle of wine. I poured myself a small glass and took a quick drink. I inhaled several long, cleansing breaths, trying to steady my anger. Once I'd gathered myself, I returned the bottle back to the cabinet. I hadn't realized that Cade had walked up until I heard him ask, "Are you okay?"

"Yeah, I'm fine. David has a way of getting to me, and I just needed a second to clear my head."

"Wanna talk about it?"

"Not really. Besides, I need to get dinner fixed." I had no idea what I was going to cook, so I went over to the refrigerator and opened the door. When I saw a package of hamburger meat, I turned to Cade and asked, "How do burgers sound?"

As I'd hoped, Cade was totally on board for grilling. I made up the burgers while he lit the grill, and it wasn't long before we were all sitting at the table eating. I watched as Cade and Harper bantered back and forth, and if I hadn't known better, I would've thought they'd known each other for years, not just a couple of days. I was pretty much amazed by them both. Cade was just so good with her, knowing exactly how to get her to open up and make her laugh, and Harper played along with his jokes and even threw some back at him. They were quite the pair, and it made me wonder what it would be like if Cade didn't leave in a few days—if he stayed and became a permanent fixture in our lives. I knew in my heart it was just some silly fantasy. Cade was only with us because Gus had ordered him to, and since the day I shot him down at the gas station, he'd shown little to no interest in me. To think he would want to stay here with us was utterly ridiculous. I was silently cursing myself for having such ludicrous thoughts when Cade looked over to me and asked, "Is everything okay?"

"Yeah, I was just thinking." I stood up and started clearing off the table. "Do you have any idea how long Gus expects you to stay here?"

"I'd suspect a couple more days. Why? Am I already wearing out my welcome?" he scoffed.

"No, not at all," I replied quickly. "I was just curious. That's all."

He grabbed the remaining dishes and brought them into the kitchen as he asked, "Are you sure? 'Cause I can make myself more scarce if I need to."

"No, Cade." I turned to face him, and I couldn't hide the emotion in my voice when I said, "I like having you around, and so does Harper. So, please don't make yourself scarce. Okay?"

"Okay, August. Whatever you want," he said, placing his hand on my shoulder.

Oh, how I wished I could tell him what I really wanted —that I found him unbelievably attractive and lay awake at night imagining what it would be like to share my bed with him night after night. Sadly, I'd never have the guts to say those things to him. Besides, if he knew what was really going on in my mind, he'd think I'd completely lost it. Hoping I hadn't already said too much, I gave him a quick nod, then turned to Harper and said, "It's time for bed, sweetie."

"Do I haf to?"

"Yes, sweetie. Otherwise, you'll be a grumpy monkey tomorrow."

"No, I won't."

"Harper," I scolded.

With a big pout on her face, Harper climbed down from the table and started towards her bedroom. Just as she got to her door, she looked back and asked, "What bout da twick?"

"What trick?"

"Da twick wit da bawoon?"

Smiling, Cade got up and walked over to her as he said, "I'm going to need one of the balloons."

"Kay." With a wide smile, Harper rushed into her room and quickly returned with one of the balloons. As she offered it to him, she asked excitedly, "Whas da twick?"

"Hold on. I'll show ya." He notched a hole at the end, then brought it up to his mouth, inhaling some of the helium. His voice went high and squeaky as he started to sing, "Let it go ... let it go!"

Harper started laughing as she said, "You silly."

"You want to try?"

Harper nodded, and after he explained everything she'd need to do, Harper took her turn in making a silly voice. They both did it several more times, and when the balloon was finally out of air, I told her, "All right, kiddo. Time for bed."

I followed behind her as she went into her room. Once I had her tucked into bed and was sure she was sleeping soundly, I went to the living room. Cade was sitting on the sofa watching TV. I sat down next to him, and an awkwardness settled between us, making me regret that I'd ever mentioned anything about how long he would be staying. Neither of us spoke as we listened to the news anchor ramble on about the upcoming mayor's campaign. I had no idea how long we'd been sitting there, giving each these quick side glances like a couple of high school teenagers, when I heard a strange noise outside. Curious, I got up and walked over to the side window. "Did you hear that?"

"Hear what?"

"I don't know. It just sounded like someone was out there."

"Move away from the window," Cade ordered as he took his gun out of his ankle holster. He opened the door and said, "Stay put."

Fear washed over me as he disappeared into the darkness. I stood frozen in the middle of the living room, waiting for some sign that Cade was okay, and no one had come to take Harper from me again. I couldn't bear the thought and was overcome with relief when he returned ten minutes later and said, "All clear."

"Are you sure?"

"Yeah." He made his way over to me, then said, "It must've been a cat or something, 'cause there was no sign of anyone out there."

"What if they come after Harper again?"

"I'm here to make sure they don't."

I could feel the panic building deep inside of me as I asked, "But what happens when you're gone?"

"I'm not leaving until we're sure that's not gonna happen, August." He brought his hands up to my face, cupping my cheeks as he whispered, "I'm not going to let anything happen to either of you."

I let his words sink in, and slowly my anxiousness started to subside. I expected him to release his hold on me, but he didn't. Instead, he just stood there with his gorgeous eyes locked on mine. Before I realized what was happening, he'd leaned towards me with his mouth just inches from mine. Our breaths mingled as he hovered over me, and just when the anticipation was becoming too much to bear, he pressed his lips against mine, kissing me passionately. God, he felt so good, smelled so good, and I couldn't help but let myself get swept away. My hands roamed over the perfectly defined muscles of his glorious chest, then around to his back as I inched closer. It had been so long since I'd been in the arms of a man, but even then, it never felt like this. Never so arousing, so intoxicating. I was no longer concerned with the rest of the world. David, those men who'd taken Harper, and everything in between became nothing more than a blur that was banished into the far recesses of my mind. The only thing that mattered was touching him, kissing him, and feeling the heat of his body against mine. Without thinking of the consequences, I reached for the hem of my t-shirt and quickly pulled it over my head, tossing it to the floor. He did the same, and then we started kissing once again. The kiss quickly became heated, and we both were losing all sense of control when Cade eased back, breaking free from our embrace as he rested his forehead against mine. *"Damn.* I'm sorry, August. I didn't mean for that to happen."

"Why are you apologizing?" I looked into his eyes, pleading for him to understand, as I whispered, "Don't you see? I want this, too."

"It doesn't matter what we want. We can't do this … we can't. You're Gus's …" He shook his head with exasperation. "I'm supposed to be here protecting you."

"And you are. You've done exactly what he's asked you to do. He doesn't have to know about this. In fact, nobody has to know. It's just you and me." I stepped towards him and placed the palms of my hands on his chest as I continued, "It's just one night."

"I don't know if I can do that, August." The man who'd shown nothing but confidence seemed so uncertain as he stood there looking down at me. His voice was low and raspy, filled with so much angst and need, and I felt as if my soul had been set on fire when he finally said, "You've got no idea how much I want you ... how much I've wanted you since the first moment I laid eyes on you. It's been fucking torture for days, and I'm telling you now, there's no way in hell one night is ever going to be enough. *Not even close.*"

"Maybe you're right, but maybe you're not." As I took his hand in mine and started leading him down the hall, I smirked and said, "There's only one way to find out."

GUNNER

Ohen we reached the foot of her bed, she turned to face me, and my eyes never left hers as she slipped her arms around my neck. She studied me for a moment, then drew me closer, softly pressing her mouth against mine. *Damn.* I wasn't just losing the battle. I'd already lost it. Hell, I was practically waving the white flag of surrender when we kissed earlier. But this kiss? No, this one was something different all together. This kiss was filled with a hunger that matched my own, and I simply wasn't strong enough to resist the temptation, especially when she kept inching closer. Her body melted into me as her tongue brushed again mine, and then it was over. I'd had all I could take. I was done fighting it. I'd wanted August James since the moment I laid eyes on her, and I was damn well going to have her. To hell with the consequences.

A soft whimper escaped her lips as I pulled her body closer to mine. My hand reached for the nape of her neck as I eased back and whispered, "You sure about this?"

"Yes." She nodded as she confirmed, "No overthinking things. Like I said … this is just for tonight."

Her hands reached behind her back and removed her black lace bra, exposing her perfect, firm breasts. Damn. She didn't shy away from me as I watched her start unbuttoning her jeans, slowly inching them down her long, slender legs. She just stood there wearing only a pair of black panties with her long hair flowing down around her delicate shoulders. So fucking sexy. "There you go again. Getting to me. You're becoming good at it. Too good."

"Is that a bad thing?"

"Ask me that again tomorrow."

"Well, in case you didn't know … you're getting to me too."

She stood there staring at me with needful eyes, waiting for me to make my next move. Damn. It was one surprise after the next with her. I could hardly restrain myself with her standing there, looking so undeniably beautiful. The only thing that got me through was seeing that spark of anticipation in her eyes as she watched me start to undress. The tip of her tongue slowly dragged across her bottom lip as I lowered my jeans and boxers down my hips and tossed them to the side.

With her eyes locked on mine, I took my aching cock in my hand and gave it a hard squeeze, trying to relieve some of the throbbing pressure that had been building since the moment we'd first kissed. I could feel my pulse raging against my fingers as I slowly stroked it, groaning out a curse as I felt it continue to harden in my grip. August took a step closer, her eyes focused totally on the motion of my hand as she made her way over to me. She lowered herself to her knees, replacing my hand with her own as she took hold of my cock. "Do you mind?"

I felt the warmth of her tongue rake against me right before she took all of me into her mouth. Her caresses were long and firm as she took me deeper, making it damn near impossible not to come right then and there. I wouldn't let that happen. "Fuck," I groaned.

After just a few more strokes, I reached for her and lifted her to her feet, tossing her sexy little body onto her bed. Her hands dropped to her hips as she quickly lowered her panties, inch by inch, down her long, sexy legs. I held her gaze as she kicked them off of the bed. She lay there with her naked body sprawled across the bed as she waited for me to come to her, and I couldn't imagine a more beautiful sight. I looked down at her, every fiber of my being aching to touch her, and asked, "Do you have any idea how incredible you are?"

I didn't wait for her to answer as I lowered myself between her legs. I needed to taste her, to see for myself just how turned on she really was. She started to squirm beneath me as I tormented her with my mouth. The warmth of her naked body enveloped me, and I could feel my need for her building, burning deep inside my gut. *Fuck.* My hands slid under her ass, pulling her closer to my mouth as the taste of her drove me wild. Her fingers dug into the sheets and her back arched off of the bed as I pressed the flat of my tongue against her sensitive flesh. She was close to the edge, and I couldn't wait a minute longer. I had to be inside her, so I reached for my jeans and took a condom out of my wallet. Once I'd slipped it on, I lowered my body between her legs and watched as a small smile of relief spread across her face.

"Yes, Cade. Yes!" she moaned as I centered myself at her entrance. She wrapped her legs around my waist, pulling me to her, and coiled her arms around my neck. I felt her tremble beneath me as I slid deep inside and paused for several breaths as I relished her warmth. I'd imagined the moment many times in my head, each one more detailed than the last, but never had I dreamed it would feel so fucking good. I started to move, rocking against her until I found the steady, hard pace that would drive her over the edge. I wanted to see her orgasm take hold, to watch her body grow rigid as she found her release, and to hear scream out my name. I began to drive deeper, harder, and her head reared back as she moaned, "Oh, please ... Don't stop!"

That was it. That was exactly what I wanted to fucking hear. Her nails dug into my lower back as her hips bucked against mine, meeting my every thrust with more force and more intensity. I could feel the pressure building, forcing a growl from my chest.

"Fuck," I groaned as she tightened around me. She panted wildly, and her thighs clamped down around my hips when I tried to increase my pace. I knew she was close, unable to stop the inevitable torment of her building orgasm. The muscles in her body grew taut, her chest stilled as she held her breath, and finally I heard the sound of air gushing from her lungs as her body fell limp in my arms. I continued to drive into her, the sounds of my body pounding against hers and echoing throughout the room until I finally came inside her.

I lowered myself down on her chest, resting for a brief moment before I rolled to my side and pulled her over to me.

The room stilled as she nestled up next to me and rested her head on my shoulder. After several moments our breaths started to slow, and just as the lustful haze started to fade, August looked up at me and said, "So ... I think you might've been right about the one night thing. It's definitely not going to be enough."

I smiled as I told her, "I tried to warn you."

"Yes, you did, but in my defense, I had no idea it could be like that."

Surprised, I asked, "What do you mean?"

"Sex." She shrugged slightly. "I didn't know it could be like that."

"Like what?"

"Oh, nothing." She shook her head with embarrassment. "I don't know why I said anything."

"August ... *Tell me.*"

"It had never been that good before," she admitted. "Like, it was really, really good."

"Yeah. It was pretty fucking incredible," I said, then leaned towards her and kissed her on the forehead. "But then ... I knew it would be."

"Oh, really?" she asked with surprise. "And how did you know that?"

"Because you're you. That's all I needed to know."

"See?" She looked up at me and smiled. "I was right. You are sweet."

"You're gonna have to stop saying that ... at least not where anyone can hear." I chuckled. "It would kill my reputation."

"You don't have to worry." She giggled, then added, "I'll do my best to keep your bad-boy reputation intact."

"I'd appreciate that."

The room fell silent as her fingers trailed over the scar on my chest, then over to the one on my shoulder. She eased up on her side as she studied them for a moment, then asked, "So, you really do have a thing for getting shot, huh?"

"Yeah, but I'm still here. It'll take more than a bullet to knock me down for good." I eased up and tossed the condom in the trash, then reached for my boxers. "Are you leaving?"

I motioned towards the door and said, "I wouldn't want Harper to wake up in the night and come in looking for you."

"You don't have to worry about that. Harper is a sound sleeper. A tornado could come through here and it wouldn't wake her up," she assured me.

"You saying you want me to stay?"

"Yeah … If you don't mind … at least until I fall asleep?"

I leaned in and kissed her, long and hard, then said, "I'll stay as long as you want me to."

Once I'd settled back in the bed, August curled up next to me and rested her head on my chest. Damn. I couldn't believe how fucking good it felt to have her lay there in my arms. It was a feeling I'd craved longer than I'd even realized, and I didn't want it to end—not tonight, not ever. I had no idea how Gus would feel about me falling for his daughter, but I owed it to him to be honest about my feelings—even if that meant risking everything, including my place in the club. It was an unsettling thought, but as I closed my eyes and listened to the peaceful sound of her breathing, I had no doubt in my mind that she was worth the fucking risk. I lay there for a couple of hours, waiting until I knew for certain that she was asleep, then I carefully eased out of bed, making sure not to wake her. Once I'd pulled on my boxers and gathered my remaining clothes, I went down to Harper's room. I eased the door open, and just like August had mentioned earlier, she was sleeping soundly. I closed the door, then headed outside to check things around the house. As soon as I saw that everything was clear, I went back to my room and got in bed. It didn't take long for my exhaustion to take over and I fell fast asleep.

The next morning, I woke up to the smell of fresh brewed coffee and cinnamon rolls. I could hear August and Harper talking, but I couldn't make out what they were saying. I pulled on my jeans and a clean t-shirt, then went into the bathroom to brush my teeth and splash some cold water on my face. After I was done, I headed into the kitchen and was surprised to see that August was wearing a pair of dark jeans with a dress shirt and her hair was pulled up. Damn, she looked fucking amazing. I glanced over at Harper and noticed that she was also dressed, and August had braided her hair. It was clear that they were about to leave, so I asked, "Where are you two headed off to?"

"I need to run to the office for a couple of hours, so Mom's coming by to take Harper to the zoo for a little while." She brought me a cup of coffee and gave me a shy smile as she explained, "I wasn't planning on going in for another couple of days, but my boss called earlier and he needs me to sign some papers."

"Is everything okay?"

"Yeah. It's just some projections for next month. It

really shouldn't take long." She paused for a moment, then said, "About last night ... I really had a good time."

"I did too." I gave her a quick wink and said, "We'll talk more about it later."

Before she could respond, the front door flew open and Samantha rushed in with a strange look on her face. "Honey ... there's a black BMW parked across the street that I've never seen before. I think they're watching your house."

Curious to see what she was talking about, I rushed over to the front window and eased the curtain back. My blood ran cold when I noticed that a second black BMW had pulled up with a third coming up behind it. I could feel my pulse racing while I watched one of the doors slowly open and reveal a large male carrying a Mack-10. As he stood up, he tucked it inside his suit jacket and waited for the guy in the front seat to get out of the car. It was clear these guys weren't fucking around. Unfortunately, there were too many of them for me to take out on my own. I had to get the women the fuck out of that house before all hell broke loose. I rushed over, and after I barricaded the front door with the kitchen table, I turned to August and shouted, "Grab your stuff."

"What are you doing? Who's out there?" August shrieked.

"Grab your stuff, August!" While she snatched her purse and keys, I raced over and grabbed Harper. I opened the back door and motioned for August and Samantha to go outside. "Move it."

They didn't hesitate. With wide eyes, they both raced out the door and headed into the backyard. When we made it over to the fence, I pulled back a couple of the loose boards, making an opening for us to get through. I waited as Samantha and August slipped through the fence. Once they were clear, I eased through with Harper, then quickly put the boards back in place. From there, we darted out of her neighbor's yard. When August looked over to me with fear in her eyes, I ordered, "Keep going. Don't look back."

We kept moving forward, passing several blocks before August asked, "What are we going to do? We can't just keep running like this."

"We need to find a car. It needs to be something older …"

I'd barely gotten the words out of my mouth when Samantha asked, "What about that?"

I looked over towards Samantha pointing to an old white church van with crosses on the side. While it wasn't an ideal pick, I figured it would be easy to hot-wire, so I nodded and said, "Yeah, that should do it."

Thankfully, the doors were unlocked, and we were able to get inside without drawing any attention to ourselves. When I started pulling apart the ignition panel, August asked, "What are you doing?"

"Gonna see if I can hot-wire it."

"Do you know how to do that?"

"Um-hmm."

"Wouldn't keys be easier?"

"Sure would." Trying not to get aggravated, I asked, "You got a set on ya?"

"No, but there might be a set hidden inside here." She reached up, and when she pulled down the visor, a set of keys fell in my lap. "Will those work?"

Stunned, I took the keys in my hand and shook my head. "Yeah, they'll do just fine."

I started the van, and seconds later, we were pulling out of the subdivision and onto the main road. We hadn't gotten far when I heard Harper cry, "Momma ... I weft Fwoppsie."

"It's okay, sweetheart. She'll be there when get back."

"I wan her."

"I'm sorry, sweetie. There's nothing I can do about that right now." August tried to keep her voice calm and steady. "It will be okay. You'll see."

Harper's bottom lip pursed into a pout as she looked out the window. I hated to see that she was upset, but unfortunately, there was nothing I could do about it. I had to get them to safety. I reached into my pocket for my burner cell and dialed Gus's number. As soon as he answered, I told him, "We've got trouble."

"What kind of trouble?"

"Three black BMWs just pulled up at August's place, and Gus, these guys didn't look like they were fucking around. They were packing, and there were too fucking many of them for me to take out on my own."

"Fuck! Where are you now?"

"We swiped a neighbor's van, and we're heading into downtown."

"Are Harper and August with you?"

"Yes, and Samantha, too."

"Good. You did the right thing getting the hell out of there. Get them over to the Sinners' clubhouse. I'll text you the address," Gus ordered. "The boys and I'll be there as soon as we can."

"Will do."

Thirty minutes later, we were pulling through the gates of the Ruthless Sinners' clubhouse. They were a smaller club than Satan's Fury but equally as impressive. There were tall security fences surrounding the compound with prospects monitoring all entrances and exits. The actual clubhouse was an old renovated warehouse with various rooms that were much like our own, which included lodging for the members, a family room, and a bar. I'd been there years before but only for a couple of hours, so I wasn't sure if they'd remember me. Even if they did, I had no idea what they'd think when I rolled up in a fucking church van with two women and a kid. Thankfully, the prospects motioned us through. When I pulled up, Viper, the president of the club, was waiting at the front door for us. Before I got out, I turned to August and said, "Wait here."

I opened my door, and as I walked over to him, a concerned look crossed his face. He was older, in his late fifties or so, with long salt-and-pepper hair that was pulled back into a ponytail. He was wearing a pair of jeans, his Sinners' cut, and biker boots, reminding me of Gus. "You guys all right?"

"We've been better, but yeah, we're fine."

"Gus said you ran into some trouble. You thinking these are the same guys the mayor is tangled up with?"

I shrugged. "Don't know anyone else who would be coming after her like this."

"From what I hear, these guys don't fuck around. If they're after Gus's girl, they ain't gonna stop until they find her."

"Or until we find them."

AUGUST

I'd thought I was terrified when I went to Satan's Fury's clubhouse for the first time, but that was nothing compared to the fear I felt entering the Ruthless Sinners' clubhouse. Maybe it was the fact that I had my daughter and mother with me or the fact that we were there to seek refuge from the crazy men who were after us. Either way, I was a nervous wreck as I followed Cade and a man named Viper into a small conference room. When we walked in, there were several men sitting at a long, narrow table. They were talking amongst themselves, but immediately stopped when they noticed that we'd come into the room. Viper turned to us and said, "Have a seat."

Once we were all settled, Cade said, "We appreciate you opening your doors to us."

"Don't mention it. Gus and I are old friends, and I have no doubt he'd do the same for any one of us." As he sat down at the head of the table, he motioned his hand to the man on his left as he said, "First, let me get introductions out of the way."

I nodded. It felt like I was looking at the starting lineup for the Tennessee Titans as I took in the size of the men at Viper's side, only instead of jerseys, these bulked-up linebackers were wearing Sinners' cuts and tattoos. "This here is Axel. He's our VP. Next to him is Shotgun. He's the club's enforcer, and to my right is Hawk. He's my sergeant-at-arms."

"I'm Gunner, and this is August James, Samantha Travers, and the little one on the end is Harper."

"Good to have y'all here." Viper gave them each a half-smile as he said, "Wish the circumstances were better."

Cade nodded. "Yeah, I think we're all in agreement there."

"I don't want to get into the details of everything now, especially with the kid in the room. I just wanted you all to know that we'll do whatever we can to help with the situation."

"I'm sure Gus will be pleased to hear that."

"I figure you're going to be here a while, so I'm getting some rooms lined up for you," he said, then glanced down at his watch. "In fact, they should be ready now."

Hawk stood up and offered, "I'll take them down and get them settled."

"Appreciate it, brother." Viper then looked over to Cade. "I'll have one of my boys come and get you when Gus arrives."

"Sounds good." Cade nodded as he stood up.

I picked up Harper, and Mom and I followed Cade and Hawk out of the room. He led us down a long hallway lined with doors and stopped when he reached our destination. As he opened one of the doors, he said, "These three rooms are all yours. You can decide who goes where."

"Thanks, brother."

"No problem."

Once he was gone, Mom motioned her hand to the door across from us as she said, "I'll take this room across the hall. You two and Cade can have the two adjoining rooms."

"I can take the room across the hall," Cade offered. "I'm sure you want to be with August and Harper."

"No. I'd actually feel better if you were closer to my girls." She reached for Harper and said, "If it's okay with you, I'll put her down for a nap while you two get things settled."

"That would be great. Thank you."

"But Momma ... I no haf Fwoppsie," Harper whined.

I kneeled down next to her and gave her a quick hug, "I know you don't, sweetie, but it's going to be okay. Just go rest with Gammy for a while, please?"

"Kay."

"Come on, sweetheart."

Mom reached for her hand and led her into her room. Once she closed the door, I walked across the hall. After I tossed my purse onto the bed, I turned to Cade and said, "We're supposed to be in here getting things settled, but what's to get settled? I don't have any clothes ... or even a toothbrush!"

"I know. Don't worry about that." He sounded cool as a cucumber as told me, "We'll get whatever you need as soon as Gus and the others pull up."

"This is so insane." I sat down on the edge of the bed

and tried my best to fight back my tears. "Why do you think those men were at my house? Do you think they were there to kidnap Harper again?"

"No."

"So, you think it's just me they're after?"

He didn't have to answer. I already knew the answer.

"But why would they want me. David could care less if I'm alive or dead." As soon as the words left my mouth, I knew the answer to my own question. "Oh, god. They hadn't come to kidnap me. They were going to kill me!"

"August ..."

"I can't believe that this is happening. It's just not fair. I'm not the one who broke the law. I'm not the one who got involved with the mob!" I shouted.

"August ... everything is going to be okay."

"Do you really think these men will be able to help us?"

"We wouldn't be here if I didn't." He took a few steps towards me and placed his hands on my hips as he said, "I'm not going to let anything happen to you, August. You have my word on that."

"I'm going to hold you to that."

He leaned forward like he was about to kiss me but stopped himself. He took a step back and said, "I'm going out in the hall to give Gus a call. Wanna see how far out he is."

"Okay."

When he walked out of the room, I laid down on the bed and tried my best not to obsess over the fact that my ex-husband was the scum of the earth. Unfortunately, that didn't happen. The longer I lay there, the more reasons I found to detest him, and I was furious with myself for ever thinking I could trust him. It wasn't like I hadn't seen the signs. I'd just chosen to ignore them, hoping that he'd change once he'd made it to the top, but deep down, I knew that wasn't going to happen. I should've listened to my gut and steered clear of him from the get-go. At least there was one good thing out of my time with David—my sweet Harper. She gave me the strength to keep moving forward, even when things were at their worst—just like today. For her, I would pull myself together and face whatever was coming head on.

It had been hours since Cade left to call Gus, and I was starting to get concerned. I was just about to step out in the hall to check on him when there was a tap on my door. As he stepped inside, he announced, "They should be here soon."

"Okay ... so, what happens now?"

"We'll talk with Viper and make a plan," he said then stepped towards me. "This is going to take some time, August. You need to prepare yourself for that."

"Are we talking about a couple days or longer?"

"It's hard to say, but I'd say longer. Probably much longer, but we'll know more when we talk to Gus."

My gaze dropped to the floor with frustration. Seeing that I was upset, he reached for me, pulling me against his chest. The bristles of his day-old beard brushed against my cheek when he lowered his mouth to my neck. Goose-bumps pricked against my skin when his lips softly grazed against my flesh. Having him so close set my mind at ease, and I was just starting to relax a little when there was a knock at the door. "They're here. Meet us in the bar."

He immediately released his hold on me and started to leave. "I've gotta go."

"Wait!" I demanded, stopping him in his tracks. "I'm going with you."

A serious look crossed his handsome face as he stated, "Not a chance, August."

"Cade, I'm going," I pushed. "If Gus wants me to leave, then I'll leave."

"Damn you're as stubborn as he is," he grumbled as he walked out into the hall. When we got to the bar, we found Gus sitting at one of the larger tables with several of the brothers sitting beside him and several more standing behind him. They were all talking to Viper and his crew. As we made our way over to them, I heard Viper ask, "You got any idea why Polito's men would be after August?"

"No way to know for sure. If I had to guess, it has something to do with her ex-husband, the mayor. When we were looking for her daughter, we found proof that he was taking bribes from Polito," Gus explained.

"But you got the kid back. Why does that matter now?"

"Because I threatened to expose him," I announced. "He called last night ... tried to make excuses for what happened with Harper, but I wouldn't listen. I was just so sick of listening to all of his stupid lies. I told him that I was going to tell the world what he'd done."

"Yeah, that would do it."

"This is all my fault." I hated that my actions had not only put me in danger, but now, so many others. "Maybe I can talk to David ... persuade him to let it go."

"It's too late for that." Gus's expression grew fierce as he said, "But don't you worry. We're going to handle this, and David James? He's done."

"Thank you, Gus."

"Why don't you go back to your room and see about Harper? We've got some things to sort out."

"Okay." I knew he was looking for an excuse to get rid of me. As I'd promised Cade, I didn't argue. "I'll be in my room if you need me."

When I turned to leave, Cade leaned over to me and said, "I'll be down as soon as we're done."

I nodded, then headed out of the bar and down the hall. I tapped on the door, then eased it open. When I stepped inside, I found Mom sitting at the foot of the bed watching Harper sleep with a concerned expression. My mother had always been strong, always finding the courage to face whatever came her way, but I was beginning to think this was all too much for her. Harper being in danger and now me—was a lot for her to contend with, and I wished there was something I could say or do to ease her mind. Unfortunately, there was nothing I could say that would give either one of us peace of mind. I tiptoed over to her and asked, "How do you think she's doing?"

"This is a lot to take in, and she's really upset about leaving her bunny at the house." She glanced over at Harper as she said, "But she's tough like her mother. She'll be fine."

"You think so?"

"Absolutely. Besides, we're in good hands. This will all be over soon." A concerned look crossed her face when she asked, "Have Gus and the others made it here yet?"

"They got here a few minutes ago. They're meeting with Viper and the others now."

She nodded. "Good. He'll know what to do about all this."

"I'm really sorry you got pulled into this, Mother. If I had known David would pull something like this—"

"There's no reason for you to apologize, August," she interrupted. "None of this is your fault."

"Of course it's my fault. I'm the one who brought David into our lives. This is all my fault, and I hate myself for it."

"August ..."

"Don't, Mom. I'm just frustrated." I let out a deep breath. "I'm going back across the hall to wait for Cade. Let me know if you need me."

I stepped out of her room, carefully closing the door behind me, then walked to my room. There was no sign of Cade, so I turned on the TV and laid across the bed. I felt so useless lying there, flipping through the channels. I wanted to do something to help resolve the situation with David and the men he'd sent after me, but there was nothing I could do. Gus had made it clear that he didn't want me involved any more than I already was, so I had no choice but to wait. I went back and forth from Mom's room to mine, doing my best to entertain Harper, but with each hour that passed, it was becoming more and more difficult. She was hungry and irritable, and so was I. Just as things were starting to get unbearable, Cade appeared with several large shopping bags filled with clothes and toiletries. When he placed them on the bed, I asked, "What's all this?"

"I got a few things. It's not much, but I thought it might help get us through the next couple of days."

I looked into the bags and was surprised to see that he'd bought clothes for all of us, and from what I could tell, he'd gotten all of our sizes right. "How did you do all this?"

"I had a little help, besides it's just a couple of pairs of jeans and t-shirts."

"Well, thank you, Cade. It was very sweet of you."

"No problem." His expression grew serious as he asked, "Did you happen to bring your cell phone with you?"

"I'm not sure." I reached for my purse, and after I searched for several minutes, I looked back to him and said, "I must've left it at the house."

"Good. I wouldn't want anyone to be able to track it. You'll need to make sure your mother doesn't have hers either." He reached into one of the bags and pulled out two burner cell phones. "These are for you and Samantha. Use them if you need to call me. I've already added your number, Samantha's, Gus's, and mine to each of them."

"Okay."

He took the bag that belonged to him, then started for the door. "I'll be back in a minute. I'm going to put these away, and then we can head down to the kitchen. They've got dinner ready for us."

"Okay. I'll let Mom know."

When he walked out, I went across the hall to Mom's room. She and Harper were sitting on the bed playing with a deck of cards when I asked, "Do you have your cell phone with you?"

"No. I left it in my car. Why?"

"Cade wanted us both to use these." As I handed her the burner, I told her, "They already have our numbers added to them."

"Oh, okay."

129

"And he wanted me to let you know that dinner's ready."

Harper jumped up and said, "I wanna eat."

"Me, too. Cade will be here in a second to take us down to the kitchen." When I looked over to Mom, I noticed she didn't seem as excited about the idea. "Is something wrong?"

"No, I'm fine. I think ... I'll just grab a bite to eat later. You two go ahead with Cade."

"Mom ... you haven't eaten anything all day." I could tell from her expression there was a reason behind her lack of appetite. "Is this because of Gus?"

"It's been a long time, August. I'm not sure I'm ready to see him."

"We're going to be here several days, Mom. You can't just hide out in this room the entire time." I reached for her arm and gave her a gentle tug. "Come on. I'm sure he'll be glad to see you."

"I'm not so sure about that," she mumbled under her breath.

Cade came and led us all down to the kitchen, and just like he'd promised, Viper and his brothers had fixed a big meal for us. They were all gathered around the table talking with Gus and the brothers he'd brought from Memphis. We followed Cade over to the table and sat down in the empty chairs next to Shadow. They each took a moment to greet us, then everyone continued talking and eating, except Gus. From the second my mother sat down, he hadn't taken his eyes off her. Eventually, Mom broke his silence by saying, "It's good to see you, Gus."

His eyes were still locked on hers as he replied, "Good to see you too, Samantha."

"I really appreciate everything you and the guys have done to help August."

"Glad we could help."

Her voice was filled with uncertainty as she suggested, "Maybe we could talk later ... catch up on old times."

"Oh, we'll definitely be doing that. Sooner than later."

There was something about his tone that sent a chill down my spine, making me wonder if Mom was right to be nervous about seeing him.

GUNNER

*I*t had been a long day, and it had taken its toll on all of us, so as soon as we were finished eating, I walked the girls back to their rooms. When we got to August's door, I was surprised when Harper turned to her mother and said, "I wanna stay wit Gammy."

"Harper, Gammy's tired and needs to get some sleep."

"It's fine with me, August. I'd love to have her stay with me, but only if it's okay with you."

"Pweez, Momma," Harper pleaded.

"Okay, sweetie. You can sleep with Gammy, but I want you to be a good girl and get some sleep. No staying up late watching cartoons."

"Kay."

August knelt down and gave Harper a hug and kiss as she said, "Good night, sweetheart. I love you."

"Wov you too, Momma."

Samantha took her by the hand and led her into the other room. Before she closed the door, she told August, "Obviously, you know where I am if you need me."

"Same here."

When the door closed, August and I were left standing alone in the hallway. I wanted to grab her up, carry her to my room, and spend the night making love to her, but unfortunately, that wasn't an option. "I'll let you get some sleep."

"Okay, I guess I'll see you in the morning," she said, as disappointment flashed through her eyes.

Once she'd gone into her room, I headed to my own, quickly closing the door behind me. After I got undressed and climbed in the bed, I tried to fall asleep, but as soon as I closed my eyes, my mind drifted to August. It wasn't something new. Lately, it seemed like she was always on my mind for one reason or another. I couldn't help myself. Over the past few days, I'd enjoyed the times I'd spent with her, getting to know her and seeing what made her tick, and I wanted more of it. I glanced over at the bathroom door that connected her room to mine, and I had to fight the urge to go to her. Silently cursing myself, I turned over and tried once again to fall asleep. I had no idea how long I'd been lying there when I heard the bathroom door ease open and the soft sound of footsteps coming towards the bed. When I rolled over, I found August standing at the edge of the bed. She looked absolutely stunning as she stood there staring down at me. "I'm sorry to wake you, but ..."

I eased up on the bed and told her, "I wasn't asleep yet. You okay?"

"No, not really," she confessed. "I just don't want to be alone right now. Do you mind if I lie down with you for a while?"

"Of course not." I moved over and pulled the covers

back. Once she'd made herself comfortable, I asked, "Do you want to talk about it?"

"No, I just want you to hold me. Can you do that?"

"Yeah, I can definitely do that."

I wrapped my arm around her and pulled her close. We lay there for several minutes, silently lost in our own thoughts, before she said, "The Sinners seem like nice guys and their clubhouse is pretty decent, too, but for some reason, I liked it better at yours."

"You did?"

"Um-hmm. I felt safe there. Like I do when I'm at home." She paused for a minute, then said, "I'm not sure I'll ever feel like that again."

"You will. I'll make sure of it."

She nestled a little closer, then stilled. It wasn't long before she fell fast asleep. For the first time that day, I felt the tension in my muscles subside, and as I lay there listening to the soothing sound of her breathing, everything felt right in the world. I knew it was crazy, especially considering how long I'd known her, but at that moment, I realized I wanted more than one night with August. I wanted a lifetime full of them. There was only one way that was ever going to happen. I had to talk to Gus. It was time for him to know that I was falling for his daughter, and I had no idea how I was going to tell him. I must've thought of a hundred different ways as I finally drifted off to sleep.

I woke up the next morning in the bed alone. I got up and showered, and once I was dressed, I went to check on August and Harper. When I knocked on the door, Harper answered with a big smile on her face. "Good morning, sweet pea."

"Mawn-in."

August came up behind her and said, "Hey."

"Hey. You sleep okay last night?"

"Yeah, thanks to you."

"Good. Glad to hear that. How about some breakfast?"

"Breakfast would be great. Let me check with Mom and see if she wants to go with us."

Harper and I followed her across the hall, and once we'd gotten Samantha, we headed down to the kitchen for a bite to eat. We'd just entered the room when Gus came over to me and ordered, "Need you down in the conference room."

"Okay, I'll be right there."

When I turned to August, she motioned for me to go on with Gus. "Go. We'll be fine."

"You sure?"

"I think I can handle getting a bowl of cereal on my own," she scoffed. "Once we're done, we'll go back down to the rooms and wait for you."

Before I could respond, Hawk came up behind us and said, "I'll keep an eye on them. As soon as they're done eating, I'll take them to the family room. Axel's kids are in there watching TV and playing video games. I'm sure they'd enjoy some company."

"That sounds great. I know Harper will love that." August smiled as she said, "Thank you so much."

While it was a nice enough offer, I didn't like the way Hawk was eyeballing August. It was clear from the way his eyes slowly skirted over her that he wasn't just being friendly to his guest. He was interested in her. I wanted to set him straight, tell him to *back the fuck off,* but I couldn't say shit—not until I had the conversation with Gus. Until then, I couldn't do a damn thing. I just had to swallow my pride and watch as he winked at her and said, "No problem, doll."

"I'll come check on you when I'm done meeting with Gus."

"Take your time. We'll be fine."

Knowing Gus was waiting for me, I turned and started towards the conference room. When I walked in, Gus was sitting at the table with Riggs, Murphy, Shadow, Blaze, T-Bone, and Gauge. It was strange not seeing Moose sitting there with my brothers, but he'd stayed behind with several brothers and prospects to keep an eye on things at the clubhouse. As soon as I sat down, Gus said, "I wanted a chance for us to speak alone before we meet with Viper and his brothers. I know I'm asking a lot having you boys come all the way here to tend to a problem that isn't yours, but I wouldn't ask if it didn't mean something to me. I can't tell you why ... at least not yet, but I'm asking you to give me one-hundred percent on this."

"Always," Blaze replied. "Whatever you need us to do. You know that."

"We're gonna need to be careful when it comes to resolving this situation with Polito. We want as little blowback as possible, and that shit isn't going to be easy, not when we're dealing with the Italian mafia."

"I say we kill every last one of those motherfuckers and be done with this shit once and for all," Murphy growled. "Then, we don't gotta worry about any blowback."

"I second that," I said and looked over to Gus. "If we don't wipe these guys out, they're just gonna keep coming back. And that goes for that piece of shit, David, too."

"I agree with you there, but we can't take out the mayor of a city like Nashville without drawing too much attention."

"Then, we find another way to take him down," I replied. "Make the douchebag wish he was fucking dead."

"We'll get to David, you can count on that. But for now, we need to focus on the immediate threat and that's Polito." Gus turned to Riggs and asked, "What about those properties he owns? Do you still have them?"

"Yeah. They're on a file on my laptop. They're four in all—a house, a small office building, and two warehouses," Riggs answered. "They were purchased under a fake company name, but with some digging I was able to connect them all to Sal Carbone."

"Good. We're going to need to get eyes on every one of those locations. Viper's crew can help with that." He thought for a moment, then said, "We need a headcount of all the men he has on his payroll. I want to be able to track Polito's every move."

"I'll get with Hammer and see what we can get set up."

"Good." Hammer was the Sinners' computer whiz. While he wasn't nearly as savvy as Riggs, he'd definitely be able to help Riggs with anything that needed to be done. "We brought artillery from back home, but if we need more, Viper will help us out."

"When you planning on us meeting with them?"

"I told Viper to give us ten minutes, so they should be here soon."

Moments later, we heard them coming down the hall. Once they arrived, Viper took his position at the head of the table with his brothers filing in around us. Gus thanked Viper once again for taking us in and helping us deal with Polito.

We spent the next few hours trying to hash out a plan to take down Polito and his crew. With all the different thoughts and opinions from the Sinners' as well as our own, it took us longer than expected to agree on how to get eyes on our target. Riggs and Hammer would try to hack into their security systems and infiltrate their cameras, enabling us to see inside. Since we had no idea how many men Polito had working for him, we'd have to set up cameras at all the properties that he owned. It was the only way to be sure that all areas were covered and every one of his men were accounted for at all times. Riggs would also try to hack into Polito's cell phone, so we'd be able to track his movements.

A strong plan was starting to unfold, but we couldn't move forward until Riggs and Hammer got the cameras up and working. Knowing we were all waiting on him, Riggs got straight to the task at hand while the rest of us did what we could to prepare for war. I helped Shadow and Murphy go through all the weapons and ammunition we'd brought from home while Viper's guys went through theirs. Once we'd done all we could for the day, we met for dinner, then headed into the bar for a drink. I was sitting at the bar with Gus, T-Bone, and Murphy. It was after nine, and Harper was already down for the night. I knew August needed some time out of that room, so I arranged for one of the Sinners' girls to keep an eye on Harper while she slept. Gus was on his third shot of Jäger-meister, and he hadn't taken his eyes off of Samantha since she walked through the door with August. Without directing his attention at any one of us, he mumbled,

"How is it possible that after twenty-five fucking years, she can still get to me? That shit doesn't seem right."

"That's a woman for ya," T-Bone scoffed as he took another shot. "Always fucking with your head."

"You reckon they know what they're doing to us?" Gus asked. "'Cause if they do, that's even more fucked up."

"I think some do, but the good ones ... *the good ones* have no idea." I glanced over at August, and my entire body tensed when I saw that Hawk was standing next to her. They were talking, and even though I had no idea what was being said, I could tell from his expression that he was trying to make a move on her. Anger surged through me as I sat there staring at him. "But that only makes it that much harder."

"You're right about that shit." Gus turned and looked at me. When he noticed that I was glaring at Hawk and August, he said, "Fuck me. I've seen that look before."

"Huh?" I quickly turned my attention back to him, and that's when I realized he was talking about me. "Prez, I've been meaning to talk you about her, but—"

"Knowing what you know, you gotta have balls to go there," he growled.

"Not like that ... You gotta know, I didn't mean for it to happen," I explained. "Hell, I tried to fight it the best I could, but she got to me. Got under my skin like no woman ever has. The kid, too."

"I trusted you."

"I know you did, and I wouldn't do anything to fuck that up," I tried to assure him. "I care about her, Gus. More than I even realized."

"Fuck, Gunner. I got too fucking much to deal with right now. I don't need this shit, too."

"I get that. I wish I could tell you that I would walk away if that's what you wanted, but I just can't do that." I glanced back over at August, and my chest tightened when I found her staring back at me. She looked so fucking beautiful, with her long dark hair down around her shoulders, and seeing her in those fucking jeans made my entire body ache with need. As she stood there gazing at me, her lips curled into a sexy smile. I'd never seen a more beautiful sight until that ass-fucker, Hawk, said something to her, drawing her attention back over to him.

"She'll end up breaking your heart." Gus warned. "The good ones always do."

"I'm willing to take that chance, besides … the damage is already done. I want her, brother. Nothing I won't do to have her."

"Suit yourself," he said, then his expression grew fierce. "But you fuck this up—you hurt her or Harper, and you'll have to deal with me."

I looked him directly in the eye as I replied, "Understood."

"I've always thought a lot of you. You're like a son to me, Gunner. Don't fuck that up."

"I won't. You have my word."

"Good." He motioned his hand in August's direction. "Now, it looks like you have some business to tend to. Wouldn't want Hawk thinking she was free for the taking."

"Yeah, I have every intention of setting him straight."

When he saw Samantha walk out of the bar and head down the hall towards her room, he downed his shot, then stood up. "I've got some business to tend to myself."

AUGUST

I'd been in the bar for just under an hour, and Hawk had been talking to me the entire time. He was a nice enough guy, charming and handsome. He was tall with pretty green eyes and blond hair. I had no doubt that plenty of women would love his undivided attention, but there was only one person I wanted to spend my time with. Unfortunately, he was at the bar with Gus and the others, and he hadn't even seemed to have noticed that I was in the room. I wanted to think that it was because he was just busy helping his brothers find a way to save my life, but something told me it was more than that. He'd been distant since the moment Gus and the others showed up at the Sinners' clubhouse, and the fact that he hadn't said a word to me since breakfast had me wondering if there was something more going on. I would've tried asking him about it, but between him talking with Gus, and Hawk hovering over me, I hadn't gotten the chance. I glanced over in Cade's direction, and when I found him staring at me, I couldn't help but smile.

Sadly, that was all that became of our little interaction because Hawk started talking again.

"Since you live here in the city, we should get together some time. I could take you out for a ride on my Harley."

"I don't know. I'm pretty busy with work and Harper."

"Surely, you can slip away for a couple of hours," he pushed. "Have you ever even been on a motorcycle?"

"No. Can't say that I have," I admitted.

"Then, you gotta let me take ya. I know you'll love it."

I didn't want to be rude, especially considering the fact that he and his brothers were helping with the situation with David, but the guy just wasn't taking the hint. I feigned a smile and replied, "You're very sweet to offer, but like I said earlier, I'm really busy."

"It's just a ride, August."

I hadn't realized that Cade had come up behind us until I heard him say, "She gave you her answer, brother."

"You got a problem with me asking the lady to take a ride?" Hawk asked.

"As a matter of fact, I do." Cade's eyes narrowed as he looked at Hawk and said, "The lady is taken."

"That's funny." Hawk glared back at Cade as he snarled, "I don't see a fucking ring on her finger or a patch on her back."

"Look, brother. I don't want a problem, but you keep going with this and we're gonna have one."

Hawk took a step towards him with a menacing look and asked, "Is that right?"

"Yeah, that's right." Even though Hawk was bigger than him, Cade didn't back down. He didn't look away or seem frightened in the least. Instead, he looked like he was ready to rip Hawk in two. "Trust me when I say, you don't wanna go there with me."

"Okay, boys. You can stop this right now 'cause I'm not impressed with this whole 'who's the bigger badass' thing you two have going on." I was tired and in no mood to watch these two fight over me like I was some stupid prize. "In fact, I find this whole thing ridiculous. I'm going to bed."

Leaving them both dumbfounded, I turned and walked out of the bar. Even though I wasn't sure why, I was practically fuming as I headed down the hall. It didn't make any sense. I liked Cade. I liked him a lot. In fact, over the past few days, I'd actually started to fall for him, which is something I never expected to happen. After my tumultuous relationship with David, I'd decided that I couldn't go through that again and had sworn off men. Sure, there were moments when I had my doubts, especially when I was around couples or when I was lying in bed alone—night after night. But I didn't have to worry about being lied to or mistreated. I figured if I ever considered dating again, it would be with a super sweet guy that worked in an office, like an accountant or engineer. The guy wouldn't be all that handsome, just an average Joe, but he would be good to me and Harper. I never once dreamed I would fall for a hot biker who took down mobsters and God knows what else. It was at that moment when I realized how little I actually knew about what went on in that motorcycle club. I was busy thinking about what I'd add to the list of different things I needed to discuss with Cade when I finally made it to my door. As I was about to step inside, I heard Gus's voice coming from my mother's room and he didn't sound happy. In fact, he sounded downright pissed.

Curious, I stepped closer to her door and heard him shout, "Why didn't you just have the decency to tell me that I wasn't who you wanted?"

"I did want you, Gus. I wanted you more than anything in this world," Mom cried. "You just don't understand. You'll never know how hard it was for me to walk away."

"Then, why don't you explain it to me, because that note you left on my pillow twenty-five years ago didn't tell me a damn thing!" he roared. "I went to bed thinking we had a good thing. Woke up to you gone, and I never even knew why. You got any idea what that does to a man, Samantha? When you rip their heart out and don't even tell them why?"

"I didn't have a choice, Gus. I knew if I stayed and told you what was going on, you would've tried to convince me to stay. You would've tried to work it out, but there was no way that could've happened. My mother would've ruined you, and you would've ended up hating me. I couldn't let that happen," she tried to explain.

"Your mother? What the hell does she have to do with you leaving?"

"It's a long story," Mom clipped.

"Under the circumstances, I think I deserve to hear it, don't you?" Gus pushed.

"Fine. I'll tell you, but you aren't going to like what I have to say." She paused for a moment, then started, "You might remember that my father was campaigning for governor when we were seeing each other. He'd made a lot of sacrifices to get to that point in his career. We all had. The media was watching his every move, and not just his. They were watching us all, so when my mother found out that we were together, she was furious with me. She thought it would hurt my father's reputation if his daughter was seeing a biker. I tried to explain to her that you were a good man and I loved you, but she wouldn't listen. I know it sounds ridiculous, but she was adamant that I end things and was furious when I refused."

"You never told me that she felt that way."

"I didn't think it mattered. I loved you and wanted to be with you. I didn't care what she thought or what the media thought." My heart ached for them both as I heard Mom say, "I thought, in time, she would learn to accept our relationship, but that didn't happen. Instead, she found a way to make sure we could never be together."

"What the hell are you talking about?"

"She had someone watching you." The room fell silent for a moment, and then Mom continued, "It was a long time ago. I'm not sure if you remember, but you were having some troubles with the club. You wouldn't tell me what those problems were, but I knew they were bad. I just didn't know how bad."

"You're gonna have to give me more than that, Samantha."

"The guy … he had a video of you and the guys at some warehouse. I have to admit, I was surprised by what I saw on that video. You never shared that part of your life with me." She inhaled a deep breath and let it out slowly. "It was hard to see everything, but there was a lot of gunfire. It showed you shooting a man. And not only you. Moose, T-Bone … were all involved in the shooting. Together, you killed six men, but you didn't stop there.

You also burned down the warehouse to cover your tracks. It's all on that video. Mom threatened to take that video to police if I didn't stop seeing you."

"*Fuck.*"

"I knew if I told you about it, you'd say you didn't care ... that we'd find a way to work it out. But I knew my mother, Gus. She'd made up her mind that she didn't want us together, and with her and my father's connections, she would've made it impossible for us to keep seeing one another." My mother's voice was filled with anguish as she said, "You would've ended up in jail. You and your brothers. You would've lost everything you worked so hard to build, and they would've blamed you for it. They would've known that your connection to me cost them their freedom and everything they cared about. I couldn't let that happen. I loved you too much."

"You should've told me."

"What difference would it have made? The end result would've been the same," she replied. "At least, this way you were able to have your life. Your club. Your brothers."

"But I didn't have you ... and I didn't have my daughter!"

"You know about August?"

"Her birthday ... her name. Yeah, it didn't take much to connect the dots. The fucked-up part of all this? I would have never known I even had a daughter if Harper hadn't been in danger."

"I think that's one of the reasons I sent her to you ... I was hoping that you would find out. That the truth would finally come out."

"That's one hell of a way for the truth to come out. Not only do I find out that I have daughter, but also a granddaughter, and that she was missing. You got any idea what that did to me?" I couldn't believe my ears. I was such an idiot. I couldn't believe I hadn't figured it out sooner. All the clues were there. They were like a huge flashing sign saying that I was Gus's daughter, and I totally missed it. Now I understood why he freaked out that day I showed up at the clubhouse. I couldn't imagine what he must've thought—what he was still thinking. It was too much to comprehend. I could hear his footsteps as he paced back and forth across the room. "Twenty-four years I've missed with her. Three years without my granddaughter. That's time I will never get back!"

"Gus ... you have to understand. I did what I thought was best for all of us. I was trying to protect you, and when I found out I was pregnant, my parents pushed me to marry Denis. He knew I didn't love him, but because he thought so much of my father, he went along with my mother's wishes ... pretended that August was his own." Her voice grew soft as she told him, "We had a good life, but he always knew my heart belonged to another. That never changed, and when my parents died, his commitment to me died along with them."

"And yet ... you still didn't come to me. You kept your secrets all to yourself. You didn't even tell August the truth. Made her think that piece of shit Denis Rayburn was her father. You've lied to her all these years just like you did to me!"

"I know. I know all of this, Gus. I'm so sorry I hurt you. I'm sorry that I lied to her, and I kept you both apart for so long," Mom cried. "I just didn't know what to do. By the time my parents died, too much time had gone by.

I didn't know how I was supposed to tell you. It was easier just to pretend that the lie was real."

"Easier for who? You? Me ... August? Exactly, who was it easier for, because where I stand, you were the one who had it easy."

"You might think that, but you're wrong. None of this was easy for me. Every time I looked at August, all I could see was you. Your eyes. Your smile. Even your stubborn spirit. These little pieces of you were a constant reminder of what I'd left behind, and I had to see them every day of my life."

"But you still had her. You got to be there ... to be a part of her life. Do you got any idea what I would've given to be there? To see how beautiful you looked carrying our child. To watch her grow in your belly. To see her the day she was born?" His voice was filled with heartache and anger, and I could feel the tears streaming down my face as I listened to him say, "I would've given the world to see that girl grow up, to be a part of her life, but you took that from me. You say you did what you thought was best for all of us, but you were wrong, Samantha. I should've been there. August should've had a father who loved her, not just some fucking fill-in your mother chose."

"And how were you going to be that kind of father to her if you were behind bars? That would've been no kind of life for you or for her. You can blame me all you want, but the truth remains ... My mother would've made sure you and your brothers spent your life in prison if I didn't walk away. Don't you get that!"

I was furious with my mother for lying to me and for lying to Gus. She'd robbed us both of a real relationship, and I wasn't sure I would ever be able to truly forgive her for that. But at the same time, I understood why she'd done it. While I'd always cared about her, I knew how my grandmother could be. She expected nothing but the best from my mother and others around her, and there would be hell to pay if she didn't get it. She was demanding and often cruel, always going for the jugular whenever she didn't get her way. I had no doubt that she would've used that video to put Gus and his brothers behind bars, especially if it meant getting my mother away from Gus. I remember those nights when I heard my mother crying herself to sleep, but I never understood why she was so upset. Now I knew the truth.

My heart ached for Gus when he said, "Maybe, but at least then I would've known the truth. I would've known why you'd left … why you'd kept my child from me. I wouldn't have spent the last twenty-five years thinking that I wasn't what you wanted, that you didn't love me the way I loved you."

"I loved you with all my heart and soul, Gus. I loved you more than I thought was humanly possible, that's why I did what I did! I sacrificed everything … my happiness, my chance at love, the life I wanted, so *you* could have those things. I loved you that much!" She started to sob as she said, "If you want to tear me down and make me pay for the choices I've made, you can rest easy because I've suffered plenty. I spent my entire life loving a man I couldn't have."

"I don't know what you expect me to say, Samantha."

"I don't want you to say anything, Gus. I just want you to understand why I did what I did. I made my mistakes. I know I did. I know there is so much wrong with this whole situation, but I gave up everything for you. I never loved another. Never had more children because I couldn't bear the thought of carrying another man's child. I only wanted you, and I had to spend every day and night knowing that I'd lost you. It was hell, Gus. It still is. I've never stopped loving you. Even now, I still have all those same feelings for you, and I don't know what to do with that. In my mind, I know I can't change what I've done, that we can never go back, but my heart still longs for you."

"Dammit, Samantha." There was a moment of silence and I thought Gus was about to waver, but then he said, "I can't do this. I just can't."

He started storming towards the door, and before I had a chance to slip back into my room, he appeared in the hall. His eyes locked on mine, and I had no doubt that he could tell that I was crying. Knowing that I'd overheard his conversation with my mother, he stepped towards me and was about to say something when I held up my hand, stopping him in his tracks. "I'm sorry, Gus, but I can't talk about this right now. It's all too much. I need some time to wrap my head around it."

He nodded. "I'm here whenever you're ready."

With that, he turned to leave. I was left sobbing in the hallway alone, heartbroken and utterly confused, and to make matters worse, I could hear my mother crying in her room. We were both a mess, and as much as I wanted to go and console her, I just couldn't do it. I was too mixed up in the head to take on her grief with mine. I started for my door but stopped when I remembered that Harper was sleeping soundly in my bed. Knowing she'd sense that I was upset, I knew I had to collect myself before I went inside. I was wiping the tears from my eyes when I heard Cade say, "August ... are you okay?"

"No," I admitted. "I'm not okay."

"Is this about earlier in the bar?"

"No. This has nothing to do with that." I turned and looked at him. "I mean, we should probably talk about that. Just not now. Right now, I can't even think straight."

"Why? What happened?"

"Oh, nothing much ... I just overheard Gus talking to my mother. If you could call it that. There was more shouting than actual talking, but basically, I just found out that my whole life was a lie."

"I'm not sure I'm following."

"I just found out that Gus is my father."

Without responding, he took my hand and led me into his room. After he closed the door, he wrapped his arms around me and just held me. Nothing more. Nothing less. It was exactly what I needed.

GUNNER

*A*s usual, Gus's gut was right. He knew from the start that August was his daughter. He just needed to confirm his suspicions with Samantha. I hated that August had to find out the way she did, but I was glad the truth was finally out. I knew it would take some time, but August was strong. I had no doubt that she'd find a way to get through this, and I would be there to make sure that she did. As she sobbed against my chest, I didn't speak. I just held her, gave her the time she needed to collect herself, and after several moments, she looked up at me and said, "I can't believe my mother never told me."

"I'm sure she had her reasons."

"Oh, yeah, she definitely had her reasons."

August walked over to my bed, and after she sat down, she told me her mother's reason for walking away from Gus. It was hard for me to hear. I could only imagine how hard it was for August, and it had to be utter torture for Gus. Finding out that she'd given up her own happiness to protect him and his brothers must've been tough, but at least now he knew the reasons behind her leaving all those years ago. I could hear the anguish in August's voice as she said, "I can't believe she sent me to see him without even telling me."

"Maybe she was hoping you would figure it out on your own."

"Yeah. She mentioned something like that when she was talking to Gus, but honestly ... who does that? She sent me here without any clue who Gus was. She didn't even tell me that they were involved, just that they were old friends and she knew he'd help me. The whole thing is crazy."

"You know what they say, 'you can't judge someone until you've walked in their shoes.'" I sat down next to her. "It's clear your mother loves you, August. It couldn't have been easy for her to send you here. She had to know there was a chance the truth would come out. Maybe that's what she wanted. Maybe she just wasn't strong enough to say the actual words. If it was me, I would've built it up much bigger in my head than it really was. I would've assumed the very worst, and for her, that would mean not only losing Gus, but losing you too."

Wiping the tears from her cheeks, she whispered, "She wouldn't have lost me."

"No, but she didn't know that ... at least, not for sure."

"So, what am I supposed to do now?" She sighed. "Do I just forgive her and try to move on?"

"Only you can answer that, August." I took her hand in mine as I said, "You've been through so much. You're still going through it. Just give yourself some time to figure it all out. Samantha will still be here when you do."

"How did you get to be so smart?"

"Hmm, I don't know." I chuckled. "I guess I have my moments."

"What about earlier in the bar with Hawk? Was that one of your moments?" she teased.

"Yes and no," I scoffed.

"O-kay." Her brows furrowed. "I'm not sure I know what you mean by that."

"Let me see if I can explain it to ya." I looked into those gorgeous dark eyes and let out a deep breath as I tried to find the right words to say. "Do you remember the day I came up to you at that gas station?"

She nodded.

"There was something about you that drew me to you, and I knew right then that I wanted you, August. Damn, I couldn't imagine wanting anything more. You were the most beautiful woman I'd ever laid my eyes on. I had to at least try to get close to you, but of course, you shot me down. Didn't even care that you broke my heart," I teased.

"Cade! I didn't shoot you down, and I certainly didn't break your heart. I was freaking out about trying to find the club and—"

"You shot me down," I interrupted. "But that's okay. I'm not a man who gives up easily."

"Well, that's good to know."

"Anyway … later that day, you showed up at the club-house and I thought I was going to get my second chance… But then I found out why you'd come and there was a possibility that you were Gus's daughter."

"So, you knew that Gus was my father?" she asked, then stood up and walked across the room, putting some distance between us.

"I knew there was a chance he was your father, but

nothing had been confirmed." I wanted to be as honest as I could be, so I told her, "Regardless, I couldn't pursue you knowing that was a possibility."

"I don't get it. What difference would it make if Gus was my father?"

"Partly because Gus is the president of the club, and partly because I've always thought of him as a father. I look up to him ... respect him in ways I never could my own."

I could see the wheels turning in her head as she asked, "You didn't want to cause a problem between the two of you?"

"No. For many reasons."

"I get the part about him being like a father to you, but what's the issue with him being the president of the club?"

"You're the president's daughter, August. I know that doesn't mean much to you, but in our world, that's a big deal. You're like royalty in our eyes."

"What?" She crossed her arms and looked at me like I'd lost my mind as she asked, "You do realize how crazy that sounds, right?"

"It is what it is." I shrugged. "Crazy or not, there's nothing the brothers won't do for you, even if that means laying down their lives for you."

"I would never expect anyone to die for me, Cade ... not because I'm Gus's daughter."

"I get that, but we're here for you nonetheless."

"Okay, so I'm the president's daughter. It wasn't like I was pushing you away. Clearly, I was interested, too."

"The president's daughter is off limits unless he gives his consent, but even if he does, it's not always the end of it. If something goes awry, there will be hell to pay," I explained. "But I wasn't worried about that when I spoke to him. I just wanted his blessing. The rest won't be an issue."

"You don't think so?"

"Nope."

"Why's that?" she pushed.

"I have every intention of doing whatever it takes to make you happy," I answered with determination. "Because ... in the end—if you're happy, I'm happy. Simple as that."

"You make that sound easy. I know firsthand, relationships are never easy. Even the best ones have their issues." Her eyes glassed over as her mind drifted for a moment. I was afraid she was going to send me walking until she asked, "So, did you get it?"

"Get what?"

"Gus's consent."

"I did ... right around the time Hawk started making his play on you." I smiled as I told her, "I might've gotten a little carried away, but I had to set things straight with him."

"You had nothing to worry about ... at least not where another man is concerned. You're the only one I'm interested in." Her eyes filled with concern as she continued, "But are you sure you want to take this chance with me? My life is pretty much a mess right now. I have the mafia trying to kill me because my ex-husband is an egomaniac with no conscience. And not only that, I also just found out that the man I thought was my father my entire life isn't, in fact, my father, and my mother has been lying to me for the past twenty-four years."

She looked out the window as she wrapped her arms

around herself and stared out, searching for answers that I wished I could give. Her soft, deep sigh made me ache to touch her. I knew time was the only thing that would help her process the pain and confusion that she had to be feeling. I knew it was a lot to take in and that I should give her space to sort things out in her head, but I'd be damned if I let her go through it alone. I wasn't leaving her side. She was mine, and I would do anything to protect her and give her peace.

I walked over and stood behind her. When she didn't turn around to look at me, I slid my arms around her waist and pressed my chest to her back. "I can tell you this … you definitely make life interesting."

"Cade!" she fussed.

I wanted to be the one to take away her pain and show her how much she meant to me. I lowered my mouth to her ear as I whispered, "I think you're an amazing woman. You're a wonderful mother. You're not only smart, you're easy to talk to. You're a knockout and an unbelievable kisser. Who could ask for more than that?"

"You're crazy. You know that, right?"

"Where you're concerned? Yeah, I'm absolutely crazy, but I know a good thing when I see it."

Her tone softened as she replied, "See … I knew you were sweet. I've known it all along."

"Damn, woman. You're going to kill my reputation talking like that," I teased.

"Well, it's true."

As I held her close, I was relieved when I felt her body begin to relax in my arms. In that moment, it felt like my entire world was centered right there with her in my arms. I was completely lost in her—the scent of her hair, the feel of her heart beating against her chest, the taste of her skin. She hung her head to the side as she leaned back, letting her weight settle against me. Her hair fell from her bare neck, and I thought again that I would never see anything as beautiful as her. I lowered my lips to the soft skin on her neck and kissed her gently.

This time I heard a lighter sigh as her breath quickened. Slowly, painstakingly, I trailed my kisses from the nape of her neck up to the bottom of her ear. I could hear her breathing louder now, almost panting. I smiled against her warm skin as I continued to nip at her. My hands slid from her waist to her flat stomach, reaching underneath her shirt to caress her bare flesh.

She laid her hands on top of mine as I began to move them higher to cup her breasts. The soft lace of her bra made my cock stir and press hard against my jeans. I kneaded her perfect tits with my palms, plumping them and teasing her taut nipples. I could feel her heart hammering in her chest excitedly as I moved my hands lower to the waistband of her jeans. I quickly undid her zipper before slipping my hand inside the front of her black thong. Her breath caught in her chest as I gently parted her folds and ran my fingertips along the length of her center, spreading the wetness to her clit. She raised her arms above her head as she wound her hands in my hair, holding on while I teased her.

My lips went to her ear as I whispered, "Let go, August. Let me give you what you need."

Her moan filled the room as she writhed against my hand. Her hips rocking in rhythm as her ass ground into my crotch. My cock was struggling against the fabric of my jeans. I throbbed with need for her, but I had to be patient. She was so close, and I needed to send her over the edge.

As she began to tremble, I tightened an arm around her waist to support her and continued to drive her towards the brink. I could feel her body tense and her hands grip my hair harder as she began chanting, "*Yes. Yes. Yes!*"

August moaned and shuddered, "Oh, god."

Her legs wobbled slightly as I released my hold on her and she turned to face me. "Better?" I asked with a smirk.

A devilish darkness filled her eyes as her gaze fell to the growing bulge in my jeans. "Getting there ..."

I raised my eyebrows and grinned. "See what you do to me, gorgeous?"

Her voracious sexual appetite was one of the things I loved about her. I knew that if she'd have me, I would fulfill her every desire until my last breath. I reached behind her, grabbing her ass and lifting her up. Her legs automatically wrapped around my waist as I carried her to the bed. When I dropped her down onto the comforter, August grabbed her jeans and began to shimmy them down over her hips. I finally eased them off and tossed them on the floor, growing more impatient to be inside her with every passing minute. She watched eagerly as I pulled my shirt over my head and dropped it. I made quick work of my jeans, kicking them onto the floor beside hers. As I reached for my boxer briefs, I saw her wet her lips before biting down hard on her full, pink bottom lip. Grinning mischievously, I slowly worked off my boxers, enjoying her eyes fixed on my cock. Once I was standing naked before her, I took it in my hand and pumped it suggestively. "Now, let's see if we can make you feel even better..."

A soft smile crossed August's face as I approached the bed, but when I yanked her panties to the side and spread her thighs wide on the mattress, her face instantly went serious. Her eyes darkened with desire as her mouth opened with a small gasp. I knelt between her thighs and reached into the nightstand for a condom. It took only a moment for me to roll it on and position myself at her entrance. I paused, looking deep into her dark eyes.

"If you let me, I'll make you happy, August. I won't let you down ... I won't hurt you. I'd die before I let that happen."

"Cade," she gasped as she pulled me to her and pressed her lips against mine. As soon as they touched mine, I knew that was true. She was everything I'd ever wanted, and I'd lay down my life for her. Polito and his men weren't getting anywhere near her. My brothers and I would make sure of that.

I poured every ounce of passion I had for August into a slow, tantalizing thrust. I watched as her back arched off the bed and her mouth stretched into an exaggerated O. Again and again, I thrust into her, picking up a punishing rhythm. Our bodies fused into one tangle of pleasure. Her body clenched around my cock, squeezing me with every contraction of her muscles. I made love to her over and over for the next hour. Every orgasm brought her closer and closer to total blissful relaxation. We might not be able to solve all our problems tonight, but the least I could do is help her forget about them for a while.

August's body jerked underneath me, and she cried out one last time in ecstasy. As I came with her, she wrapped her arms around me and clung to me tightly, like she was afraid I might pull away. Her voice was filled with emotion as she whispered, "Cade."

"Right here, baby. I'm right here," I assured her.

With a relieved sigh, her eyes closed and she curled up next to me. It wasn't long before her breath slowed and her entire body relaxed next to mine. There were so many things I wanted to tell her, but I didn't say a word. Instead, I just held her close, relishing in the feeling of her body next to mine as she drifted off to sleep.

AUGUST

*A*s much as I hated to leave Cade and his warm bed, I didn't have a choice. I had to get back to Harper. When I got back to my room, Jae was lying on the bed next to her, half-asleep and watching a movie. After I thanked her for staying with Harper, she slipped out of the room and closed the door. As I looked down at Harper sleeping, I was worried that I might wake her when I crawled in the bed next to her, but she didn't even budge when I laid my head on the pillow. I was too exhausted mentally and physically to even think, and thankfully, I was able to fall right to sleep.

The next morning, I woke up with Harper hovering over me, her eyebrows furrowed and her bottom lip pursed into a pout. "I wanna go home."

"Why? What's wrong?"

She shrugged. "I no wike it here. I miss Fwoppsie."

"I'm sorry, sweetie, but we can't go home right now." Harper was a smart child. I knew I had to choose my words wisely, or she would keep pushing. "But we will get to go home soon, and then you can get Floppsie back."

"Why we can't go now?"

"We just can't." I eased up on the bed as I told her, "It isn't safe for us to be there right now, but Cade and his friends are going to fix that. As soon as they do, we'll go home."

"Kay."

I looked down at my watch and was surprised to see that it was almost eleven. Figuring that she was hungry, I asked, "How about we go get something to eat, and then go to the playroom? We can see if your new friends are there."

"I wan some ce-weal."

"You got it." I sat up on the bed and threw the covers back. "Let's get dressed, and then we can go."

Smiling, she hopped off the bed and rushed over to the bag of clothes Cade had brought, quickly picking out an outfit. After I'd done the same, we both got dressed, brushed our teeth, and started out of the room. When we stepped out into the hall, I stopped and found myself staring at my mother's door. I hadn't spoken to her since I'd learned the truth about Gus, and while I wasn't ready to have that discussion with her, I knew I couldn't go eat without asking her to join us. I walked over and tapped on her door. When she answered, her eyes were puffy from the night before, but she was dressed and feigned a smile. "Good morning, girls. Did you two sleep well?"

"We slept fine," I answered flatly. "We were about to go grab something to eat if you want to join us."

"Sure." She stepped out into the hall, and after she

closed the door, she picked up Harper. "How's my sweet girl this morning?"

They bantered back and forth all the way to the kitchen. When we walked in, I was surprised to see that none of the guys were around, only Jae and a couple of the other Sinners' girls. They greeted us as we each made ourselves a bowl of cereal, but left soon after, leaving us completely alone in the kitchen. My mind was racing as I sat across the table from my mother. I had so many questions I wanted to ask her, but I didn't want to bring it up with Harper sitting there. As soon as we were done eating, we took Harper down to the family room, and I was relieved to see that several of the kids were there. Without skipping a beat, Harper rushed over and started playing while Mom and I sat down on the sofa.

We were watching Harper play when Mom turned to me and asked, "Is something wrong?"

"I heard you and Gus talking last night."

"You did?" she asked as the color drained from her face. "What exactly did you hear?"

"Everything." I could feel all the hurt and anger building in the pit of my stomach as I whispered, "I know Gus is my father."

"I'm sorry, August. I didn't want you to find out this way."

"How did you want me to find out? Were you planning on telling me, or were you hoping that you could keep it a secret forever?" I could tell from her expression that she wasn't sure how to reply. "I had every right to know the truth, Mom. You shouldn't have kept this from me."

"I know. I made a mistake … a big, terrible mistake, and I would change it if I could."

"I just don't get it. Did everyone know, but me?" When she didn't respond, I knew her answer. "So, grandmother knew Denis wasn't my father?"

"Yes, sweetheart. She knew everything. The minute she found out I was pregnant with you, she started pushing me to marry him. I never expected for Denis to actually go along with it, but he was working with your grandfather and hoped that marrying me would help further his career." She turned and looked down at the floor with embarrassment as she told me, "I don't think that's the only reason why he went along with it. I'm pretty sure he was in love with your grandmother."

"What?"

"I know that sounds crazy, but he was always so different around her. His eyes would light up when she walked into the room. His tone changed whenever he spoke to her. I don't know. You would've had to see it for yourself to know what I'm talking about." She gave a half-shrug before saying, "When she died, he was devastated—way more devastated than he should've been."

"Oh, Mom," I gasped. "You should've told me."

"I didn't know how. I'd kept the secret locked away, hoping one day it would just go away. But it never did. Instead, it just grew bigger and bigger, to the point I didn't know what to do with it. When Denis left, I know it was hard on you, especially when he never called or came by to see you, but honestly I was relieved that I didn't have to pretend anymore."

"Mom." I sighed at the thought. "You didn't have to carry all that alone."

Her gaze drifted to the ceiling as she thought to herself

for a moment. After a long, cleansing sigh, she finally muttered, "Things could've been so different."

"You didn't have a choice." I placed my hand on her arm as I said, "I heard you tell him what Grandmother did ... how she forced you to leave him."

"She hated him, but she had no idea what kind of man he really was."

"But what kind of man was he, Mom?" Remembering what she'd said about the video, I asked, "Did he really kill someone?"

"It's complicated, August."

"How can killing someone be complicated, Mother? He either did it or he didn't."

"The man he killed ... those men who they all killed, were members of a vicious gang who did horrible, unimaginable things, and they were trying to hurt Gus and his brothers. Gus got to them before that happened." She looked over to me with a fire in her eyes as she said, "Right or wrong, he was protecting the people he cared about the most. That's what he does. That's how I knew he would help you get Harper back. I knew he'd figure out that you were his daughter, and there was no way in hell that he would let any harm come to you or his granddaughter."

"Did you tell Grandmother about any of this?"

"I tried, but she didn't care. She wouldn't listen to me when I told her how good he was to me, but even if she did, it wouldn't have mattered. Back then, what I wanted was irrelevant. It was always about her and what she wanted, just like it had been my entire life."

"I'm sorry, Momma. I really am." I placed my hand on hers. "You really loved him, didn't you?"

"Yes. I loved him very much. The crazy thing is, I still do." Tears filled her eyes as she said, "I should've been stronger. I should've stood up for myself, but I was scared of what my mother might do in retaliation. I couldn't take a chance on her causing something that would hurt Gus."

"I can understand that. I really can. I might've even done the same thing if I was in your shoes, but not telling me that Gus was my father ... that I don't understand, especially after Grandmother died."

"I was afraid I would lose you ... that you would hate me for keeping the truth from you." She squeezed my hand as she said, "I couldn't bear it if I lost you, August. You mean the world to me."

"Mom, you're not going to lose me. Not now. Not ever," I assured her. "I love you, but it's going to take me some time to forgive you for this with Gus. Even though I understand why you initially did it, I can't help but feel betrayed and lied to. I'm sure he feels the same way."

She started crying again as she muttered, "He does."

"Give him time. Give us both some time. It will work out ... that is if Polito and his band of thugs don't get to me first," I huffed.

"August! That's not funny," my mother scolded.

"I wasn't trying to be funny." I glanced behind me, looking for some sign of Cade, but there was none. "Is it just me, or does this place seem oddly quiet to you?"

"I'm sure they're in one of their meetings trying to figure out how to deal with David and those awful men he's working with."

"You're probably right."

We both settled back and watched Harper as she played with her little friends. Every now and then, I would glance down at my watch, checking the time. When it came time for her nap, Mom and I took her down to my room. While I put her down, Mom went across the hall to get some rest of her own. Two hours later, Harper was up and ready for another bite to eat. It all seemed so mundane as Mom and I took her back to the kitchen, grabbed a late lunch, and then headed back to the playroom. I was fighting utter boredom as one hour rolled into the next. It was well after four, and I'd still seen no sign of Cade or the others. Becoming frustrated, I looked over to Mom and asked, "Do you mind watching Harper? I'm going to try and find Cade and see what's going on."

"Of course."

As I stood to leave, I waved over at Harper and said, "I'll be right back. Gammy is going to watch you for a bit."

Harper nodded, then quickly turned her attention back to the little girl she was playing with. I stood there watching her for a minute, and I tried to imagine what I would've done if I was in my mother's shoes. I wanted to think that I would've told her the truth, but deep down, I wasn't so sure. Feeling more confused than ever, I walked out into the hall to go find Cade. I hadn't gotten very far when I heard men's voices coming from the conference room. I didn't want to interrupt, so I turned to go back to the family room. I hadn't gotten far when I heard someone call out my name. When I turned, I found Hawk walking in my direction. I forced a smile as I said, "Hey, Hawk."

"Hey." A look of discomfort crossed his face. "I wanted to apologize about last night."

"That's not necessary. There's nothing to apologize for."

"Yeah. It's definitely necessary. I didn't know you and Gunner were a thing, otherwise I wouldn't have—"

"Hawk … it's really okay." I smiled as I told him, "Your intentions were good, and under different circumstances …"

A smirk crossed his face as he chuckled and said, "My intentions were anything but good, August."

"Oh."

"Come on, August. You're a beautiful woman." He leaned towards me with a smirk that would make any other woman swoon. "You can't blame me for at least trying to get you to go out with me."

"If you say so." I glanced over his shoulder and asked him, "Have you seen Gunner?"

"Yeah. We were all just meeting about … *things*." I knew he wouldn't tell me any more than that, so I wasn't surprised when he quickly changed the subject. "Where's that cute kid of yours?"

"She's in the family room playing with some of the other kids. My mother is with her."

He nodded. "Glad she found some friends here. I'm sure all this hasn't been easy on her."

"No, it hasn't."

"August?" Gus called as he started walking in my direction. "I was hoping you would be around."

"Oh, yeah?"

"Wondered if you had a few minutes for us to talk?"

I knew I couldn't put him off forever, but I was hoping that I would have more time to prepare for our inevitable conversation. Dread washed over me as I asked, "Now?"

"Unless you've got somewhere else you need to be?"

"No ... Mom is watching Harper, so I don't have anywhere that I need to be, at least not for a little while." I shrugged with a smile. "So, yeah. I guess I'm free to talk."

"Good." He motioned for me to follow as he said, "Let's find a place where we can talk privately."

When he started down the hall, I did as he'd asked and followed. I expected him to take me to an empty room or the bar, but he led me out of the Sinners' clubhouse and into the parking lot. We both continued walking until he stopped next to a big black Harley motorcycle. He took a helmet out of one of the saddlebags and offered it to me. "Wait ... You're wanting me to ride on that?"

"Yeah." He grabbed his off the backseat and slipped it on his head. "Haven't you ever been on a motorcycle before?"

"No, not exactly."

"Well, there's a first time for everything."

After he got on, he offered his hand and helped me climb on behind him. I was a little nervous about riding a motorcycle for the first time, but the thought of my first ride being with my father seemed bittersweet. I placed my hands on his waist and moments later, we were on the road. With the warmth of the sun my face and the cool breeze blowing in my hair, I quickly relaxed and was amazed at how free I felt. As crazy as it sounds, I felt more like myself than I ever had. We'd been riding for about forty-five minutes or so when I realized that we were headed to Radnor Lake State Park. It was just outside of the city and had incredible views. We continued into the park, and when Gus found the perfect spot by the water, he pulled over and parked the bike. We both got off and headed over to a small picnic table.

Once we were seated, I looked over to him, watching as he stared out onto the lake, and it was hard to believe that I hadn't seen it sooner: his dark, almost black eyes, the arch of his brow, the subtle wave in his dark hair, even the tiny crook in the corner of his mouth when he smiled. We shared so many similar traits, making it impossible to deny that he was, in fact, my father. When he turned to look at me, I could see the pain and anguish in his eyes—an emotion he tried so hard to hide from others. I knew the feeling. I'd spent my entire life trying to hide the hurt I felt so deep inside, and I wished there was a way I could take it all away ... for both of us. Gus's voice was strained as he said, "I have so many things I want to say to you, but I don't have a clue where to start."

"I know. I feel the same way." I inhaled a deep breath then said, "I wish things could've been different ... that you didn't have to find out about me like this."

"We both know Samantha had her reasons for keeping you from me, and I'm trying to come to terms with those, but I just can't stop thinking about how different things could've been if I'd just followed my gut and had gone after her."

"Why didn't you?"

Gus reached into his pocket for his wallet. He flipped it open and pulled out an old, folded sheet of a paper. He offered it to me, and as soon as I opened it and saw the handwriting, I knew it was from my mother.

AUGUST 19, 1994

GUS,

I've been lying here watching you sleep for hours, just thinking about the time we've shared together. This summer has been the best few months of my life. I can honestly say I've never been happier, and that's all because of you. I love you, Gus. I love you with every fiber of my being. You mean so much to me, more than I thought possible. With you, I've learned how it feels to truly love and to be loved. That's why this letter is so hard to write.

I've done a lot of thinking over the past few weeks, and I've come to realize that it doesn't matter how much I love you or you love me. It just isn't enough. We're from two different worlds, headed down two completely different paths, and if we stay together, we're only going to end up destroying one another. I can't bear for that to happen. I love you too much. It breaks my heart to say this to you, but I'm leaving Memphis. I am asking you to please respect my decision. Don't try to find me. Don't call me. Let me find a way to move on, and I will do the same for you. It's the only way either of us will ever make it through this.

This wasn't an easy decision for me. In fact, it's killing me to walk away from you, but deep down I know it's the right thing to do. Please remember—I love you today, I loved you yesterday, and I will love you tomorrow and always. That will never change.

LOVE,
    Samantha

After reading the letter, I could only imagine the heartbreak that my mother was feeling as she wrote those words to Gus. Even though she knew the truth about him, it was clear that she loved him terribly. It must've been gut-wrenching to know that she had to leave him and the life that they could've had together in order to protect him. Tears were steadily streaming down my face as I muttered, "Oh, Gus."

"I bet I've read that letter a million times over the years." He looked out onto the lake, watching as the waves crashed along the bank, and sighed. "Now, it finally makes sense why she didn't come back to me."

"You really did love her, didn't you?"

"I did. I think I always will. I tried to move on, tried to forget about the time we had together, but in all my years of searching, I never found anyone who made me feel the way she did."

"So, you never married?"

"Never." He shook his head. "Didn't seem right to tie myself to someone that I couldn't truly give my heart to."

There's not many men in this world who would've made the choices he'd made. Most would've just denied their true feelings and married someone who they didn't fully love. It would have made it easier to move on and forget the past, but Gus knew that would only bring him more heartache. I couldn't help but respect him for that. "I can see why she loved you so much."

His eyes met mine as he said, "I want you to know that if I had known about you, I would've—"

"I know, Gus," I interrupted. "And so would I, but we can't go back. We've just gotta find a way to move forward from this. *We all do.*"

"You got any idea how we do that?"

"No, but I'm sure we can figure it out."

"I certainly hope so." He placed his hand on my arm as he said, "You're everything a father could want in a daughter, and I really hope you'll give me a chance to get to know you and Harper better."

"I'd like that." I knew I was walking on sensitive ground when I asked, "What about Mom? Do you think you could forgive her ... that you two could find a way to work past all this?"

"I'd like to say we could, but I honestly don't know." He turned his attention back to the water. "There's been so much hurt, years and years of it, and not just for me. Samantha endured plenty of heartache of her own. I just don't know how we move on from that."

"If you both still love each other like you say you do, then you'll find a way."

"I guess only time will tell." He glanced down at his watch. "We better be getting back. I need to help get things prepared."

"Prepared for what?"

"Can't say. That's club business," he answered flatly.

"So, you don't discuss club business?"

"No, not with anyone except the brothers."

"Not even with the president's daughter?" I asked with a smirk. "Besides, something tells me that this particular business has something to do with me."

"That might be true, but it doesn't change anything." His tone turned serious as he said, "Discussing details only puts you and Harper in danger, August. Not going to let that happen."

"Okay, I understand."

As he stood up, he glanced over at me and said, "I'm guessing since you mentioned the president's daughter thing, that you and Gunner had a conversation."

"We did. In fact, we had a lengthy conversation." I followed him over to his motorcycle, and as I got on behind him, I put on my helmet and said, "In case you didn't know, he really thinks a lot of you."

"I think a lot of him as well." After he put on his helmet, he glanced over his shoulder at me. "You got yourself a good one with him."

Without giving me a chance to respond, he started the engine and drove out onto the main road. The sun had just started to set as we started back towards the Sinners' clubhouse. I tried to focus on all the beautiful scenery, but I couldn't stop thinking about what Gus had said about helping the others get prepared. I was curious to know if his getting prepared had something to do with the men who were trying to kill me. I couldn't help but wonder if he would kill them just like he had the gang members who'd threatened his brothers so long ago. It was then that I realized I simply didn't care how he dealt them. I just wanted it to be over. I wanted to get on with my life and get my daughter home to her own bed and to Floppsie. When we arrived at the clubhouse, I thanked Gus for taking the time to talk to me and for the amazing ride. It was great to get away, even if it was just for a little while.

Once we said our final goodbyes, I went back to my room to check on Mom and Harper. To my surprise, I found Jae sitting on my bed with Harper, watching cartoons. "Oh ... Hey, Jae. I didn't know you were watching Harper."

"Your mother asked me to sit with her for a little while," she explained.

"Did she happen to say why?"

"No." Jae got up off the bed and walked over to the side table. She picked up a notepad and said, "But she did leave you this note."

When I read that she'd gone to the house to get Floppsie, my heart started to race with horror. All I could think about were those men charging towards my house and how they'd come to kill me. There was a good chance that at least one of them was still there watching to see if I would return. I couldn't believe that she'd do something so foolish, especially over something as silly as a child's toy. Knowing she could be in danger, I rushed over and grabbed the burner cell phone Cade had given me and dialed her number. I let it ring several times, and when she didn't answer, I called her again. And again. Still no answer. Damn.

GUNNER

$\mathcal{T}$he sun had barely begun to rise when Gus called my brothers and me into a meeting with Sinners. As hoped, Riggs and Hammer had managed to hack into the security feed at each of Polito's properties, which was an integral part to taking Polito down. We spent the entire morning and most of the afternoon going over the video feed. By doing so, we were able to start gathering a head count of all of Polito's men, and each of their comings and goings of the four properties. He had fifteen in his main warehouse, and eight more holed up in his office building along with Polito himself and his right hand, Sal Carbone.

From what we could tell, the smaller warehouse was mainly used as storage and had only two guards posted. Unfortunately, we still had no idea how many Polito had inside the house. With the cameras being on the exterior of the home, we couldn't get a good visual on what was going on inside. After hours of trying to get a decent view, Blaze became frustrated and grumbled, "This shit isn't doing us any good. We can't see a damn thing with these fucking cameras."

"I'm sorry, brother, but it's the best I could do," Riggs replied.

"We gotta find a way to get a look inside or we're gonna be fucked," Murphy warned.

Knowing he was right, I offered, "I could go over and check it out."

"It's too dangerous," Viper warned. "If anyone sees you, this whole plan could go up in flames."

"We need cameras inside the house," Murphy pushed. "That's the only way we can be certain of what we're walking in to."

"He's right," Riggs interjected. "If Gunner and I could get close enough, I could install a couple of micro-cameras on a couple of the windows. If positioned right, we could get a better idea of what's going on in there."

Gus looked over to him and said, "Get it done. Murphy ... Go with them in case they need a hand."

Without a moment's hesitation, Riggs, Murphy, and I stood and walked out of the conference room. We followed Riggs down to his room, and once he had every-thing he needed, we got in the SUV and headed to Polito's home. He lived several miles out of town in one of those gated communities with houses that were three times the size of most with meticulous landscaping and overstated décor. I pulled up to the curb across the street from Poli-to's and killed the engine. Other than a couple of cars parked in the drive, there was no one in sight, making it impossible to know if anyone was around. I looked over to them and said, "We're gonna need a distraction."

Murphy scanned the area for a moment, then said,

"There's a fire hydrant. We could run it over ... fake an accident."

"Hmm ... Yeah, we could do that, but then, we'll have to deal with not only the fire department but also the cops. I'm thinking that might be too much of a distraction." I motioned to the house across the street. "You think they've got security system?"

"From the looks of it, you would think so."

"Can't you do your voodoo and trigger the alarm?"

"Yeah, I can do that."

"Make it a good one ... one that will bring the cops and the fire department." I looked back over at Polito's place as I said, "Give our friends something to watch for a while."

Riggs pulled out his laptop, and within minutes the loud, pulsing sound of a security alarm was going off. Knowing the cops would be there soon, I started the SUV and drove over to the street behind Polito's. We got out and started to make our way to his backyard. Once the cops showed up, we jumped the fence and rushed over to the hedges. Adrenaline was pulsing through me as we went from window to window, mounting the cameras where we could get a decent view inside the house. We were just finishing up when two fire trucks pulled up across the street, giving us the distraction we needed to get the hell out of there.

Murphy whispered, "It's time to move!"

My heart was pounding a mile a minute as we got back in the SUV and tried to catch our breaths. With a proud smirk, Riggs announced, "I can't believe we pulled it off."

Murphy dashed his excitement when he replied, "We

don't know for sure that we did. We still need to see if the cameras show anything."

"You're right. Let me check." He grabbed his laptop from the dash, and after a few clicks, he looked back over to me and smiled. "We're golden."

"Good deal." Murphy seemed relieved as he said, "Let's get back and tell them we're in."

I started up the SUV and headed towards the Sinners' clubhouse. I was eager to see August. Even with everything that had been going on, she was on my mind all day. Remembering how upset she was about hearing the news of Gus being her father, I needed to lay my eyes on her and make sure she was okay. When we pulled up to the clubhouse, we all got out of the SUV and headed towards the front door. As we stepped inside, I turned to them and said, "You go ahead. I'll be there as soon as I check in on August."

"Will do."

I was just starting down the hall when I spotted August rushing towards me. Her eyes were filled with panic as she gasped, "Mom's gone, and I'm afraid that something's happened to her."

"What do you mean *gone?*"

"She left Harper with Jae and went to the house to get Harper's bunny. She's been begging for that crazy thing since we got here. I guess all the whining got to Mom, and she decided to go do something about it." August let out a frustrated sigh. "I don't know what she was thinking! Doesn't she know how stupid it is for her to go back to the house?"

"Maybe she's okay. Have you tried calling her?"

"About a hundred times, but I never got an answer."

Her eyes were wide with panic as she stammered, "So ... I went to check her room, and that's when I found her phone on her desk. She'd left it here!"

"Damn." Knowing she had no means of transportation and she'd have to get through the guard at the gate, I asked, "How the hell did she even leave? She's got no car."

"I have no idea," she huffed. "If I had to guess, I'd bet she called a cab or an Uber."

"Okay ... That's possible, but how the hell did she get through the gate? There's always a prospect on guard."

"Who knows? She's always been pretty crafty when she puts her mind to it."

"Damn." I ran my hand through my hair as I thought about my next move. I knew he wouldn't like hearing the news, but I had to tell Gus—the sooner the better. I reached for August's hand, leading her down the hall and said, "Come on. We gotta talk to Gus."

When we got to the conference room, Gus was sitting at the table with Riggs and the others, watching the surveillance feed, and none of them even noticed when we walked up behind them. I cleared my throat, drawing Gus's attention over to me as I said, "We've got a problem."

"What's going on?"

"It's Samantha ... She's left the clubhouse."

"What the fuck are you talking about?"

"Samantha left August a note saying she was going to the house to get something for Harper. August's looked for her, but she's nowhere to be found."

"Damn it!" Gus stood up and interrupted me as he roared, "How the hell did she get out the fucking gate?"

"I don't know, but I'm sure as hell gonna find out!"

Viper turned to Hawk and asked, "Who's monitoring the fucking gate?"

"Bolt's on duty until midnight."

Rage washed over Viper, making him look like he was about to explode as he roared, "Get his ass in here, now!"

Hawk stood and quickly walked out of the room. With a hopeful expression, Gus looked over to Riggs and asked, "Can you trace her burner?"

"There's no point in trying to trace it," I told him. "She left it on her desk."

"Well, damn," Gus grumbled.

"What are we going to do now?" August gasped. "What if they have her? What if they hurt her?"

"I know you're worried, but we'll find her, August." I reached for her, pulling her towards me as I wrapped her in my arms and held her tightly against my chest. *"We'll find her."*

I was still holding her when Hawk returned with their prospect, Bolt. Viper stood and charged towards him as he growled, "Were you watching the gate today?"

"Been standing at my post since two this afternoon," Bolt answered.

"Did you happen to see Mrs. Rayburn leave the premises?"

"Yes, sir. I did. She left around five or so," Bolt answered, completely unaware of the wrath that was about to come his way.

Viper grabber the collar of his t-shirt, fisting it in his hand as he jerked Bolt forward and snarled, "And you just let her walk out of here!"

"She told me that she got the okay, Prez." His voice

trembled as he added, "I just assumed that she was telling me the truth."

"And you didn't think you should check with me before you just let her waltz out of here!" Viper roared.

"Like I told ya … I-I thought she was telling the truth, sir," he stammered. "Under the circumstances, I didn't think she'd make that shit up."

"Goddamn it! How could you be so fucking stupid!" The vein in Viper's neck pulsed with rage as he said, "Get your shit and get the fuck out of here. Your days with the Sinners are done."

"But Prez. It was an honest mistake!" Bolt pleaded.

"I'm no longer *Prez* to you. Now get your ass out of my clubhouse!" Viper demanded.

Looking completely defeated, Bolt lowered his head and walked out of the room. We were all so busy listening to Viper let loose on Bolt that none of had noticed that Riggs had been steadily working on his computer. He muttered something under his breath, then turned his laptop monitor in our direction. "Umm, Gus … you're gonna want to see this."

When I looked down at the screen, Riggs had pulled up the live feed from Polito's main warehouse. When I saw two men entering a building with a woman in their grasp, I knew immediately it was Samantha. She was blindfolded and struggling to keep up as they thrust her into the center of the room. Seconds later, one of the men grabbed a chair and placed it behind her, then gave her a hard shove, forcing her to sit. I was watching her tug against her restraints when I heard August cry, "Oh my god! Mom!"

Gus quickly turned to me and demanded, "Get her out of here!"

I took a hold of her arm and gave her a gentle tug, leading her out into the hall. Knowing that Harper was likely in August's room, I took her down to my room. Once we were inside, she wrapped her arms around my neck and tucked her head under my chin, clinging to me tightly. I ran my hand down her back and tried to keep my voice steady and calm as I told her, "August, you gotta know Gus isn't going to let anything happen to her."

"This just keeps getting worse and worse! I just want it all to end!"

"It will. You just gotta hang in there a little longer. Can you do that for me?"

"I can try." She looked up at me with anger-filled eyes as she said, "I know this might make me sound like an awful human being, but I want you to make them pay ... Each and every last one of them!"

"We will. You can count on that." I kissed her on the forehead. "I need to get back in there. Are you going to be okay while I'm gone?"

"I'll be fine." She released me from our embrace as she looked up at me and pleaded, "Just ... please get her back for me."

"I'll do my best."

I kissed her once more, then headed back to the conference room. When I stepped inside, Gus and Viper were hovering over Riggs' computer, watching as Polito entered the room. Gus clenched his fists and slammed them down on the table as he barked, "We gotta get over there now!"

"We do, and the whole fucking plan goes down the fucking drain," Viper warned.

"I don't give a fuck about the goddamn plan!" Gus shouted with frustration. "I'm not going to just sit here while Samantha's life is in danger!"

"We could move ahead with the plan we already have," Murphy suggested. "We've worked out all the details. We all know what to do and when to do it. We just need to get the job done sooner than later."

"He's right," I added. "We spent hours going over every detail."

"There's one thing we didn't cover," Blaze announced. "I get that we're dividing up, going into each property simultaneously, and wiping these motherfuckers out, but after? If we want it to look like Polito dropped off the face of the earth, we can't leave any remains behind."

Blaze had a valid concern. We'd worked hard to come up with a plan where we wouldn't have to worry about any backlash for either of our clubs. The most crucial part of making that happen was to be sure there was no evidence that tied us to Polito's death. While he didn't go into detail, Viper looked over to Blaze and replied, "Don't worry about cleanup. We've got that covered."

"Good," Blaze said and stood up. "Then, let's do this thing."

Gus and Viper both nodded, giving us all the order to move forward. Knowing time wasn't on our hands, we all rushed out of the conference room and went straight to the Sinners' garage. We had to load our artillery into the SUVs, along with anything else we might need to forge our attack on Polito. Each of us quickly checked every single weapon, ensuring that they were all in working order, and gathered enough ammo to wipe out an entire army. We were making good time, and everything was just about set to go, when I noticed Gus walking back into the clubhouse. Knowing Gus like I did, I realized exactly where he was headed. I just hoped he'd find the right words to say to help her through these next few hours.

AUGUST

$\mathcal{I}$ was trying my best not to cry. Hell, I'd spent enough damn time crying over the past week, and I was sick of it. I decided right then and there that I needed another emotion to get me through all of this—anger. It wasn't exactly difficult to make the transition. I had plenty of things to be angry about: the fact that my ex-husband got in bed with the mafia, that his ties with them caused my daughter to be kidnapped, and now, my own life was in danger. That was plenty, but the fact that now my mother's life was in jeopardy was enough to send me completely over the edge. I was entering a full-on rage when I heard a knock on my door. I opened it and was surprised to see Gus standing in the hallway. My mind went directly to a horrible place, thinking that something awful had happened to my mother. I tried not to completely lose it as I asked, "Did something happen?"

"No. Not that we are aware of." He paused for a moment, then said, "I just wanted to let you know that we're leaving, and if I have anything to say about it, we won't be coming back without Samantha."

"Thank you, Gus. I can't begin to tell you how much I appreciate you all helping us like this."

"You're family, August," he answered emphatically. "There's nothing in this world I wouldn't do for either of you."

"It's easy to see why my mother cared so much for you, Gus." Feeling the need to be close to him, I stepped towards him and wrapped my arms around his waist, hugging him tightly. "You really are a good man."

"Not as good as you might think, but I take care of what's mine." He gave me a quick squeeze, then took a step back, releasing me from our embrace. "I better get going. The guys are waiting."

"Okay."

He started towards the door, then stopped and turned back to me. "Rev and Link, a couple of the Sinners' prospects will be out in the hall watching over you and Harper while we're gone. Just let one of them know if you need anything."

"I will. Thank you." When he started to leave, I called out to him, "Gus?"

He turned to face me. "Yeah?"

"Be careful."

"Always."

With that, he walked out of the room and closed the door. I stood there for a moment, trying to figure out my next move when I heard a commotion in the next room. It wasn't until that moment I remembered that Jae was still watching Harper. Feeling guilty for leaving her for so long, I rushed through the connecting bathroom into my room. When I walked in, I was surprised to see that Jae had already given Harper a bath and had gotten her into her pj's. They were both sprawled out on the floor playing with a deck of cards. Jae looked up at me with concern as she sat up and asked, "Did you find your mom?"

I didn't want Harper to worry, so I said, "Gus has gone to get her."

"Okay. Good."

When I went over and sat down on the edge of the bed, Harper got up and crawled into my lap. "Me and Jae pway go-fish."

"That's great, sweetie." I glanced over at Jae as I told Harper, "She's very sweet to play with you like that."

"I enjoyed it. Harper is a special little girl."

"Yes, she is." When she stood to leave, I smiled and said, "Thank you for watching her, Jae. I really do appreciate it."

"Anytime." Jae ran her hand over Harper's head as she said, "I'll see you tomorrow, kiddo. You be good for your momma."

Harper nodded with a smile.

As she walked out of the room, I said, "Goodnight, Jae."

"Night!"

As soon as she closed the door, Harper eased over to her spot on the bed and slipped under the covers. When I got up to change, Harper sat up and asked, "Where's Gammy?"

"She went to run an errand."

A curious look crossed her face as she lay back on her pillow. "It's dark out."

"Yes, it is." I took off my jeans and t-shirt, then put on the sleep shirt Cade had bought me. As I walked back over to the bed and crawled in next to Harper, I told her, "She'll be home soon."

"Cause Gus go get her?"

"Yeah. He'll bring her back." I leaned over and gave her a kiss. "Now, try and get some sleep."

"But I not sweepy." She gave me her best little pout. "Can we wash a movie?"

"We don't have a way to watch a movie, sweetheart." I reached for the remote and turned on the TV. "But I'll see what's on."

I started flipping through the channels, and after several minutes of searching, I found an old children's movie about a fairy I thought she might like. Seemingly pleased with my choice, she curled up on her pillow with her eyes glued to the television screen. I tried to ignore the anxious feeling that was growing in the pit of my stomach and focus on the quiet moment with my daughter, but it just couldn't be done—not when I had no idea what was going on with Mom. I had no idea if they had hurt her or even if she was still alive. Every time I thought about one of those men putting their hands on her, my stomach would turn and nausea would wash over me. I lay back on my pillow, and as I stared up at the blank ceiling, I started thinking about all the things my mother had done for me over the years. She'd helped me find my first apartment, supported me without judgement when my marriage fell apart, and was always there whenever I needed a hand with Harper. It had always been that way, even more so when I was a child.

I could still remember how she would come watch me cheer at every football game, attend every single awards program at school, and never missed a single performance when I was in the school play. Denis Rayburn, the man I'd spent my entire life calling *Dad*, was a different story. He was rarely ever there during those special moments in my life. He was always too busy with work. As I lay there lost in my thoughts, I found myself thinking back to a trip we all took to the beach during my summer break. I was eleven or twelve, and he'd rented us a house right on the water. I was so excited that we were all there together, and I couldn't wait to swim in the ocean for the first time.

As soon as we were unpacked, I put on my swimsuit and rushed into the living room. Mom was busy in the kitchen putting our groceries away while he was sitting on the sofa reading over some papers. Normally I wouldn't interrupt him when he was working, but since I was eager to get out on the beach, I went over to him and asked, "Can we go swimming?"

Without looking up, he answered, "Maybe later."

"But you promised that we could go."

"And we will." Still focused on his papers, he huffed, "I've got some work to do first."

"Leave your father be, August. I'll take you in a minute," Mom promised.

I wanted so desperately to argue, but I knew it wouldn't do any good. Once my father started working, it would be hours before he stopped. Trying my best to be patient, I went out on the front porch and stared out at the water. It was the most beautiful sight I'd ever seen. I was watching the waves crash along the sand when I heard my mother talking to my father. It wasn't until that moment when I realized I hadn't shut the sliding door all the way. With the wind and the waves, it was difficult to hear exactly what they were saying, but I could tell from the tone in her voice that Mom was upset. "It wouldn't kill you to at least pretend that you want to be here."

"Don't start, Samantha. I can't help it that I have work to do."

"Your work can wait," Mom scolded. "That little girl loves you, Denis. She's excited about being here and wants to swim with her father."

He mumbled something incoherent under his breath, then snapped, "I'll go with her later."

"Fine. Suit yourself." Mom opened the sliding glass door and feigned a smile as she told me, "I'm ready when you are."

I could see the sadness in her eyes, but I was too young to truly understand why it was there. I nodded, then walked over to her and gave her a hug. "I love you, Momma."

"I love you, too, sweet girl." She gave me a quick squeeze, then said, "Now, let's go for that swim!"

Too excited to even think, I grabbed my towel and rushed to the front door. Mom grabbed our chairs and umbrella, then followed me out onto the front porch. When we got down to the beach, Mom started setting up our spot. Seeing that I was about to bust a gut, she smiled and said, "You can go ahead and get in, but don't go too deep. I'll be there in a minute."

Before she had a chance to change her mind, I took off running towards the water. I could still remember the feeling of the utter joy I'd felt the moment I first stepped into that gorgeous blue ocean. It was so warm, and the sand felt so strange between my toes. I absolutely loved it. I waved at my mother as I urged, "Come on, Momma!"

"I'm coming! I'm coming!" Moments later, she was at my side, and we were fighting against the monstrous waves as we tried to get into the deeper water. Once we'd gotten waist deep, I dove in, kicking and splashing as I swam around my moth-

er's legs. I was pretending to be a mermaid, swimming along with all my fish friends when I came across a shell in the shape of a circle. I was studying it when Mom glanced over my shoulder and said, "Look at that! You found a sand dollar."

"What's a sand dollar?"

"It's a little sea urchin, but if you look at it real close, some people say it resembles Christ on the cross. It's supposed to be good luck if you find one."

"That's so cool."

"Yes, it is." Mom pointed towards the shore as she asked, "Why don't you go show your father?"

I'd been so excited about finally getting to swim in the ocean, I hadn't even noticed that he'd come down. When I started towards him, I noticed that he had on his swimsuit and sunglasses. I'd hoped that meant he was going to come swim with us, but I'd quickly learn he had other plans. "Hey, Daddy. Look what I found!"

"Hmph. A sand dollar." He took it in his hand and studied it for a moment, then his nose crinkled as he announced, "This one's broken."

"It is?" I asked as I leaned in to see.

"Yeah. The edge is broken off." He slipped it into the pocket of his t-shirt, then smiled as he said, "Why don't ya go see if you can find another one?"

"Okay."

Feeling a little disappointed, I went back to the water next to my mother. I searched for over an hour, hoping to find another sand dollar that wasn't broken, but never did. When I finally came back for air, Mom asked, "Do you want to swim some more or make a sandcastle?"

I glanced up at the shore at my father sitting in his chair. I watched as he brought his beer up to his mouth and took a long drink. "I want to swim some more."

"Okay. Then, let's swim."

Mom and I spent another half hour swimming and jumping the waves. We would've stayed longer, but my dad motioned for us to come back. When we approached, he looked over to Mom and said, "I'm ready for dinner."

"Okay. Just give me a minute to get this cleaned up."

She quickly wrapped a towel around me and then herself before collecting our chairs and umbrella. Dad grabbed our chairs, and without saying a word, he started walking towards the house. I watched as she followed behind him, never saying a word as they trekked through the sand and up to the front porch. They both disappeared inside, while I played in the sand. It wasn't long before my mother called me inside to eat. Once I'd changed clothes, we all gathered around the table. I was still feeling excited about being at the beach, so I started in with the typical kid questions. "What are we doing tomorrow?"

"We'll go back to the beach and swim."

"And look for more sand dollars and shells?"

"Yes. We can do that. We're here for several days, August. We'll have plenty of time to do whatever we want." Hoping to get me to settle down, she turned to me and said, "Now, eat your dinner before it gets cold."

"Yes, ma'am."

I sat there watching as Mom picked at her dinner, and Dad devoured his. As soon as he was done, he got up, never saying thank you or helping to clear the dishes. He just went back to his work while she cleaned the kitchen. Once she was done, she didn't join him in the living room. Instead, she took a book out on the porch and read until bed.

Thinking back on it now, I remember it always being

like that with them. They rarely ever kissed or held hands. I couldn't remember the last time I'd actually seen them talk or laugh together. There were times when he would talk with me, and even hug me and kiss my cheek, but there was a distance there—one I never really understood, at least not until now. Knowing what I do now, I get why he never truly invested himself in his marriage or with me. We were never truly his, and he was never truly ours. He wasn't my father. He was simply a stand in.

As I thought about that broken sand dollar I'd given Denis, I realized that he'd never given it back to me. If I had to guess, I'd say he'd tossed it as soon as I returned to the water, never giving it a second thought. I couldn't help but wonder what Gus would've thought about my little, broken treasure. Remembering how he'd lined his walls with broken motorcycle parts, I couldn't help but think that he would've held on to it, keeping it as a memento of a wonderful memory we'd shared. Unfortunately, I'd never truly know how he would've reacted.

I glanced down at Harper and wasn't surprised to see that she was sound asleep. I was far too wound up to even think about sleeping. I wouldn't be able to relax until I knew my mother was back, safe and sound, so being careful not to wake Harper, I eased out of bed. It had been two hours since the guys had left, but I hadn't heard anything from anyone. Curious, I opened the door and peeked my head out into the hall. Just as Gus had promised, Rev and Link were standing guard. "Any sign of them?"

"No, ma'am. Not yet."

"Okay. Please let me know if you hear anything."

"Will do."

I closed the door, leaned my back against it, trying to muster whatever strength I had left in me to make it through the next few hours. I closed my eyes and let Gus's words play back in my mind. *"We won't be coming back without Samantha."* Having no other choice, all I could do was hold on and pray that he would stay true to his word.

GUNNER

The plan was simple. Divide and conquer. We'd hit all four of Polito's properties simultaneously, hoping to catch him and his crew off-guard. While Gus was with Shadow and his team of twenty at the main warehouse, T-Bone and Hawk had six men covering the office with Gauge. Blaze and Axel had six more at the other warehouse, while I was at Polito's home with Viper, Murphy, Riggs, and four other Sinners. As much as I wanted to be there to get August's mother back safely, I didn't have a choice. Knowing we were familiar with the property, Gus wanted me at the house with Riggs and Murphy. At exactly, 8:42 p.m., we would enter each of our designated locations and wipe out anyone who was present, including Polito and his front man, Carbone.

Tensions were high as we waited on Riggs to check the surveillance feed one last time, making sure we didn't have any surprises, especially ones that could be avoided. Even after he'd given us the go ahead to proceed, we all knew we'd have to be extra careful when we entered Polito's home. We were in a neighborhood full of possible onlookers, and on top of that, the cameras we'd installed only gave us a view of the ground floor, making it impossible to know what was going on upstairs. For August and Samantha, I was willing to take the risk. We all were.

The time had arrived for us to proceed to our locations. We were masked in darkness as Viper, Riggs, and I made our way up to the front door. As we hid in the stillness of the night, Murphy and a few of Viper's boys slipped around back. The countdown had begun. I glanced over at Riggs, and for just a brief moment, time stood frozen. We both knew what lay ahead, what we were putting on the line, but knowing my brothers had my back, I was ready to face whatever was waiting for us behind that closed door. I wanted this shit to come to an end, and for August to finally be free of Polito.

As we put the silencers on each of our weapons, Riggs' eyes flicked from mine over to Viper's. Once he was certain we were ready, he gave the nod, letting us know it was time. I watched as he pulled out his gun and shot the lock on the front door. Adrenaline surged through me, engulfing my entire body with a mix of fear and excitement as he kicked the door open. As soon as we stepped inside, two men in suits came charging towards us with their weapons drawn, making it impossible to survey my surroundings. They were the same two men we'd seen on the surveillance video, tall and bulky, wearing business suits, and they both seemed stunned to see us standing there. I used that moment of shock to my advantage and started shooting, taking out the biggest of the two with the first shot and wounding the second. Viper charged over to the guy I'd shot in the chest and placed the barrel of his gun at his head. "Who else is here?"

"You're dead asshole. All of you," the guy barked.

"Answer the fucking question!" Viper demanded.

"I'm not telling you shit, motherfucker!"

"Have it your way, dickhead." Viper pulled the trigger, killing the guy instantly. We were checking to see if anyone else was close, when gunshots were fired in the back of the house. Having no idea what Murphy and his boys were facing, Viper turned and started towards them. As he disappeared into the next room, he shouted, "You two, get upstairs."

As ordered, Riggs and I started up the staircase. The house was like something out of one those magazines for the rich and famous with elegant pictures on the walls and large crystal chandlers. The stairs curved upward, making it difficult to see as we made our way up to the second level of the house. We'd almost reached the top when a shot was fired, and I felt a familiar searing pain flash across my bicep. I glanced down at my arm, and even though it was just a simple graze, I was pissed I'd actually been hit—*again*. "Goddamn it!"

The second I saw the asshole who'd shot me, I aimed my 45 directly at his head and fired, killing him. His life-less body dropped to the floor with a loud *thud*. Riggs smirked as he glanced back at me and asked, "You all right?"

"Yeah, I'm fine." I glanced over at the body on the stairway and said, "Next time, that motherfucker will think twice before shooting me."

As he stepped over him, Riggs chuckled. "Yeah, you taught him a lesson for sure."

"Damn straight I did."

Like the rest of the house, the upstairs was decorated in all kinds of fancy shit—a large statue standing beneath the window, expensive paintings lining the hallway, and more crystal chandeliers. When we approached the first bedroom, Riggs turned to me as he reached for the doorknob and said, "Cover me."

I nodded and watched as he opened the door and stepped inside the oversized room. There was a king-sized sleigh bed along with several large, ornate antique pieces of furniture, but there was no one to be seen. I covered his every move as Riggs checked the closet and adjoining bathroom. Once we were certain no one was inside, I looked over to him and said, "It's clear. We need to get moving."

He motioned his hand towards the door, then said, "Across the hall."

I nodded, then stepped out of the room and into the next. Like the one before, it was completely empty. We continued forward, checking the next two rooms with no sign of anyone. I was beginning to think we wouldn't find anyone at all, but I was wrong. When we went to the next room, the door was different from the others. There was a door panel lock with a keypad. Having no idea why an inside door would have such a lock, I turned to Riggs and asked, "What the fuck is this?"

"Might be a safe room or something?" He turned the doorknob, trying to get inside as he said, "No telling who or what's on the other side of that door."

"How the hell are we supposed to get in there to find out?"

Riggs took a step back, aiming his 45 at the lock, and

shot off several rounds. When there was nothing except a few wood fragments left behind, I lifted my foot and kicked the door down. We were both expecting to find more men waiting to take us down, but instead, we were greeted with complete silence. The room was dark, making it difficult to see as we stepped inside.

I had a strange feeling we weren't alone, and that feeling was confirmed the second I heard a strange sound drag across the floor. My heart rate started to quicken as I aimed my weapon and prepared to take my shot. Just as I was about to pull the trigger, Riggs moved to my side, allowing the light from the hallway to cast a dim light into the room. It was at that moment when I saw the source of the strange sound. A large chain was mounted to the floor. I followed the links across the room and found that it was attached to the ankle of a beautiful young woman, who was cowering in the corner, trembling in fear. I could hear the surprise in Riggs' voice as he asked, "What the fuck?"

Trying to shield her face, the girl held up her hands as she cried, "Please don't shoot."

"We won't as long as you don't give us reason to," I told her. "You got a name?"

"Gabriella."

The second she said her name, I knew exactly who she was. I'd often wondered what had happened to the girl who was locked away in the room with Harper back when Polito had taken her. Now I knew. "Damn."

"What?" Riggs asked, "Do you know her?"

"No, but Harper does." I knelt down beside the young woman as I asked, "How long have you been here?"

"Weeks … maybe months. I don't know anymore."

"Well, we're getting you outta here tonight." I grabbed a thin blanket off the bed and used it to wrap around her. "I'm gonna need to remove this chain."

"Okay." I looked over to Riggs and said, "See if you can find a light."

When he started searching, Gabriella told me, "There's not one."

"They've just left you sitting here in the fucking dark?"

"Yes. There's just the window, and the light that comes from under the door."

I couldn't help but think of how scared Harper must've been when she was locked away in that godforsaken room for all those days. The thought angered me to no end, making me want to kill Polito with my bare hands. Without telling me where he was going, Riggs stepped out of the room, only to return moments later with a lamp. He plugged it in, and for the first time, I got a good look at Gabriella. She was pretty and young, maybe twenty or so, with long, curly hair. Even though she was a little on the skinny side, you could tell by her muscle tone she was athletic. With her olive skin, it was difficult to see the dark circles under her eyes, but they were there none the less. I had no idea what the girl had been through, but it was clear that being locked away in that room had taken its toll on her. I tried to keep my voice low and non-threatening when I said, "I'm going to need you to cover your eyes for just a minute."

She nodded, then looked away and covered her head with the blanket. Hoping it would be enough to shield her from any of the fragments, I aimed my gun at one of the chain links and pulled the trigger. Riggs gave it a tug, then said, "That got it."

"Good."

While I hadn't managed to get it completely off of her ankle, I'd made it possible for us to get her out of that fucking room. I eased over to her and was about to pick her up when Riggs said, "We need to make sure the rest of the house is clear."

As much as I hated to leave her there, I didn't have a choice. "We're going to have to go check the other rooms, and then we'll be back to get you."

"No," she said, as tears filled her eyes, "please don't leave me in here alone. Not again."

"I'm sorry, but we don't have a choice." I stood up and told her, "We have to make sure it's safe so we can get you home."

"Um ... There's a woman. She's across the hall."

"Okay. We'll check it out."

"Be careful ... She's his mother or something," Gabriella warned.

I nodded. Before we walked out, I turned back to her and said, "Don't worry. We'll be back for you."

I closed the door, then followed Riggs across the hall. When he tried to turn the doorknob, he discovered it was locked. He was about to knock it down, when a bullet pierced through the wooden door, quickly followed by two more. "Fuck. The bitch is carrying."

Wasting no time, I lifted my leg, slamming my foot into the door. As it flew open, I dodged to the side, avoiding the next few rounds that were shot in our direction. Several more shots were fired, followed by a brief moment of silence. Taking a chance, I inched forward, just enough to see inside the room, and immediately spotted the source of the shooting. It was an older woman, sixty or even older, with long gray hair, and she was wearing one of those old lady dusters, making her look like a typical grandmother—but there was nothing typical about *this* grandmother. She was packing heat and was prepared to take us out without a second thought. As she cursed under her breath, she exchanged clips and was about to take aim when I shouted, "Hold it right there."

Paying no mind to me, she released the safety. Her eyes were dark and menacing, and she was practically foaming at the mouth as she snarled, "You two are as good as dead."

"You need to calm down, lady. Put the gun away."

"Not a chance. I'm gonna fill your puny, little heads full of metal!" she growled. It was clearly not the first time this lady had taken someone out. Just looking at her made me realize why Polito had turned out to be such an evil bastard.

"Just put the gun down!" I ordered.

Ignoring me, she aimed her weapon in my direction. Before she had a chance to shoot, Riggs fired his weapon and nailed her square in the chest. We both watched as she flailed backwards and fell to the ground. I glanced over at Riggs. His face was twisted with anguish. While I knew he hated that he'd had to shoot not only a woman, but an elderly woman at that, it had to be done. "Thanks for covering my ass, brother."

He nodded, then walked over to the elderly woman and knelt down beside her. He placed his fingers at her neck, checking for a pulse. Once he knew without a doubt that she was gone, he got up and motioned for me to follow. He went across the hall to the last remaining room. We both knew it had to be checked, but after facing the *grand-maw from hell*, neither of us were looking forward to seeing what was behind that closed door. Unfortunately, we didn't have a choice, so I turned the knob and eased the door open. When we stepped inside, there was an enormous bed with a headboard that reached the ceiling, massive side tables, and a dresser that filled the entire side wall. An oriental carpet covered the floor, and there was a mirror covering the ceiling over the bed. Obviously just as surprised as I was, Riggs' mouth dropped open as he muttered, "Holy shit."

"This is gotta be Polito's room."

"Definitely."

We continued into the room, searching for anything out of the ordinary. While Riggs checked in the closet, I went to have a look in the bathroom. The second I stepped into the room, I was greeted with a punch to the gut, followed by a quick blow to the head. My gun fell to the ground as I stumbled back, leaving me to fend for myself. My head was spinning and I was struggling to take in a breath, but I wouldn't let myself fall down, knowing if that happened, I was done. I was trying to inch my way up to a standing position when I noticed a pair of men's dress shoes approaching me.

While I had no idea who the fuck they belonged to, I kept myself low and charged towards him, trying with all my strength to tackle him to the ground. I quickly discovered that the guy was built like a Mack truck, and he barely budged. With ease, he lifted his elbow and slammed it into my shoulder, forcing me to release my grip around his waist. I barely had a chance to think before he was on me, driving his fist into my ribs, back, and head. Knowing the motherfucker was about to get the best of me, I reared back my fist and slammed it into his balls. His knees buckled, forcing him to hunch downward, and I used the opportunity to ram the back of my head into his nose, breaking it instantly. He was momentarily dazed, so I punched him in the gut and then once more in his jaw. To my relief, the sonofabitch fell backwards, knocking his head on the edge of the tub. I was about to lay into him again when I realized the motherfucker was out cold. Even though he was out, the guy was still breathing. Knowing that wasn't a part of the plan, I reached down and picked up my 45 off the bathroom floor, then shot him twice.

It was at that moment I noticed Riggs leaning on the doorframe with a smirk. "You done fucking around now?"

"Would've been done sooner if you would've given me a hand," I grumbled.

"Yeah, but what's the fun in that." He patted me on the shoulder and said, "You know I would've stepped in if I thought you really needed me."

"Um-hmm." I walked out of the bathroom and back into the bedroom. "Let's get Gabriella and get the fuck out of this place."

We went back down the hall where Gabriella was being held, and when we opened the door, we found her in the same spot where we'd left her. I could see the relief in her eyes when I offered her my hand and said, "It's time to get you out of here."

She nodded as she took a hold of my hand and rose to her feet. "Thank you ... whoever you are."

"We'll explain all that later. For now, let's get you somewhere safe."

"Okay."

She followed us out of the room and down the hall. As we continued down the steps, Gabriella seemed oddly unfazed by the dead bodies sprawled out on the floor. If anything, she seemed pleased by the sight. I can't say that I blamed her. If I'd been locked up in that room for as long as she had, I'd want the assholes dead too. There were no more of Polito's men left in the house. We'd dealt with them all. When we finally made it down the stairs, we found Viper, Murphy, and the others standing around talking among themselves. I thought they would've been trying to clear the mess we'd made, but instead, Viper was talking to someone on the phone while the others waited for him to give the next order. The room fell silent when he ended the call. Once he'd put his phone away, he looked over to me and asked, "Who's the girl?"

"Her name's Gabriella. I don't know much more than that."

"Then, how do you know she's not one of them?" he pushed.

"Cause she was chained to the fucking floor like some animal," I barked. "Had her in there for weeks."

"Fuck." He ran his hand over his thick beard as he pondered his next move. "Let's get her back to the club-house. We'll talk to Gus and see what he wants to do about her."

"Sounds good."

Viper looked over to Bull, one of his prospects, and told him, "Get her out to the SUV and stay with her until we get there."

As ordered, he walked over to Gabriella and gently took her by the arm, leading her out of the house. Once they were gone, I turned my attention back to Viper. "You heard from Gus or the others?"

"Yeah. Talked to them a few minutes ago. Everything went as planned. Polito and Sal are done, along with all his men. Same for the office and the other warehouse." Before I could ask, he said, "They've got Samantha and are headed back to the clubhouse."

"Good. Did they run into any trouble?"

"No more than what was expected." He motioned towards my arm as he said, "What about you? You need to have Doc look at that?"

"I'm good." I glanced down at my blood-soaked shirt and said, "It's just a graze."

Out of the blue, there was a knock at the front door. I was expecting it to be the cops, especially after the psycho grandmother shot several rounds at us, but Viper seemed unconcerned as he walked over and opened the door. Instead of men in uniform, there was a man carrying a large duffle bag. He was wearing dark jeans with a neatly pressed, white button-down shirt and brown penny loafers. His hair was combed to the side, and he was sporting a pair of wire-rimmed glasses. Behind him were several other men, also carrying large duffel bags. I had no idea who the fuck these guys were, but Viper certainly did.

With piqued interest, I listened as Viper told the first guy, "That was fast. I wasn't expecting you so soon."

"I was waiting on your call."

Without invitation, the guys dropped their bags at the door and started walking through the house. As they walked by me, I leaned over to Brick, one of the Sinners, and asked, "Who the fuck are these guys?"

"That would be 'Billy the Butcher' and his crew."

"What the fuck are they doing here?"

"He's the cleaner," Brick answered. "He's the shit. You won't find another guy around that's as good as he is."

When the Butcher and his guys were done looking around, they each went back over to their duffle bags and simultaneously pulled out bright yellow hazmat suits. As the Butcher started to step into his, he said, "Looks like your boys made quite a mess."

"That they did, and this isn't the only mess we're going to need you to clean up." Clearly anxious about his reaction, Viper tugged at his beard as he told him, "We have three other locations that need to be cleared by morning."

The Butcher had his hazmat suit on and was ready to zip it up when he answered, "No way I can make that happen, Viper."

"We'll make it worth your while. You know that."

"I won't make you any promises, but if we manage to pull it off, it's going to cost you," the Butcher warned.

"Just do what you do, and if you need a hand from any of my boys, just say the word."

He thought for a moment, then reached back into his bag for a pair of large yellow gloves. By now, the Butcher's crew were all dressed in their hazmat suits, silently waiting for their boss to decide if they were going to move forward. As he started to slip on his gloves, he told Viper, "I work better with just my guys, but it would speed things up if you would help load *your friends* into the back of my trailer."

"Yeah, we can do that."

"Good. I've backed the trailer up to the garage. You can load from there without the neighbors being able to see," he suggested. "I would do it quickly. It won't take long for someone to become suspicious."

The Butcher reached back into his duffle bag once again, pulling out spray bottles, boxes of garbage bags, and scrub brushes. I watched with intrigue as the rest of his crew did the same, so intrigued in fact, that I didn't hear Viper order, "Let's get moving boys."

Instead of following the others, I just stood there watching as the strange men in the yellow suits went over and got busy cleaning a large pool of blood on the floor. I was still watching when my attention was drawn over to Murphy when he yelled, "Yo, Gunner. Give me a hand!"

He was trying to lift one of the bodies off the floor, but the guy had at least a hundred pounds on him.

"Yeah. Coming!"

Pulling myself out of my daze, I rushed over and helped him get the guy out to the garage. When we finally hauled him out to the trailer, I was surprised to see that it was a white, six-by-twelve-foot moving trailer—large enough to move a houseful of furniture. Once we had him loaded, I followed Riggs back inside to get the next guy. Within minutes, we had all Polito's men and his mother loaded up, and we were on our way back to the Sinners' clubhouse to meet up with Gus and the others.

AUGUST

$\mathcal{I}$ can't begin to describe the relief I felt when I saw my mother and Gus coming down the hall. Rev and Link had told me that he and the others had gotten her safely out of the warehouse, but I didn't truly believe them until I saw her with my own eyes. The second I spotted her, I rushed over and wrapped my arms around her, hugging her tightly. After discovering that Polito had taken her, I didn't know what to think. I imagined the most horrific things and had almost convinced myself that I would never see her again. I simply couldn't believe that she was standing there, safe and sound, that I could see her beautiful face, smell the soft scent of her perfume, and feel the familiar touch of her arms around me. Finally accepting the fact that she was truly okay, I squeezed her even tighter and whispered, "Thank god, you're okay."

"I'm so sorry, sweetheart. I'm so sorry for all of this." She stepped back, looking at me as she cried, "I never meant for any of this to happen."

Before I had a chance to respond, Hawk and several of his brothers came walking through the door. Gus lifted his hand, letting them know that he was coming, then turned his attention back to me. "I need to meet with them for a few minutes. You okay to get her back to her room?"

"Of course."

A softness crossed his face as Gus placed his hand on Mom's shoulder and said, "I won't be long. When I get done, we'll talk."

"Okay, I'd like that."

They stood there for a brief moment, and just by the way they were looking at one another, I knew something was going on between them. When he turned to leave, I called out to him. "Gus?"

"Yeah?"

"What about Gunner? Is he okay?"

He smiled, then answered, "Yeah, darlin'. He's just fine."

"Thank goodness. I hadn't heard, so … Anyway, thank you for bringing Mom back to me."

"No need to thank me, August." He glanced over at Mom. "Not even the good Lord himself could've stopped me from going after her."

He gave me a quick wink, then walked away. I took Mom's hand and led her back to her room. Harper was sleeping soundly across the hall, so I left the door open as we entered her room. Once we were both sitting on the bed, I asked, "What happened?"

She ran her hands down her face and sighed. "Where do you want me to start?"

"The beginning would be good."

"Well, you know how Harper's been begging for Floppsie?"

"Yes, but she's—"

"She's a little girl in a strange place," Mom interrupted. "She wanted something that would make her feel safe again. I know it sounds crazy, but I wanted to give that to her. With you and Gus so upset with me, I wanted one person who didn't think I had screwed everything up."

"Oh, Mom. I don't know what to say."

"You could say that I was crazy for doing something so stupid, that my actions put you and Harper in even more danger," she cried.

"It wasn't the best idea you've ever had, but I understand why you did it."

"I was so stupid to go over to that house. I knew there was a chance that those men were still there, but I went anyway."

"Is that where they got you?"

"Yes. I'd gone in through the backyard ... used that spot that was broken in the fence and slipped through. We hadn't had the chance to lock the backdoor, so I was able to get inside." Her eyes dropped to the floor as she said, "I found Floppsie on the sofa and was just about to rush back out when two men came in through the front door. They grabbed me, blindfolded me, and after they tied my hands behind my back, they took me to some strange warehouse or something."

"Did they hurt you?"

"No, but I have no doubt that they would have. The second he took off my blindfold, I knew I was in trouble. Anthony Polito was there along with a bunch of his guards and some guy he called Sal. There were these fancy cars parked inside, and an office-like room surrounded in glass upstairs. They were all standing around, watching as Anthony asked one question after the next. I'd never been so terrified. You should've seen him, August. That man was pure evil, and I could feel it radiating off of him."

"What did he do?"

"They kept asking me all these questions about you and where you were." Tears filled her eyes as she said, "I knew what would happen if they found you, so there was no way in hell I was going to tell them anything. He threatened to hurt me ... to do god-awful things to me if I didn't tell him, but I still refused. His patience was wearing thin, and I had no doubt that he was going to make good on his promises when all hell broke loose."

"What do you mean?"

"I was sitting in that chair ... my hands bound behind my back in this big, open, metal building. He'd just raised his hand to slap me when one of the men dropped to the floor. At first, I didn't realize that he'd even been shot, but then a second man fell and then another."

"Gus."

"At first, I had no idea who it was. My brain just wasn't registering anything. I was too scared to think, especially when all the shooting started." I could see the horror in her eyes as she thought back on everything she'd seen and heard. "I wanted to run and hide, but I couldn't move. I just had to sit there and watch."

"You must've been so terrified."

"I was ... but then I spotted Gus. As soon as I saw him, I knew everything was going to be okay. I knew he wouldn't let those men hurt me, and he'd get me home safe."

"But what happened to Anthony Polito?"

"Hmm ... Well, Gus was headed in my direction when Anthony shouted across the room, ordering his men to stop him. They rushed towards him but didn't get very far. It wasn't long before there were no guards left, just Anthony and Sal. These two powerful men ... men who'd done unthinkable things to so many, were truly terrified."

"So, what ended up happening."

"In all the chaos, Anthony had managed to get over to me. He had the barrel of his gun pointed at my head, and he threatened to kill me if Gus and the others didn't walk away. What he didn't know was that Shadow had come up behind him." She paused for a moment and let out a deep breath before saying, "He killed him, and seconds later, Gus killed Sal."

It was hard to believe that my father had killed those men, and while I didn't know for certain, I had a feeling that Cade had had his own part in taking out Polito and his men. That, in itself, might've made me feel differently about them both, but I knew in my heart they would never hurt anyone without good reason. It all came down to the simple fact that they both were good men who would do whatever they had to do to protect those they loved. This time was no different. My mother's life was in danger, and they did what they had to do to bring her back to me. "We owe Gus so much. I don't know how I will ever be able to thank him."

"I'm sure you'll find a way. We both will."

I thought back to their brief moment in the hall, and I

L. WILDER

was still curious about what had happened between them. Hoping she'd tell me, I asked, "What about you and Gus?"

"What about me and Gus?"

"Come on, Mom," I pushed. "Did y'all make up?"

"I wouldn't go that far, but I'm hopeful."

I was just about to give her a hard time when Cade appeared in the doorway. I rushed over and reached for him, hugging him tightly. "When did you get back?"

"Just a few minutes ago." He kissed me on the crook of my neck. "You okay?"

"I'm much better now." I could've stayed there in his arms for the rest of the night, but quickly remembered we weren't alone. I took a step back, releasing him from my grasp. That's when I noticed his arm. "What happened to you?"

He glanced down at his bloodstained shirt and shook his head. "It's nothing."

"It doesn't look like nothing!" I argued.

"It's just a graze, August. I'm fine."

"You were shot!

"It's just a scratch," he assured me. "I'm fine."

"You weren't kidding when you said you had a thing about getting shot, were you?" Not giving him a chance to answer, I carefully raised his sleeve and gasped when I saw the black burnt-like wound. "We need to get a doctor to—"

"I'll have Viper's guy check me out in a bit. Right now, Gus wants to see you in the conference room."

"Why?"

"He has something he wants to talk to you about."

"Oh, okay."

When I turned to Mom, she smiled and said, "Go ahead. I'll keep an eye on Harper."

I nodded, then followed Cade out of the room. As we walked down the hall, I couldn't stop staring at Cade's wound. It made me sick to think that he'd been hurt because of me. I hated it. I hated everything about what happened that night, and it was all because of David. Thankfully, I would soon find out that he would get what was coming to him. When we walked into the conference room, I was surprised to see that Gus wasn't alone. In fact, all the brothers of Satan's Fury were there. They all waited patiently as Cade and I sat down at the table next to them. Once we were settled, Gus said, "I'm sure by now you know that Polito has been taken care of."

"I do." I looked at the men sitting around that table as I said, "I've already said this to Gus, but I want you all to know how much I appreciate what you did tonight. I know you put your lives in danger for us, and I will always be indebted to each and every one of you for doing so."

"Like I already told you, that's what we do. We protect what's ours. That's why we asked you to come down here and talk to us." His tone grew even more serious as he said, "We have one last matter to contend with."

"Okay. What's that?"

"David," he answered flatly. "We have to decide what we're going to do about him."

"I honestly don't care what you do to him." I wanted to make him pay for all the hell he'd put us through, so I told him, "I'd kill him myself if I could."

"As much as I would love to put a bullet in that man's head, I don't think that's our best move. He's the mayor.

There's no way in hell we'll be able to take him out without blowback."

"Okay, then. What do you suggest we do?"

"We gotta get him where it hurts." Gus cocked his eyebrow and he asked, "What's most important to him?"

"Well, that's easy," I scoffed. "His career."

"Then, we take it from him, but we don't stop there." His eyes narrowed as he said, "We take everything from him, including his freedom."

"That sounds great to me, but how?"

Riggs leaned forward and said, "We were hoping you could help us with that."

"I'll do anything you need me to do."

"We have everything we need to prove that David was taking bribes." Riggs pushed a folder over to me. When I opened it, I saw page after page of large sums of money deposited into his campaign accounts. "Each one of those deposits can be tracked back to Polito or Carbone, but not just them. David was in bed with several big names. We just need to get this information into the right hands."

"Why couldn't I simply take it to the police?"

"You gotta remember, we don't know who David has in his pocket," Riggs explained. "We just can't take the chance on this getting brushed under the rug."

"I hadn't thought about that."

Shadow added, "The election is just a couple of months away, right?"

"Yeah?"

"And he's running against that Brent Walker guy?"

"He is."

"All right then. I'm sure he would be very interested to know that the guy he's running against is a crook. Hell, his campaign would be made with information like this. If we can get this folder in his hands, then I'd bet he'll do all the work for us."

"You're absolutely right." Excitement washed over me. "I know plenty of people who'd be able to help us out. I'll just need to call in a few favors."

"We were hoping you'd say that." Gus stood up and said, "You get the names we need, and we'll make sure they get everything they need to not only sink David but also put him behind bars."

I smiled as I told them, "This could actually work."

"It's one hell of a payback for all the shit he's pulled."

"It's late," Cade announced. "She's had a long night. I'm going to walk her back down to her room."

Gus nodded, and then Cade took me back down to my room. When we got to my door, he stopped and pulled me close, kissing me softly. As glad as I was that my troubles with David were coming to an end, I knew it wouldn't be long before we all left the Sinners' clubhouse. Harper and I would return home, while Cade would head back to Memphis. I'd gotten used to him being around. I liked having him close, but it was more than that. I'd fallen for him, really fallen for him, and I wasn't ready for us to be apart. I could tell by the way he kissed me, so possessive and full of need, that he felt the same way.

GUNNER

Once I'd gotten August to her room, I went back to the conference room with the others. As I headed down the hall, I knew I was in for a long night. While we'd been successful in ending Polito and getting Samantha back safe, there was still a great deal of work to be done. Once the Butcher and his crew finished with the house, he called Viper to let him know that he was on his way to the warehouse. Our goal was to make it look like Polito and Carbone skipped town in a hurry, leaving everything he owned behind. Riggs spent the next few hours monitoring all the police scanners, making sure that no one called in with concerns about a possible break-in. From where I stood, everything seemed to be going as planned, and I had no doubt that a big part of that was due to the Butcher. We'd never dealt with anyone like him before, but after hearing Viper sing his praises and seeing his work firsthand, we felt confident that he would erase any and all evidence of the attack.

The sun was just starting to rise when he called to let

us know that the job was done. With all that had gone down, it was hard to believe that there'd been no major snags—no snooping neighbors, noise complaints, or patrolling cops. Knowing we still had to contend with David and Gabriella, Gus gave the order for us to return to our rooms for a few hours of shut eye. As much as I wanted to go see about August, I knew she would still be sleeping and I was utterly exhausted, so I went straight to my room and crashed.

I had no idea how long I'd been sleeping when I felt someone crawling into bed with me. I knew right away it was August and pulled her close, relishing in the feel of her body next to mine. I liked having her there next to me, and I wasn't looking forward to having to leave her. Unfortunately, I didn't have a choice. She had her own life here in Nashville, and I couldn't force her to leave that all behind for me—at least not yet. If this thing between us was ever going to work, I'd have to be patient and give her time to decide her next move.

As she nestled in closer, her hand brushed against the bandage on my arm, causing her to still. I leaned over and kissed her on the forehead as I said, "I got it checked out. I'm fine."

"Are you sure?"

"Absolutely."

"Good." She nestled a little closer, and after several moments she let out a sigh. I knew something was on her mind, but I wasn't expecting her to say, "You know, I'm sure this is going to sound all kinds of crazy, especially after everything's that happened … and you getting shot, but a part of me is sad that it's almost over."

Even though I knew exactly what she was talking about, I asked, "Why's that?"

"Because that means it's time for you to go back to Memphis, and I'm not ready for you to go." Before I had a chance to interject, she said, "I know you have to go, but … I don't want to lose you."

"No way in hell that's gonna happen," I tried to assure her.

"But how can you be so sure?"

"Because I am." I eased up on my side and looked down at her. When her gorgeous eyes met mine, my gut twisted into a knot. I was crazy about this woman, and it was time to let her know exactly how I felt. "I need you to listen to me, August."

Her brows furrowed as she replied, "Okay?"

"You're not going to lose me, and I have no intention of losing you." I lowered my mouth to the crook of her neck, and trailed kisses along her shoulder as I whispered, "I meant it when I said I'd do whatever it took to make you happy. I know it won't be easy, but we'll figure it out."

"You promise?"

Answering her the best way I knew how, I dropped my mouth to hers, kissing her long and hard. Her mouth was warm and wet, and all of her little moans and whimpers made my cock ache with need. I reached for the hem of her t-shirt and slipped it over her head, exposing her perfect round breasts. I was done. I couldn't wait a moment longer to have her. After making quick work of my boxers, I slipped her panties and leggings down past her ankles, leaving her completely bare. She looked like the perfect wet dream as she lay there sprawled out on my bed, waiting for me to take her. So fucking beautiful. It was hard to believe that she was mine. I watched the goosebumps rise along her skin as I settled myself between her thighs.

Hovering over her, I placed my mouth close to her ear and whispered, "You're mine, August. Now and forever."

Without saying a word, she pressed her lips to mine in a possessive, demanding kiss as she wrapped her legs around my waist, pressing my cock against her. I spent the next hour making love to her, and if I hadn't needed to talk to Gus, I would've stayed there in that bed with her all morning. After one last kiss, I forced myself out of the bed. As I started to pull on my boxers, I looked over to her and said, "I gotta run and check in with Gus."

"Oh ... Well, umm." A smirk crossed her face as she said, "I think he might be in my mother's room."

"Is that right?"

"Yeah." She reached for her t-shirt and slipped it on. "Before I came to see you, I went over to check on her. I was just about to open her door when I heard his voice. I might've tried to eavesdrop, but I wasn't sure what was going on in there."

"Oh, yeah?" I pulled on my jeans and chuckled. "You think they were up to something?"

A funny look crossed her face. "Uh ... I don't know, and I don't want to know."

"I totally understand." When she finished getting dressed, I asked, "Where's Harper?"

"Jae took her down to the kitchen to get some breakfast. I should probably go see about her."

"I'll go with you." I was running on just a few hours of sleep, so I told her, "I could use a cup of coffee or two."

When we walked out of my room, I noticed August

glancing over at her mother's room with a smile. While we both had our suspicions, neither of us knew what was going on in that room, but it was clear from her expression that she hoped that Samantha and Gus would find a way to work things out. I felt the same way. I hoped that they'd be able to put their past behind them, because after all these years, they deserved their second chance at happiness. When we got down to the kitchen, there was no one there, so we each grabbed a cup of coffee and headed to the family room to see if Jae and Harper were there. As soon as we walked in, I spotted Harper sitting on the sofa with Jae and Gabriella. Harper was in Gabriella's lap, talking a mile a minute. I couldn't remember seeing her look so happy. August leaned over to me and asked, "Who's that with Harper?"

"When we got her back from Polito, do you remember her telling you about being locked in a room with a girl named Gabriella?"

"Yeah."

"Well, that's her. We found her locked away in one of Polito's bedrooms." I remembered how shocked I was when we'd found her chained in that room. I felt so bad for her and was relieved to see that she seemed to be doing much better now that she was free. As we started towards them, I continued, "She'd been there for weeks."

"Oh, god. That's awful."

"At least now we can finally find out what happened while Harper was gone." When we got over to Gabriella, she looked up at us and smiled. "Looks like you've found a friend."

"Hi, Momma!" A big smile crossed Harpers face as she announced, "Iss Gab-we-ella."

"Well, hello Gabriella. I'm August, Harper's mother."

Gabriella extended her hand and said, "It's really nice to meet you, August. Your daughter is an amazing little girl."

"Yes, she is," August replied as she shook her hand. "Harper told me a little about you, but not much about the time you two spent in that room together."

"I'm not sure why Harper was in there with me, but they were much nicer to her than they were to me. It was clear that they didn't want any harm to come to her."

"Well, that makes me feel a little better, I guess." August sighed as she studied Gabriella for a moment. "As sorry as I am that you were locked in that room, I'm glad Harper had you with her. I have no doubt it made the experience at least tolerable."

"Harper was a blessing to me as well. I was about to lose my mind when they brought her into that room with me." Gabriella looked down at Harper with such adoration as she ran her hand over her head. "I was so tired of being alone and scared. It was nice to have someone to look after ... even if it was just for a little while."

"Do you know why he took you like that?"

She shrugged. "I don't know for sure, but if I had to guess, I would say it had something to do with my father. He and Anthony Polito weren't exactly friends. You would've thought killing my father was enough, but it wasn't. Anthony was an evil man who would stop at nothing to get what he wanted."

"We've had our own run-in with him," August told her. "I know how awful he can be."

"What about your family, Gabriella?" I asked. "Is there someone we can call for you?"

Anguish crossed her face as she replied, "There's no one ... at least, not anymore."

"So, you have nowhere to go?"

"No." For a moment, it looked like she was going to cry, but she managed to pull herself together as she continued, "But I'll figure something out."

"We'll figure out something together," I said as her eyes met mine. "You helped Harper through a tough time. The least we can do is show you the same courtesy."

"Thank you. I really appreciate that."

"No thanks necessary." I glanced down at my watch, and when I noticed the time, I said, "I need to go check in with Riggs and the others."

"Oh." After pulling me to the side where the others couldn't hear, August reached into her pocket and pulled out a slip of paper. As she offered it to me, she said, "Here are the names and the emails that Riggs needed. The first one is Brent's campaign manager."

I took it from her hand. "I'll be sure he gets it."

After giving her a brief kiss on the cheek, I waved to Harper and Gabriella, then walked out the room. When I got down to the conference room, Riggs and Murphy were sitting at the table talking to Viper, Hawk, and Axel. I was surprised that Gus wasn't with them. He was usually the first one up and going, but I had a feeling he'd been otherwise detained. I sat down next to Riggs and handed him the piece of paper August had given me. "Morning."

"Morning," they each replied.

There were papers scattered on the table, and Riggs was hammering away at his computer. Worried something might be up, I asked, "What's all this?"

"We're doing what can to erase all signs of Polito in

Nashville." Riggs looked over to me as he continued, "I'm trying to get the deeds to his properties transferred over to a new dummy company ... one that we have full control of. At some point, we'll move ownership over to Viper and his club as reimbursement for their help. We just need to wait until we're certain David has been dealt with."

"Speaking of David ..." I pointed at the paper I'd just handed to Riggs. "Those are the names August said she'd get for you. The first one is Brent's actual campaign manager. The others work with him on his campaign."

"Good. I'll get moving on this next."

"How you planning on getting that information to them without tracking it back to us?"

"I'll set up an email with an untraceable IP address." He turned his attention back to his computer as he said, "They'll have no idea who it came from or if it's true, but it won't be hard for them to check things out for themselves."

I looked back over to Viper as I asked, "Any issues arise from our visit with Polito last night?"

"Oddly enough, there hasn't been anything. Looks like we might've actually pulled it off," Viper answered proudly.

I was just about to respond when Gus replied, "Good. That's exactly what I wanted to hear."

He, Blaze, and Shadow came over and sat down next to me. As they got settled in their seats, I couldn't help but notice that there was something different about Gus. I couldn't put my finger on exactly what it was; that tough-as-nails expression he normally wore was there, yet it seemed toned down. While I couldn't be sure, I figured it had something to do with his morning with Samantha. Viper looked over to Gus and boasted, "We make a pretty damn good team, that's for sure."

"That we do." Gus nodded. "We can't thank you enough for your help, Viper. You boys really pulled through for us. You got a good thing going here, but I knew that coming in. We all did."

"Appreciate that, brother, but we were more than happy to help."

"Well, as soon as we tie up some loose ends, we'll get out of your hair and let you get back to business as usual." Gus turned to Riggs and asked, "You got the ownership to the properties moved over?"

"Almost."

"And David?"

Riggs nodded. "August supplied the names we needed, and I'll be getting everything sent over to them within the hour."

A satisfied look crossed Gus's face as he leaned back in his chair and said, "Then, that should just about do it."

"There's just one more thing we need to figure out," I told him.

His eyes narrowed as he asked, "And what's that?"

"Gabriella." With all that was going on, we hadn't had a chance to discuss what we were going to do about her. "We need to get things sorted with her."

"Fuck, I forgot all about her." Gus thought for a moment, then asked, "I know she was with Harper, but have we got any idea who this girl actually is?"

"Not much. I was talking to her this morning, and she told me that Polito killed her father, then kidnapped her. No idea what he was planning on doing with her," I explained. "She didn't say much more than that, but she made it clear that she's got no place to go."

"Well, the decision is completely up to her, but she's welcome to come back to Memphis with us," Gus offered. "We can help get her on her feet, and she can decide what to do from there."

"I'll let her know."

"But I don't want any surprises. If she does decide to come back with us, we'll need to find out who she really is and why Polito killed her father," he said then turned to Riggs. "Once we get more information from her, I'll need you to see what you can find out."

"Will do."

"So, when are we planning to head out?" Murphy asked, sounding eager.

"That depends on how much time Riggs needs," Gus answered.

"I'm about to wrap things up." Riggs looked down at his watch as he continued, "I should be done within the hour."

A pained expression crossed Gus's face, and I knew exactly why it was there. Like me, he wasn't looking forward to leaving. Not only had he just started to get to know the daughter he never even knew he had, he'd finally gotten Samantha back. It wouldn't be easy for him to leave her behind, but if I knew Gus, he would be seeing them again sooner than later. He quickly rebounded and said, "Then, I say it's time to start packing up. You boys get ready to roll out."

"You don't have to tell me twice," Blaze teased as he stood and started for the door. "Momma, I'm coming home!"

The room rang out in laughter as he strutted out of the room with Shadow and Murphy following close behind. I stood to follow them but stopped when Gus said, "I'm gonna need you to hang back with August and Harper for a couple of days. Just until we know David is no longer a risk. You good with that?"

"Yeah, I'm definitely good with that."

"I thought you would be," he scoffed. "I'm expecting you to take good care of my girls."

"You know I will." I stood up and started for the door. Just before I walked out, I turned back to him and said, "I won't let you down, Prez."

"I know that, son. I've known it all along."

AUGUST

J'd never been a fan of goodbyes, especially when it's someone I truly care about. I was always worried that I would never see them again, so I wanted to hold on to them and prolong the time we shared together. Even though I knew that wasn't the case with Gus and the brothers of Satan's Fury, saying goodbye to them was just as hard. Once we'd gotten packed up, we loaded everything into the SUVs. I'd just put our bags away when Gabriella come over to us. She knelt down beside Harper, and with a soft smile, she told her, "Hey, cutie. Before I left, I wanted to tell you goodbye."

Harper's brows furrowed as she asked her, "W'ere ya going?"

"To Memphis with the guys for a little while."

"Why?"

"They're going to help me find a place to live and do grownup stuff. Things that you don't have to worry about just yet." Gabriella wasn't your typical beauty. She had a way about her that was endearing and comforting to those around her, but my gut told me that she was hiding something. I just had no idea what it was. After all she'd been through, I hoped her secrets wouldn't end up causing her even more trouble. Gabriella wrapped her arms around Harper and gave her a hug. "I'm really going to miss you."

Harper's eyes filled with tears as she returned Gabriella's embrace. "I miss you, too."

"Maybe your mom can bring you by to see me when you come to Memphis."

Harper nodded, then Gabriella gave her a quick kiss on the cheek before turning her attention to me. As she stood, she said, "I hope you both have a safe trip home."

"Thanks, Gabriella. You, too." I gave her a quick hug as I said, "If you ever need anything, just give me a call."

"I will."

She gave Harper a little wave goodbye, then turned and started towards Blaze and the others. Harper didn't take her eyes off of Gabriella as she got into their SUV and closed the door. Seeing that she was upset, I picked up Harper and tried to console her. I was just starting to make her feel better when the guys started coming over to tell Harper and me goodbye. Each time they gave me a hug, I had to fight back the tears. These men had risked their lives for us, and not only that—they had also made us feel like we were a part of their family. While it wasn't easy, I'd managed to keep it together until Gus came over to me. The second he approached me, I could feel the tears starting to sting my eyes. A tender smile crossed his face as he said, "You know this isn't goodbye."

"I know, but that doesn't make this any easier."

"Can't disagree with you there." He reached for me,

hugging me tightly as he said, "I never knew how much I wanted a daughter until I met you. Now that I have, I'm gonna do my best to make up for lost time."

Hearing those words from him moved me in a way I didn't expect. I thought back to my childhood and the years I'd spent with Denis, and he'd never once made me feel as loved as Gus did in that moment. In the short time we'd spent together, Gus had shown me the kind of compassion and understanding that only a father could, and I knew without a doubt that he meant it when he said he would make up for the time we'd lost. I loved him for that. With tears streaming down my face, I hugged him back and said, "I'm going to hold you to that cause I kind of like having you around, and I want Harper to know her grandfather."

"That's a good thing 'cause I have every intention of spending as much time as possible with her." Then he took a step back and looked over to Harper and said, "You be good for your momma, and I'll see you two soon, okay?"

"Kay." Her brows furrowed as she asked, "When?"

"When will I see you?"

Harper nodded.

"Very soon if I have anything to say about it. That all right with you?"

Harper nodded with a smile, then held her arms out, letting him know that she also wanted a hug. Gus quickly obliged, lifting her into his arms and giving her a tight squeeze. When he was done, he gave her a kiss on the cheek and handed her over to me. "I'll be in touch."

"I'll be looking forward to it."

When he walked away, I turned to put Harper in

Hawk's SUV. Since Cade's was still at my house, he offered to run us home. I'd just gotten Harper settled when I noticed that Gus had gone over to talk to Mom. She was waiting for him on the other side of the SUV, so I couldn't hear what either of them were saying. I didn't have to. I could see the love they felt for each other. It was written all over their faces, and it pained me to know that they had to say goodbye once again.

My chest tightened when I saw Gus wrap his arms around her, pulling her close as he whispered something in her ear. She clung to him, quietly sobbing as she buried her head in his chest. They remained like that for several minutes, and then he brought his hand up to her chin, forcing her to look at him. Anguish marked his face as he said a few more words to her, then kissed her tenderly. While it was brief, the kiss was effective, and my mother finally smiled. It was clear that their conversation was coming to an end, so I slipped into the SUV next to Harper and closed the door. Moments later, she started towards us and got inside the SUV.

Once she was buckled in, Hawk started the engine and we were on our way. As we headed out of the parking lot, I realized that the church van we'd *borrowed* was nowhere in sight. Curious, I leaned towards the front where Hawk and Cade were sitting and asked, "What happened to the van?"

"One of Viper's boys took it back before anyone had a chance to report it stolen," Cade answered.

"Okay. Good."

When we pulled through the gate, I noticed Mom turning back to see Gus one last time. I knew she was heartbroken over having to leave him, so I suggested,

"Hey, Mom ... Why don't you stay with us for a few days? Just until things start to settle down."

"Oh, honey. I appreciate the offer, but I really don't want to impose." She feigned a smile as she said, "I know you want to get back home and into your own routines."

"Mom, I wouldn't have asked you to come if I didn't want you there. Besides, you don't need to be home alone right now, especially with David still on the loose."

Before she could argue, Cade turned to look at her and said, "She's right. Gus would want you to be there with us."

"Okay." She turned to look out the window and sighed.
"

When we pulled up at the house, Cade and Hawk went inside to check things out. After a thorough search, they came back out and said, "It's a bit of a mess, but it's safe to go in."

"Thank goodness." After I grabbed my bag from the back of his SUV, I went over to Hawk and said, "Thanks again for everything."

"No problem. Glad we could help."

"We really do appreciate everything y'all did for us," Cade told him. "If you're ever in Memphis, be sure to give us a call."

"You know I will."

They gave each other a quick man hug, then Hawk turned and got in his SUV. Once he was gone, we all went inside. I thought it would feel good to finally be home, but I felt out of place. Even with Cade there to watch over us, I didn't feel safe, but it was more than that. I had no idea why, but it simply didn't feel like home anymore. I wasn't the only who was feeling out of sorts.

Floppsie was lying on the floor, just waiting for Harper to snatch her up, but she didn't. Instead, she passed right by the stuffed bunny and headed outside. I walked over to the window and was watching Harper as she climbed up in her swing when Cade came up behind me. "You okay?"

"I'm getting there." I raised the bags in my hand as I said, "I'm going to put all this away. I'll be right back."

"Take your time. I'll be outside with Harper."

"Okay." I eased up on my tiptoes and kissed him on the jaw. "I'm glad you're here."

"Me too. More than you know."

I was feeling pretty good about things when I went to put my stuff away, but as soon as I walked into my room, I spotted my cell phone sitting on the bedside table. I dropped my bags on the bed, then picked up the phone to see if I had any messages. Dread washed over me when I saw all the texts and missed calls from work and several of my friends. I even had a couple from David. I don't know what I was expecting. I'd been MIA for days, so it only made sense that they'd wonder where I was. I knew I should call and let them know that I was okay, but I wasn't ready to deal with it. I figured one more day wouldn't hurt, so I just tossed the phone back down on the table and started putting my things away. Once I was done, I headed to the kitchen to see if we had anything I might be able to fix for dinner.

I opened the fridge, and just as I'd expected, there was nothing to be found. What few groceries I had were out of date or just simply not appealing. I closed the refrigerator and went back into the living room where Mom was sitting on the sofa. The TV wasn't on, but she was staring blankly at the screen. I hated to see her so withdrawn, so I went over and sat down beside her. "Are you okay?"

"No, but I will be."

I tried to comfort her by saying, "You'll see him again, Mom."

"I know. I'm just upset with myself for waiting so long to set things straight between us," she said then started to cry. "I've spent so many years wishing things could've been different. I should've done something sooner, and then I wouldn't have wasted so much precious time."

"You can't change what's been done, but you and Gus have a second chance at happiness together." I placed my hand on hers as I said, "I know he cares a great deal for you, Mom. He's not the kind of man who's just going to let you slip through his fingers again."

"Would you think I was crazy if I told you I was thinking of going to Memphis for a while?" she asked as a look of apprehension crossed her face.

"What do you mean 'for a while'?"

"A few months ... just long enough to see if there's anything left of what we had all those years ago?"

I'd had similar thoughts about Cade, so I told her, "No, I don't think that sounds crazy at all."

"I'm not saying that's something I would actually do, but it's something to think about." I could see her spirits lifting as she went on, "I've always loved Memphis, and I have friends there ..."

"Mom, it's a good idea. You should do it."

"I think I will then," she said, as a smile crossed her face.

"Good!" I leaned over and hugged her. "I want you to be happy, Mom."

"I want the same thing for you." She glanced out the window and watched Cade as he pushed Harper on the swing. "He's a good boy, August, and he's clearly crazy about you and Harper."

"I'm pretty crazy about him too," I said then stood up. "I better get out there and give Cade a hand."

"Okay."

When I walked outside, Cade was still pushing Harper on the swing while she sang one of her silly nursery rhymes. It was good to see her smiling, and I hoped that she would be pleased when I asked, "So, what do you two think about having pizza and watching a movie tonight?"

"Can we watch *Fwozen*?" Harper asked with excitement.

"Umm," I mumbled. "Any chance we could watch something else?"

She thought for a moment, then turned to Cade and asked, "You wanna watch *Fwozen*?"

"How about we watch something else first, and then we can watch *Frozen*?"

Knowing she'd never make it through two movies, I smiled and said, "That sounds like a great idea. What do you think, Harper?"

"Kay."

"Great." As I sat down on the swing next to her, I noticed several dark clouds rolling in. "It looks like we might get a little rain tonight. There's nothing like a cozy night inside when it's storming."

"I have to agree with you there," Cade replied, "especially when I'm with my two favorite ladies."

Harper smiled as she looked over her shoulder at Cade. She didn't say a word, but I knew what she was thinking. Cade had made quite the impression on her during the time he'd spent with her. I was pleased to see that she liked him as much as she did. In fact, her liking him made me fall for him even more. We stayed outside for a little longer, and when it finally started to rain we went inside and I ordered our pizzas. Once they arrived, we all piled up in the living room and started our movie. Harper and I curled up next to Cade on the sofa while mom lay back in the recliner. With the dark room and the storm rolling outside, I didn't make it through the whole movie before I fell fast asleep. I was completely out of it when Cade picked me up and carried me to bed. As he kissed me on the forehead, he whispered, "I've already taken care of Harper. She's in her bed asleep."

With my eyes barely open, I nodded and said, "Thank you."

"Goodnight, beautiful."

"Goodnight," I mumbled, then fell right back to sleep.

I woke up the next morning with the sound of rain and thunder rumbling outside, making it hard to get up. I just wanted to lay there and enjoy a moment of quiet, but once I remembered all those missed texts and messages, I just kept getting more and more anxious. I'd put it off long enough, so I reached for my phone and opened up my messages. I had no idea how long it took me to go through them all, but I'd saved the worst for last—my boss. When I finally returned his call, he made it clear that he wasn't pleased that I'd never made it to the office to sign the projections for next month. He was even more upset that I hadn't been back to the office since Harper's return. He'd assumed that I was just taking vacation time to be with her, and I wasn't in the position to correct him.

When he asked me to come in to see him the following week, I knew there was a good chance that he'd fire me, but honestly, I just didn't care. There were other jobs to be had. I was about to start sorting through my emails when Cade appeared in my doorway. "Hey, you're gonna wanna see this?"

"What?"

"Just come on. You need to see it for yourself," he urged.

I got up and followed him to the living room where Mom was sitting on the sofa watching the news. Her eyes were glued to the screen and didn't even notice when I sat down beside her. Curious to see what had her so enthralled, I turned my attention to the news. That's when I saw several police officers and David coming out of the courthouse. David's hands were cuffed behind his back, and news reporters were all in his face, asking questions and taking pictures. It looked like a madhouse. Cameras flashed over and over as the officers led him to one of their squad cars. I was too overwhelmed by what I was seeing to hear anything the anchor woman was saying, so I looked over to Cade and asked, "What's going on?"

"Turns out, David was already under investigation for taking bribes and possible embezzlement from his campaign funds. The information we leaked to his counterpart only confirmed some of their suspicions. They also mentioned Harper, too."

"Harper? What about her?"

"That even though she's been returned home safely, there's talk that he might've had something to do with her kidnapping." With a look of satisfaction, Cade continued,

"They're saying David will be impeached and unable to run for office again. They're also talking about a lengthy jail term."

"So, we did it?"

"Yeah, baby. We did it."

Too excited to control myself, I leapt off the sofa and rushed over to him, jumping into his arms as I cried, "It's finally over!"

"Yeah." His tone changed as he repeated, "It's finally over."

I released my hold on him as I stepped back and looked at him. When I saw his face, I knew he'd have to leave me soon. "How long do we have?"

"I'll stick around until tomorrow. Just to make sure he doesn't get out on bail." His eyes met mine as he said, "I'd stay longer, but I really need to get back."

Even though I was ecstatic that David finally got what was coming to him, my heart sank at the thought of Cade going home so soon. I thought we'd have longer, at least a couple of days, but that clearly wasn't going to happen. I inhaled a deep breath, trying my best to hide my disappointment, and I thought I was pulling it off until Mom said, "I think you two deserve a little time to celebrate on your own. Why don't you let me take Harper home with me for the night? That way you can have the night to yourselves?"

"Are you sure?"

"Of course, I'm sure." Mom smiled as she stood up. "Besides, I love spending time with Harper, and honestly, I really want to be in my own home."

"Well, okay then. I'll go get her a bag together."

"No need," Mom fussed. "I'll get her ready. You just

relax and see what you can find out about what they have on David."

When she rushed out of the room, I made my way back over to the sofa and sat down. As I stared at the screen, I mumbled, "I just can't believe it. They actually got him."

"Yeah. I'd hate to be in his shoes right now."

We sat there watching the news for another hour or so. Mom and Harper made it over to her house, leaving Cade and I completely alone for the first time. For a brief moment, I wasn't sure how to act, but Cade made it easy. He suggested that we get out of the house for a bit and have dinner downtown. Excited by the thought of having a night out with him, I quickly took a shower and got dressed in my sexiest black dress. After I did my makeup and hair, I slipped on my heels and headed into the living room to find Cade. He was waiting patiently on the sofa, and when I walked in, his eyes widened with surprise. "Damn, you look amazing."

"Thank you." I smiled as I watched him stand and start walking towards me. He looked so good in his dark fitted t-shirt and jeans that I almost considered asking him to just skip our night out, but I resisted. Instead, I asked, "You ready to go?"

"Give me a minute." Cade's eyes roamed slowly over me, and a sexy smirk crossed his face. "I'm trying to decide if I can make it through dinner before I take that dress off of you."

"I'm sure you can manage," I teased.

"Maybe, but it won't be easy."

After a brief, but heated kiss, he reached for my hand and led me out to his SUV. He drove us to the east side of town, and we ate outside at a little place where they had tiny white lights hanging in the trees above us. It couldn't have been more perfect. There weren't many people around, and we were actually able to talk. The waitress had just brought our drinks over when I asked, "I know we've talked about *us* and I'm pretty sure we both love what's happening between us, but how do you see things playing out?"

"Well, let me ask this first ... What do you think about moving to Memphis?"

It was something I'd already considered, so I answered, "I wouldn't have a problem with it. I can find a job there or whatever, but I would need time to get things sorted. And we're still getting to know each other."

"I'm in no rush. I can wait until you're ready," he said then reached for my hand. "Until then, I want to see you as often as I can."

"So, weekend visits and phone calls."

"I know it doesn't sound all that great now, but we'll make it work," he tried to assure me.

"You know, I'm gonna hold you to that," I teased.

"I sure as hell hope so."

Once we were done with dinner, we talked about going downtown to walk the strip but decided we didn't want to waste our time together fighting the crowds. Instead, we went back to the house where it was quiet. As soon as we walked through the door, we both took off our shoes and headed into the living room. We were about to sit down on the sofa when I turned and just looked at him. My heart swelled as I studied his handsome face. *I loved him.* I knew that without a doubt, and I couldn't stand the thought of being away from him, even for a little while. At the same time, I was well aware of how much his club and brothers meant to him. Even though I wanted to, I couldn't ask him to walk away from them. My voice trembled as I told him, "I can't believe you're really leaving tomorrow."

He wrapped his arms around me and held me close to his chest as he whispered, "It's only for a little while, August."

"I know," I sniffled.

"I'll be back before you know it," he whispered as he wiped a tear from my cheek.

"I know," I nodded, fighting back tears. "I'm fine, really."

"Good, 'cause I have every intention of making the best of this time we have together."

He took a step towards me and lifted his hand to the nape of my neck, pulling my mouth to his. The touch of his lips set me on fire. In all my life, I'd never felt such a hunger for a man, and from the way he was kissing me, there was no doubt he felt the same. His rough palms slid effortlessly over my skin as he unzipped my dress and let it fall to the floor, leaving me in just my lace panties.

A rush of heat rolled against my skin as he stood there staring at me, appraising me. I'd never wanted anyone like I wanted Cade—I couldn't breathe, couldn't think. Reaching out, I grasped the hem of his t-shirt, and he bent forward so I could pull it over his head. Once I'd tossed it next to my dress, I laid my hand on his heart, relieved to feel that his beat was fast and hard like mine. "I want you to think about me when you're gone."

"You know I will."

His lips brushed against mine, but not gently like

before. Instead, it was hot, passionate, and demanding. I moaned into his mouth, stealing the last of his restraint. I gasped when Cade lifted me up and held me tightly, making me feel safe and secure in his strong arms as he carried me down the hall. Seconds later, I was on my bed with his body covering mine. His weight pressed against me as his hands, rough and impatient, roamed over my body. I felt utterly possessed by him as his mouth closed over my breast, scraping his teeth across my sensitive flesh. My fingers tangled in his hair as he flicked his tongue against my nipple, sending goosebumps prickling across my skin. My breath caught as his hand slid between my legs. He ran his fingers along my center while his other hand cupped my breast. Every nerve in my body tingled from his touch, making me impatient for more.

Unable to resist, I reached down, tugging at his jeans as I pleaded, "Now."

He lifted off of me and quickly removed them. Cade was beautiful. Standing there in all his naked glory with those perfectly defined abs and pronounced *V* had me writhing with anticipation. He was the ultimate seduction. When he caught me gazing at him, his eyes danced with mischief as he asked, "Like what you see, beautiful?"

"Mmm-hmm" and a brief nod was all I could muster.

He pulled out a condom from his jeans pocket, then slowly slipped it over his long, hard shaft. The smirk he was sporting quickly faded as he looked down at me sprawled out on the bed. His voice was low and raspy as he growled, "Mine. All mine."

Before I had time to respond, he was back on top of me, centering himself between my legs. He hovered over me, the heat of our breaths mingling between us until the anticipation became too much and his mouth crashed down on mine. His hand dove into my hair, grasping at the nape of my neck as he delved deeper into my mouth, our tongues twisting and tasting each other with all the passion and desire that had been building between us. He broke from our kiss just long enough to whisper, "You'll never know how much you get to me."

His hands drifted down my thighs as he lowered my panties. Once they were gone, without warning, he rolled to his back, carrying me with him so I was on top. After straddling my knees on either side, I reached for him, placing his cock at my center as I took him deep inside. After a brief moment of adjusting to him, I set my hands on his chest and slowly began to move as I rocked my hips against him.

I'd never felt anything so incredible. I wanted to savor the moment, let myself feel every sensation, but Cade had other plans. He placed his hands on my hips, guiding me to move faster. Taking his cue, I quickened my pace, becoming more fervent and intense with each shift of my hips. The muscles in my stomach began to tighten and I knew it was coming.

With one last swerve of my hips, heat surged through me, consuming me as my orgasm tore throughout my body. I was completely sated, but Cade wasn't done. Instead, he turned us over, positioning himself on top of me so he could take control. His body slammed into mine as I gripped his shoulders and met his thrusts with my own. Our panting and moans echoed through the room as our bodies moved together. Every drive of his hips, every swirl of mine, brought me closer and closer to a second orgasm that threatened to tear me apart. My head thrashed back as I gasped, "Yes!"

He was focused and unrelenting as he drove into me again and again. A low, deep growl echoed through the room as he found his own release. After several moments, he eased off of me and rolled over on his side, pulling me close to him. I could feel his heart hammering inside his chest. Cade looked over to me, and his eyes burned with an intensity I didn't understand until he said the words, "I love you, August."

"I love you too, Cade," I whispered then I pressed my lips to his. As I trailed my fingers across his chest, I thought about him going back to the clubhouse, and all the hang-arounds who would be there, trying to make their move on him. I looked up at him with a playful smile and said, "I'm thinking you need a new tattoo."

"Oh, really? What do you have in mind?"

I giggled as I said, "How about *'Property of the President's Daughter'*?"

"Whatever makes you happy, baby."

GUNNER

*L*eaving August was even harder than I expected. After we'd spent most of the night tangled in each other's arms, I forced myself out of the bed, gave her one last, long memorable kiss goodbye, and then headed out to my truck. I sat there in her driveway for several minutes questioning if I was doing the right thing by leaving. In the end, I succumbed to the fact that I had no choice. My family, my brothers, and the club were in Memphis, and my life was there with them. I hoped a time would come where August would come to love being in Memphis just as much. Until then, we'd just have to make this long-distance thing work. Like we'd talked about, we would call one another often, and whenever possible, I would go there to see her or she'd come to me in Memphis. At the time, it sounded like a good plan, but with each mile I drove towards home and away from August, I had my doubts. Hell, I'd only been gone a couple of hours, and I was already missing her. It didn't help matters that I could still smell her scent on my skin. I had to pull myself together or my brothers would never let me live it down.

After I made it back to the clubhouse, I finally got the distraction I needed to help get August off my mind. Blaze needed some help in the garage, and we had a shit-ton of work that had to be done to prepare for our next run. All of it kept me pretty occupied, and before I knew it, the weekend was quickly approaching. Relieved that it wouldn't be long before I got to spend some time with August, I got busy trying to finish up an engine I'd been working on. I'd just finished adjusting the timing chain, when Murphy walked up and asked, "Hey, brother. What you got going on Friday night?"

"I was thinking about heading to Nashville. Why?"

"It's Riley's birthday. Grady wanted us to head over to the Smoking Gun to celebrate." Riley was his old lady, and Murphy was head over heels for her. After all these years, it was good to see him settled down. "I know she'd want you to be there."

"Of course, she would. It wouldn't be a party without me," I poked.

"Does that mean you're coming?"

As much as I hated that I'd lose a day with August, I couldn't miss Riley's birthday, so I answered, "Yeah, I wouldn't miss it."

"Good. While I'm thinking about it, I talked to Grady about Gabriella."

"Oh, yeah? What did he have to say?"

"He's going to let her waitress for a while and see if she's got what it takes to bartend later for more money. He's also got a place above the bar she can rent if she wants."

"That would be great." Gabriella had been at the club with us for several days, and as far as I knew, she hadn't told us much about herself and the full reason behind Polito kidnapping her. Curious if anything had changed, I asked, "We know any more about who she really is?"

He shook his head. "No. She's definitely being vague about her true identity, so Riggs hasn't been able to find anything on her." His eyes narrowed as he added, "If she hadn't been there for Harper like she had, Gus would've already sent her walking, but I think he feels indebted to her."

"Maybe, but he won't let that go forever."

"No, but now she'll be Grady's problem."

"That she will."

He chuckled as he turned and started back over to the truck he'd been working on. "Plan to be at the bar at eight."

"Will do."

I spent the next few hours in the garage, then headed back to my place. While I enjoyed hanging out at the clubhouse, it could be noisy, and I was exhausted. I needed some fucking sleep. I walked out into the parking lot and hopped on my bike. I'd always believed that there was no better therapy on the planet than riding a motor-cycle. It wasn't a long drive to the house, but it was enough to clear my head. When I pulled up in the drive-way, I groaned as soon as I was greeted by my overgrown, knee-high grass. My home wasn't much, just a three-bedroom craftsman that was painted dark gray with white trim. It had a small front porch with a couple of rockers and, well now, several dead pots of flowers. I went inside and cursed under my breath when I noticed all the dirty laundry and dishes in the sink. It was only a matter of time before August would come down for a visit, so I knew I needed to get the place cleaned up. But it would have to wait. After a long day, I was too tired to fool with it, so I took a hot shower and went to bed. I was just about to doze off when my phone chimed with a message.

I picked it up and smiled when I saw that it was from August.

AUGUST:

Hey, handsome.

ME:

Hey there, beautiful. Everything okay?

AUGUST:

Yes. Everything's fine. I was just thinking about you.

ME:

Oh, yeah?

AUGUST:

Yep. Seems I've been doing a lot of that lately.

ME:

Well, you're not the only one. I haven't been able to stop thinking of you in that little black dress.

AUGUST:

So, you liked seeing me in that, huh?

ME:

Almost as much as I liked seeing you out of it.

AUGUST:

Well, I'll have to remember that.

ME:

You still okay with me coming up on Saturday?

AUGUST:

Of course. I wish you were coming sooner and staying longer.

ME:

Me too.

AUGUST:

I guess I better get some sleep.

ME:

Yeah. Me too.

AUGUST:

Remember, I have to go in to see my boss in the morning.

ME:

Okay. Good luck with that.

AUGUST:

I might need it. LOL. I hope you sleep well.

ME:

You, too. Goodnight, beautiful.

AUGUST:

Nite! xoxo

I TOSSED my phone back on the nightstand and it wasn't long until my exhaustion took over and I fell asleep. The next morning, I called August to wish her good luck with her meeting, then spent some time around the house, cleaning and mowing the yard. Once I was done, I went over to the garage to finish up the engine I'd been working on. It was after six before I finished everything I needed to do, so I didn't have long to get ready to meet up with everyone at the bar. I rushed home for a quick shower, then threw on a pair of jeans, a t-shirt, and my cut, and once the boots were on, I was out the door. It was just after seven when I pulled into the Smoking Gun's parking lot. I parked next to my brothers' bikes, then headed inside. As soon as I stepped through the door, one of the waitresses came over to me and asked, "Are you here for the birthday party?"

"Yeah, I guess."

"Okay, follow me."

She led me through the crowd and up a short flight of stairs to a private seating area that Grady had arranged for us. He was Riley's cousin and best friend as well as the owner of the Smoking Gun, and he'd reserved the VIP room for all of us. When I walked up to everyone, they were sitting around talking and drinking. As expected, Blaze was with his old lady, Kenadee, and Shadow was with Alex, his old lady. I hated that August couldn't be there with me, but I decided to make the best of it. I sat down next to Riggs and asked, "Where's Reece?"

"She had some work to finish up, but she's heading over later."

"Hey, Gunner," Riley called out from the other table. "Glad you could make it."

"A team of wild horses couldn't have kept me away."

"Might've if you'd been trying to ride one of them," she said as a smirk crossed her face.

"You're not going to let me live that one down, are ya?"

"Well," she giggled, "I'm not the one who tried riding a horse to impress a girl when I didn't have a clue what I was doing."

Riggs leaned over to me as he snickered. "She's got a point, brother."

"It was that fucking horse. I would've been fine if I was riding one that wasn't crazy."

"Karma, brother," Blaze poked. "That's what you get for trying to make a move on Gigi when you knew she was Hunter's girl."

"Gigi wasn't his girl … Well, at least not yet," I replied, trying to justify my actions. "And besides, me trying to ride that horse had nothing to do with her."

"Mm-hmm. Keep telling yourself that. We all know what's what," Murphy teased.

I was about to attempt to defend myself when Grady walked up with some guy I'd never seen before. He was a big dude with a black leather jacket and a menacing stare. Just by looking at him you could tell he wasn't someone you'd fuck with, making me wonder what he was doing with a guy as easygoing as Grady. But then it all made sense. As they headed over to the table where Murphy and Riley were sitting, he said, "Hey, guys. For any of you who don't know, this is my brother, Jasper."

As soon as I heard his name, I remembered the stories about him. He wasn't a biker, but he was a badass motherfucker just the same. When Riley's father ran into some financial problems, he turned to Jasper for help. Her dad was desperate to save his farm, so he decided to try his hand at running guns. Jasper apparently had the contact her father needed to get his foot through the door, enabling him to delve into a new, substantially more dangerous line of work. When the money started rolling in, her father thought he had things under control, but he was wrong—very wrong.

A deal gone bad almost cost him Riley's life, but by then, Murphy had fallen for her and there was no way in hell he was going to let any harm come to her. The club did what we could to help, and in the end, things played out in our favor. After we all greeted him, he and Grady sat down next to Riley.

"Hey, Jasper." Riley smiled as she said, "It's been a while."

"Yes, it has."

"Are you in town for long?" she asked.

"Yeah ... Madison and I are actually in the process of moving back, but it's going to take some time," he replied.

"Madison?"

"It's a long story," Grady interjected, cutting Jasper off. "I'll tell ya all about it later."

"Okay."

Murphy looked over to Grady as he said, "Wanted to thank you again for taking on Gabriella. I owe you one."

"Not a problem." He glanced over his shoulder and watched as Gabriella took an order from the table across the room. Something about the way he was looking at her made me think that he might be interested in her. I couldn't blame him. She was a pretty girl, and from what little I'd talked to her, she seemed to have a good head on her shoulders. But she had secrets, big ones, and if Grady wasn't careful, they might bite him in the ass. Grady pointed in her direction as he said, "She seems to be fitting in just fine."

"Glad to hear it."

Grady lifted his empty beer, then announced to all of us, "I think it's time for another round."

"Hell, yeah," T-Bone cheered. "Make it two!"

"You got it."

He motioned to one of the waitresses, signaling her to bring us more drinks. We spent the next hour or so drinking and talking amongst ourselves. I loved having the time to just cut loose and enjoy the company of my brothers, but I couldn't stop wishing that August was there with me. When I glanced over at Gus, he wasn't saying much. It was pretty clear he had something on his mind. I wondered if it had anything to do with Samantha, but knowing Gus was a man who shared only what he wanted, I knew better than to ask. I finished off my beer then turned to Riggs and Blaze. "I'm heading out."

"It's barely after ten, brother."

"I know, but I'm leaving early in the morning to go see August and Harper."

Blaze's expression grew serious as he asked, "Is she the one?"

"Yeah. Without a doubt."

"Then, what the hell are you doing?" Riggs grumbled. "You finally found her, and you just leave her? What the fuck is that?"

"I didn't have a choice. She's got a life there."

"Of course, you had a choice. There's always a choice," Riggs argued. "You could've stayed there, helped her get things sorted, and bring her and the daughter back with you when she was ready."

"He's right. You don't leave a woman like August behind." Blaze shook his head. "She can have a life here, brother."

"So, you're saying I fucked up?"

"That's exactly what he's saying," Gus chimed in, then

turned and looked me in the eyes. "And I can't say that I disagree."

Well, damn. I knew in my gut they were right. I'd felt so torn, like I needed to be in two places at once, and I wasn't sure what to do. I thought I was doing the right thing by coming back, but after talking with them, I realized how wrong I'd been. I looked at Gus and asked, "You gonna be good with me staying up there for a while?"

"You gonna bring my girls with you when you come back?"

"That's the plan," I answered.

He nodded. "Then, you have my blessing."

"Thanks, Prez," I said, then stood up to leave. "I'll be back as soon as I can."

Determined like never before, I headed home, and after I packed a bag, I was on my way to Nashville. I was going to take my brothers' advice and go get my girls. With each mile I drove closer to her, I could feel all the tension I'd been carrying with me this past week start to fade. That's when I knew for sure that I was doing the right thing. I just prayed that August would feel the same way.

When I got to her house, it was just after four in the morning. I knew she'd be asleep, and I was worried that I might scare her if I just walked up and knocked on the door. I killed the engine and was trying to figure out what I should do when the carport light came on. I spotted a shadow in the window, so I decided to take a chance. I got out of the truck and headed towards the house. I'd just started up the steps when the front door flew open and revealed August standing there half-asleep in her nightgown. Damn, she looked absolutely stunning, making me wish I'd come even sooner.

"Cade!" She leapt forward and landed in my arms, hugging me as she asked, "What are you doing here?"

"Couldn't wait a minute longer to see my girl."

"God, it's so good to see you." She pressed her lips to mine, kissing me passionately. Like every time I was close to her, my hands got a mind of their own and started drifting over her body, and it wasn't long before I started to lose control. After several moments, she took a step back and released me from our embrace. "Come on in."

I followed her inside, and after she'd locked the door, she led me into the living room. When I saw that the TV was on, and her pillow and blanket were on the sofa, I asked, "Were you sleeping in here?"

"Yes and no." She looked down at her spot on the sofa and sighed. "I haven't been sleeping much lately."

"Why not?"

"It's kind of a mix of things. Mainly the fact that my boss wasn't pleased that it took me so long to come back after Harper's kidnapping, so he fired me. Now, I have no job, and I have no idea what I'm going to do about it. Things like that."

"You lost your job?" Knowing what her career meant to her, I asked, "Why didn't you tell me?"

"I'm telling you now." She gave me one of her looks and said, "Besides, that's only a small part of it. I've had all kinds of things on my mind."

"Me too."

"Really?" Her eyes narrowed as she asked, "What have you had on your mind?"

"You. Just you," I said as I stepped towards her. "I can't do this anymore, August."

"Can't do what?"

"Be away from you." I placed my hands on her hips and pulled her close. "The minute I walked out that door, I was too far away from you."

"Cade," she whispered.

"I mean it, August. I want you to keep getting to me until the day I take my last breath." Her eyes locked on mine. "I want to spend my life with you, marry you, and have a family with you, and I don't want to wait to make that happen. Call me crazy, but I want it now."

"I don't think you're crazy. In fact, I feel the same way." A smile crossed her face as she asked, "So, what do you suggest we do about it?"

"I say we do what feels right." I lowered my mouth to her neck and trailed kisses along the curve of her collarbone and whispered, "And the only thing that feels right is being together, so we find a way to do that."

"Then, we're doing this?"

"I know we have some things we've gotta work out, but yeah, baby, we're definitely doing this."

Her lips met mine, and what started off as a sweet, tender kiss, quickly became heated and full of need. Unable to wait another fucking second to have her, I lifted her into my arms and started down the hall. When we got to the bedroom, August looked up at me and smiled. "I really do love you, Cade."

"And I love you."

EPILOGUE

GUNNER

Three Years Later

I WAS STANDING in my kitchen, leaning against the door-frame as I watched the utter chaos unravel before me. I never knew a kid's birthday party could get so out of hand, but August wanted it to be perfect. After all, Tanner had just turned one and she wanted him to have the best birthday ever. From the looks of it, she'd pulled it off. Balloons and streamers were hanging from every corner, kids were laughing and screaming as they ran from room to room, and my brothers were hanging out in the living room. They were watching the football game on the big screen while their ol' ladies were in the kitchen helping August finish getting lunch ready. Everyone seemed to be having a great time, especially Tanner. He was in his high chair, shoveling Cheerios into his mouth as he watched the kids race around the room. I'd just given him a few more when Blaze came up behind me and said, "He's getting bigger by the minute."

"Yeah. Don't I know it." I glanced down at Tanner, and even though I could see so much of myself in him, I still couldn't believe he was mine. "In a blink of an eye, he'll be walking, and then there'll be no stopping him."

Just about that time, August zipped by us, looking beautiful as ever. She was just a couple months pregnant and barely showing, but she'd already started thinking that it was a girl, even trying to come up with names. Like her father, she'd always had a great gut instinct, so I just went along with it, knowing I'd be happy with whatever we had. After she placed one of the trays of food on the table, she came over to me and smiled one of those smiles —the kind that told me she was about to ask me to do something for her. So fucking adorable. "Would you mind grabbing the ice out of the freezer and putting it in the cooler with the drinks?"

"Sure. Anything else you need?"

"No. That should do it." She leaned up on her tiptoes and gave me a quick kiss. "Thanks, babe."

With that, she disappeared into the kitchen with the others. I looked over to Blaze as I asked, "You wanna give me a hand?"

"Sure." As we headed out to the garage, Blaze said, "You're gonna have your work cut out for you with having a third kid running around here."

"Yeah, but I can't wait." I thought back to the past couple of years I'd spent with Harper. From the start, she'd stolen my heart. With her father locked up, I'd done what I could to be the father she no longer had, and I was pleased that she'd let me do that. The kid was pretty damn special, and I was lucky to have her in my life. Thinking I'd learned a thing or two from helping to raise her, I said, "Maybe August is right, and we'll have ourselves a girl. Then, it'll be a little easier."

"Are you kidding me? Boys are much easier to contend with." He grunted. "Just think about when they start dating and show up with a guy like one of us. Hell, I wouldn't wish that on any father."

"Especially in your case. Damn, I can just imagine what Kenadee's father thought about you," I teased.

"At least he isn't the president of the club, and I'm not in constant worry of losing my balls," Blaze poked.

"Oh, I'm not worried about that." I pulled a couple of bags of ice out of the freezer and tossed them on the ground, breaking the chunks into smaller pieces. "I have every intention of making August happy for as long as possible and keeping my balls intact."

"I'd say you're doing a good job of that so far." As we tossed the ice on top of the drinks, he continued, "August seems pretty damn happy to me."

I was about to respond when Gus walked up behind us and said, "Yes, she does, and it's a damn good thing too."

"Hey, Prez." Blaze pretended to look down at his watch as he told him, "Running a little late, aren't ya?"

"Yeah, but for good reason." He lifted the enormous box he was carrying in his hands. "I had to run by and grab the cake for August."

"Great. You're just in time."

I opened the door for him and Blaze followed him inside. I was about to go in with them when I noticed Harper sitting on the front porch swing with my father. She was going on and on while my father hung on her every word. They were both clearly having a great time, neither of them caring that they were missing the party inside. It had been like that with them from the start. Harper had a way of talking to him, and he absolutely adored her. Knowing it wouldn't be long before we ate, I called out to them, "Hey, you two! It's time to come inside."

"Why?" Harper fussed.

"Cause we're about to eat."

I could tell by the look in her eyes that she was about to argue and was relieved when my dad took Harper's hand and led her inside. I followed behind them and was surprised to see that all the food was on the table, and the guys were already making their plates. After they got something to eat, Dad and Harper went over and sat down at the table next to my mother and Samantha. Most of the guys took their plates to the living room to finish watching the game, but Gus and I hung back, watching Tanner as he dove into his apple sauce. Gus smiled as he said, "Hard to believe it's already been a year."

"I know. It seems like only yesterday when August was telling me that she was pregnant."

"I'm glad she decided to stay home with the kids."

"Me too."

As much as August loved her new job, training to be a pharmaceutical assistant was tough, especially when you have a newborn at home. It took a little pushing from Gus and me, but she finally agreed to put work on hold and just enjoy being a mother—at least for a little while. When the line started to die down, Gus made himself a plate, then went over and sat down next to Samantha. I watched as he leaned over to her and whispered something in her ear, making her smile. It felt good to have them there—not just for Tanner, but August, too.

Once we finished eating, August brought out an enormous birthday cake with Mickey Mouse's face painted in the center. When everyone had gotten a piece, she took a smaller version of the same cake over to Tanner and placed it on his tray. Mickey Mouse was his favorite character on TV, and his face lit up when he saw him plastered on the top. Unable to resist, he reached down and grabbed a handful before smashing into his face. In a matter of seconds, he was covered head to toe in icing. I took my eyes off of him just long enough to look over to August, and the expression on her face was priceless. With complete and utter adoration in her eyes, she watched as our son made a hell of a mess, and neither of us would've had it any other way. Laughing, I told everyone, "That's my boy!"

"He sure is!" my mother teased as she picked up chunks of cake off the floor.

"Cade, take a picture for me," Samantha asked as she handed me her phone. "Get one with August and Harper too."

"You got it."

After taking pictures, I helped August and the others get things cleaned up, and then she and I headed into the living room with my brothers and their ol' ladies. Each of them were all nestled up, talking amongst themselves. August and I sat down on the end of the sofa and watched as Tanner and Harper played on the floor with some of his new birthday toys. August looked over to the rest of his gifts that I'd stacked in the corner and asked, "What are we going to do with all this stuff?"

"I have no idea, but I'm sure we'll find a place for it."

"I hope so. I can't imagine what it's gonna look like in here when we've got three kids to tend to."

"We'll manage, and if it gets too crowded, we'll find a bigger place."

"Really?"

"Whatever makes you happy, baby."

A soft smile crossed her face as she said, "In case you didn't know, you make me happy, Cade. You're all I'll ever need."

"Well then, you're set, 'cause I'm sure as hell not going anywhere."

"Good to know."

Harper got tired of playing with Tanner and went to go play with the other kids. The second she left the room, he started to cry. I was about to go get him when I noticed Gus walking towards him. My heart swelled as I watched him lift my son into his arms. Using a low, soothing tone, he started talking to him as he walked him around the room, and in a matter of seconds, Tanner stopped crying. Gus had a way of doing that to people. Hell, I could still remember the day I first met him at Danvers Pub. I'd been feeling pretty down in the dumps when he came over and sat down next to me. After talking and having a few drinks, he had me feeling a little better about things. Gus had been on his way out the door when he invited me to take a bike ride with him. I'd told him I might, but he could tell I wasn't really considering it. That's when he'd said something to me that still stuck with me even after all these years— *"We only regret the chances we didn't take."* At the time, I didn't get it. I thought they were just words, but now, thinking back on that moment, I understood exactly what he meant. That one chance opened the door to so many more, and with each one I took, I created the life I have now—a life filled with so much good that I couldn't believe it was mine.

August leaned over and laid her head against my chest. Damn. There was no better feeling than having her close to me. I kissed her on the forehead as I whispered, "You know … you still get to me."

She glanced up at me with a soft smile. "I love you."

"There you go again." I leaned towards her and gave her a brief kiss. "Couldn't love you more if I tried."

The End

For more of Gus and Samantha's story, be sure to check out *Gus: Satan's Fury MC- Memphis* releasing in mid-September. This novella will include Part 1 of Gus's story that was included in the *Love, Loyalty, and Mayhem Anthology and a* Part 2 that will include what happened between them during and after Gunner.

***If you want to know more about Jasper, (Grady's brother) be sure to check out *Day Three: What Bad Boys Do* which is already live on Amazon.
Day Three Blurb:

There's nothing more dangerous than a man with nothing to lose.
The moment I saw Madison Brooks, I knew she was different from the others. She wasn't a hardened criminal

with blood on her hands. She was innocent, untouched by my world, and undeniably beautiful.

I couldn't get her out of my head. I kept imagining what it would be like to hold her, touch her, and claim her as mine.

On day three, I found myself questioning whether or not I could complete the assignment. In fact, I found myself questioning everything.

Also coming soon!

Grady's book will release later this fall and will include more about Gabriella! You won't want to miss it!

Thanks so much for reading!

If you haven't had a chance to check out Murphy: Satan's Fury MC- Memphis, there is a short excerpt after the acknowledgments.

Be sure to sign up for my newsletter for updates on releases and chances to win giveaways. Here's the link:
http://eepurl.com/dvSpW5
Also- please follow me on BookBub:
https://www.bookbub.com/authors/l-wilder

ACKNOWLEDGMENTS

I am blessed to have so many wonderful people who are willing to give their time and effort to making my books the best they can be. Without them, I wouldn't be able to breathe life into my characters and share their stories with you. To the people I've listed below and so many others, I want to say thank you for taking this journey with me. Your support means the world to me, and I truly mean it when I say appreciate everything you do. I love you all!

PA: Natalie Weston
Editing/Proofing: Lisa Cullinan- editor, Rose Holub- Proofer
Promoting: Amy Jones, Veronica Ines Garcia, Neringa Neringiukas, Whynter M. Raven
BETAS/Early Readers: Kaci Stewart, Tanya Skaggs, Jo Lynn, and Jessey Elliott

Street Team: All the wonderful members of Wilder's Women (You rock!)
Best Friend and biggest supporter: My mother (Love you to the moon and back.)

A short excerpt of Murphy: Satan's Fury MC-Memphis Book 4 is included in the following pages. Blaze, Shadow, and Riggs are also included in this Memphis series, and you can find all three on Amazon. They are all free with KU.

EXCERPT FROM MURPHY:
SATAN'S FURY- MEMPHIS

PROLOGUE

Murphy

WHETHER IT'S BEEN A MISHAP, a heartbreak, or an unexpected turn of events, we've all had at least one of those defining moments that marked us in one way or another, changing us forever. I'd like to say that I'd only had one of those moments in my life, but sadly, there'd been more than I could count. Each time it had taken a piece of me, scarring me right down to my soul—the first one was the day my old man packed up all his shit and walked out on my mom and me.

My father was a lowlife asshole who took advantage of my mother and anyone else who'd let him, so I figured we were better off without him. My mother didn't agree. His leaving had gotten to her in ways I'll never understand. She started going out at night, partying and sleeping around like a fucking teenager. By the time I was sixteen,

I'd stopped keeping track of the men who my mother moved in and out of our house—all of them had bolted as soon as she mentioned the word marriage. I figured she'd give up on men altogether, but she never stopped trying. She was continuously on the hunt for her Mr. Right, leaving me to my own vices—which suited me just fine. I'd have rather been with Amy, my best friend and future fiancé, than anyone else in the world anyway.

Amy lived next door, so she knew things at my place weren't exactly the greatest, but she understood, especially since her home life wasn't much better. There were times when things got pretty rough for both of us, but together we'd find a way to pick up the pieces. Thankfully, things weren't always bad. In fact, we had a lot of good times together, no matter what we were doing or where we were, so it was no surprise that as we grew older, our friendship turned into something more.

We were both seventeen, naive and full of hope, sitting on her window ledge with our feet dangling out onto the roof. After several minutes of comfortable silence, I glanced over at Amy. It was clear from her expression that she had something on her mind, so I asked, "You okay?"

"Do you think your mom is happy?"

"I don't know. I guess. Why?"

"I just think it's sad that she hasn't found someone who genuinely loves her. I would think that would really hurt."

"Maybe ... but she seems to think that Joe is 'the one.' He supposedly loves her," I scoffed.

"Yeah, well ... she said the same thing about Danny, Rick, and John, but all those jerks ended up breaking her heart."

"I suppose, but you have to give her credit. She hasn't stopped trying."

"Give her credit? Are you kidding me?" Her eyes skirted over to me. "She's all but forgotten that she has a son who she should be taking care of."

"I can take care of myself."

"That's not the point, Linc. You shouldn't have to take care of yourself. That's what moms are for," she argued.

"I guess both of our moms missed that whole *good-parenting* lesson."

"You can say that again."

She looked up at the stars above, and after several moments, she asked, "Do you ever think about the future?"

It wasn't a question I expected her to ask, and I certainly had no idea what kind of answer she was hoping for, so I hesitated with my response. "Um … *yeah.* Sometimes."

"When you think about it"—her blue eyes locked on mine—"what do you see?"

"I don't know. What do you see?"

"Oh, no you don't." She leaned towards me, nudging me with her shoulder. "You can't answer a question with a question, Lincoln."

"All right, then." I gave her a quick shrug as I answered, "When I think about the future, I see *you.*"

A soft smile crossed her face. "You do?"

"Well, yeah. It's always been you and me. I can't imagine my life without you in it." I inched my arm around her waist and asked, "What about you? What do you see when you think about the future?"

"I see us in a little white house with a front porch

swing and flowers along the walkway." Her voice was low, almost a whisper, as she continued, "It's a thousand miles from here, and our parents have no idea where we are. There's no yelling ... no fighting ... and there's food on the table every night. Things are good. Things are the way they're supposed to be."

"Sounds pretty damn good to me."

"Yeah, it sure does."

I pulled her close to me and said, "I'll do whatever it takes to give you all that and more, Amy. Just wait and see."

With no means to go to college, I decided to join the military. Amy wasn't exactly thrilled with the idea about me leaving, especially for such long increments of time, but I assured her that it was the quickest way for us to get that little white house with the front porch swing. Our time apart was hard on both of us, but with each day that passed, it got a little easier. I'd only been gone a few months when Amy started nursing school. Even though she was busy, she still found time to write me every day, and we talked on the phone as often as possible. Without even knowing it, Amy had gotten me through some pretty rough spots. I'd close my eyes, think about her crystal-blue eyes and adorable smile, and I would get a temporary reprieve from the death and destruction that surrounded me. She gave me something to live for, so when I returned from my second tour in Afghanistan, I asked her to marry me. By then, she'd gotten a taste of the military life. She knew what life as a soldier's wife would be like, but she still accepted my proposal, assuring me that she loved me enough to put our life together on hold for a little longer.

While there were many things that marked me during

my four years in the Army, it wasn't until the end of my tour that I encountered my second defining moment. After spending more than a year overseas, I was finally heading home. I'd never been gone that long before and was eager to get back to Amy. She had no idea I was coming, so it was going to be one hell of a surprise. I couldn't wait to see the look on her face when she opened the door and found me standing on the other side, so as soon as the plane landed in Memphis, I got my rental car and headed over to our place. As soon as I pulled up to the house, I grabbed my bag out of the car and rushed up the front porch steps. I knocked on the door, and my heart started racing when I heard rumbling inside the house. Moments later, the door flew open and Amy appeared with a startled look on her face.

Instead of jumping into my arms, she cinched her bathrobe tightly around her waist as she gasped. "Linc? What are you doing here?"

Paying no regard to her odd behavior, I stepped forward and wrapped my arms around her waist, lifting her in the air as I hugged her tightly. "I'm on leave for the next two weeks, baby."

With a half-hearted hug, she asked, "Why didn't you tell me?"

"I wanted to surprise you."

"Well, you definitely did that," she mumbled under her breath. "I wish you would've told me you were coming. I would've met you at the airport."

"I know, but like I said, I wanted to surprise you." I lowered my mouth to her neck, and as I started to trail kisses along the curve of her jaw, I whispered, "Damn, I've missed you. I can't tell you how good it is to see you."

"It's good to see you too."

When she started to pull away from me, I quickly lowered her feet to the ground and said, "I've got another surprise for you."

I reached into my back pocket and pulled out an envelope. As I handed it over to her, she said "I don't know if I can handle any more surprises right now, Linc."

"Well, this is one that can't wait." I watched her expression as she opened the envelope. "I've wanted to do this for a long time but just didn't have the means to make it happen. That all changed this summer when I was promoted to corporal."

A look of confusion crossed her face as she stared at the two tickets to Cancun. "What is this?"

"We're eloping, baby. It's time for us to make things official."

I'd barely gotten the words out of my mouth when a man came walking down the hall. He was a tall guy with dark hair. I don't remember much more than that, other than the fact that he was only wearing a pair of boxers as he asked, "Amy ... is everything okay?"

"Who the fuck are you?" I roared.

"I'm, uh ... umm," he stammered.

He was too freaked out to answer, but it didn't matter. I knew by the look on his face that he'd been screwing around with Amy, and that's all I needed to know. Rage washed over me as I lunged towards him and growled, "You motherfucker!"

"Wait." Amy reached for me as she shrieked, "Linc ... Don't."

As soon as the asshole realized I was about to beat the

hell out of him, he held up his hands at his sides and pleaded, "Look, man. I don't want any trouble."

"You should've thought about that before you started fucking my girl!"

I reared my fist back and then punched him in the face, nearly knocking him out. His head flew back as blood spewed from his mouth. Before he had a chance to recover, I slammed my fist into his gut. He toppled forward as he wrapped his arms around his stomach, but it did little to protect him from my continuous blows to his abdomen and face. I hit him again and again, and in a matter of seconds, he was a puddled mess on the floor. Worried that I might actually kill him, Amy scurried in front of me and pushed me back as she shouted, "Stop, Linc!"

When I saw the panicked look on her face, I froze. With my heart pounding rapidly in my chest, I inhaled a deep breath and tried to rein in my anger. I grit my teeth as I snarled, "What the fuck is this guy doing in my house, Amy?"

"I'll explain everything, but you're gonna have to stop and listen to me."

"Just tell me!"

She cradled his face in her hands, and with complete adoration in her voice, she said, "This is Kevin. He's one of the doctors from the hospital. We've been seeing each other for the past few months, and—"

"What?" I motioned my hand towards the douchebag on the floor. "You've been seeing him for months, and you didn't fucking tell me!"

"I wanted to, but I just didn't know how." She looked up at me with sad eyes and said, "You have to know that I loved you, Lincoln. I wanted a life with you … the life we dreamed about, but you just kept putting me off. Just one more tour … just a few more months. I couldn't take it anymore."

"So, you go and spread your legs for some asshole doctor you've been working with?"

"It's not like that, Linc." She stood up and looked me right in the eye. "We started out as friends … He listened to me. He was there for me, and—"

"He listened to you? Are you fucking kidding me?"

"He's a good man, Lincoln."

"I'm sure he's a goddamn prince!"

"You're not being fair!" She reached for my arm, clinging to me as she said, "You knew how I felt about you leaving. I tried to get you to stay. I begged you, but you just wouldn't listen."

"So, you decided to act like a fucking whore and shack up with someone else?"

"Look, you can put all of this on me if that makes you feel better, but we both know that's not true!"

"I'm done listening to this bullshit, Amy." As I started for the door, I noticed several boxes and bags of luggage stacked in the doorway. I'd busted my ass to get her that house with the fucking swing on the front porch, but it was all for nothing. I turned and glared at her with disgust. "I want you out by morning. Leave the key in the mailbox."

With that, I grabbed my bag and stormed out of the house, slamming the door behind me. From there, I don't even know how I made it back to my rental car. I was totally consumed with emotion—rage, heartbreak, and absolute disbelief. I looked back at the house, and a feeling of anguish washed over me when I saw Amy standing there with tears in her eyes. I could've gone back and tried to talk it out with her, but I knew that wasn't gonna change a damn thing. We could never go back to the way things were. My heart would still be broken. *I would still be broken.* I glanced down at the plane tickets to Cancun and ripped them to shreds before tossing them out the window. I was done. Love was just some fucked up illusion. Unlike my mother, I wouldn't spend my life looking for something that simply didn't exist.

MURPHY

TEN YEARS LATER

*W*hile we'd won battle after battle, Satan's Fury was always at war. It was the price we paid for reigning supreme over the Memphis territory. With the Mississippi River at our fingertips, everyone knew it was a sweet spot and wanted to claim it as their own. Unfortunately for them, that meant going head-to-head with the most notorious MC in the south. While we always managed to come out on top, we'd never faced an enemy like Josue Navarro—a Mexican cartel boss with an unrelenting thirst for revenge. His brother, Rodrigo, had come to Memphis looking to score big, but he'd gotten himself killed in the process, leaving his brother clueless as to who was to blame. Even though we weren't the ones who actually pulled the trigger, the blame still fell on our shoulders, and Navarro set his sights on ending us all. We knew he had the means to destroy everything we'd worked for, but we'd never cowered down from a fight. We'd been preparing to take him head on when he was arrested for killing Jason Brazzle, his niece's best friend. We all knew he'd try to get the charges dropped, but there was no way that was gonna happen with an eyewitness and photographic evidence. Our problem was solved, but there was a catch.

The eyewitness—the person who was willing to put her life on the line to put him behind bars—was Reece Winters, my brother Riggs's old lady. She was a reporter for the *Memphis Metro* and had been working on a piece about the cartel. Hoping to get information on Navarro's brother, Reece had gone to question Jason. When she arrived at his apartment that day, she was surprised to find Navarro and his men were there. From the fire escape window, Reece had watched Navarro kill Jason and reported it to the police. Shortly after, she became their prime witness, and they asked her to testify at his trial. Knowing that she and her son were in serious danger, Gus, Fury's president, had arranged for us to get her to safety. T-Bone, Gunner, and I, along with Riggs and two of our prospects, Crow and Rider, packed up Reece and her son and headed up to Jed's cabin in the Appalachian Mountains—a place where we could protect her from Navarro's watchful eye. While we'd felt certain that Reece and her son would be safe there, I wasn't taking any chances. As the club's sergeant-at-arms, it was my responsibility to ensure everyone's safety. It was a job that I took very seriously, so I'd left no stone unturned as I set up a list of strict surveillance procedures for each of us to follow. The brothers and I would take shifts monitoring the grounds with every precaution to make sure that no one came snooping around.

After living there for over a month, we'd all settled

into our routines, and while everything seemed to be going as planned, I wasn't about to let my guard down. The trial was quickly approaching, which meant Navarro would be even more desperate to track down Reece and end her before she had a chance to testify. There was no way in hell we were going to let that happen. Not on my watch. I was on my way out to relieve Riggs from his post when Gunner came barreling in from outside. As he started taking off his hat and gloves, I asked, "Did you complete the perimeter check?"

"I did." He removed his thick winter coat and tossed it onto the back of one of the kitchen chairs. "All clear."

"And what about Crow? You check in with him?"

"Yep. He's good, as always." Gunner reached for the coffee pot, then added, "The kid has a knack for this shit. Might be time for us to consider patching him in."

"Yeah. He's a good kid. I'll be sure to mention it to Gus."

As Gunner headed straight towards the fridge, he asked, "Is there any more of that lasagna left from last night?"

"I don't think so. I'm pretty sure T-Bone finished it off for breakfast."

"Damn. We're gonna have to put a muzzle on that man before he eats us out of house and home."

"At least we don't have to worry about having a garbage disposal."

"You ain't lying there, brother." He chuckled. "There's nothing that man won't eat."

"Maybe we should get Reece to cook him up a mess of brussels sprouts and see what he does with those."

"Hell, yes. And maybe some beets and liverwurst. I'd pay money to see that."

"Knowing him, he'd scarf them down like there's no tomorrow." I pulled on my hat, grabbed my thermos filled with hot coffee, and started towards the door. "I'm gonna go relieve Riggs. Let me know if anything comes up."

"You know I will."

Just as I was about to walk out of the kitchen, he tossed his scarf over to me. "You're gonna need that. The wind is blowing out of the east, and it'll chill ya down to the bone."

"Thanks, man."

I wrapped it around my neck, but it did little to protect me from the arctic wind as I stepped out onto the porch. The fresh fallen snow glittered and shined like diamonds under the light of the full moon, which made the forest look like a winter wonderland. The only sound I could hear was the icy layer crushing beneath my feet as I trampled through the knee-deep white stuff and made my way over to Riggs. When I walked up to him, he looked up at me and smiled. "Before you ask ... Yes, I did the perimeter check, and everything's clear."

I shrugged. "Wasn't even gonna ask."

"Yeah, right. We both know you can't help yourself," he teased.

"What can I say?" I glanced back over at the house as I said, "Gotta keep Reece and that boy of yours safe."

"You got that right."

Riggs was the club hacker, and with his particular skillset, he was able to get the most updated information on just about anything. Knowing the trial was just two weeks away, I asked, "Any news about Navarro?"

"Not a damn thing." Concern crossed his face as he continued, "I gotta tell ya, brother … the closer this trial gets, the more nervous I get. Navarro knows that with Reece's testimony he's toast. He has to be feeling pretty fucking desperate right about now, and desperate people do some fucked-up shit."

"I'm sure Reece feels the same way." I shook my head and added, "She has to be nervous about testifying."

"Yeah. She's been trying to put on a brave front, but I know it's worrying her. I don't think she's been sleeping all that well. That's one of the reasons why I have something special planned for her tonight."

"Something special, huh? Well, don't keep her waiting. Get your ass inside."

"You don't have to tell me twice." As he started towards the house, he handed me the two-way radio. He hadn't gotten very far when he shouted, "It's gonna be a cold one tonight."

"No different than last night. At least the snow has finally stopped falling."

"You're right about that. I'll check in with you in a bit. Try to stay warm!"

The bitter wind howled through the trees, biting at my flesh as I headed towards the back gate. I wanted nothing more than to go back to the cabin and sit by the fire, but it would be hours before that happened. As I tromped through the heavy snow with my teeth chattering and my bones aching, I found it hard to believe that I ever enjoyed a single moment of winter, but when I was a kid, I loved the snow. Hell, I couldn't get enough of it. There was nothing better than putting on a pair of my old man's coveralls and heading out into the blistering cold with the kids from my neighborhood. We'd spend the entire day building forts and having snowball fights with our buddies. We wouldn't head home until our clothes were soaked through and our fingers and toes were completely numb. But now, I was over it, and I was thankful that I'd finally made it to my post. We'd made two enclosures on either end of the property that were similar to deer stands. Each of them gave us a clear view of the grounds while protecting us from the elements. As soon as I'd climbed inside, I reached for the binoculars and started searching the woods for any sign of intruders. I'd been sitting there for over an hour with not so much as a critter climbing a tree when I heard Crow's voice on the radio saying, "Guys ... I think we've got company."

My stomach twisted into an anxious knot as I responded, "What the fuck are you talking about?"

"I'm out here on the west bank of the creek, and there's a UTV parked back here in the woods." Everything came to a screeching halt as I listened to the sounds of his feet crunching through the snow. Seconds later, he told us, "And the engine's still warm. Whoever is out here ..."

His voice had suddenly trailed off, and my blood ran cold when I heard a faint gurgling sound in the background. I had been coming down from my post when I heard Riggs shout, "Crow ... Crow! You there, brother?"

I already knew the answer. Whoever was out there had already ended him, and if I didn't move fast, there would be more death to follow. I was racing towards the house when I heard T-Bone's voice on the radio. "Murphy's Law."

Since there was a chance that Crow's radio had been

compromised, we all changed our frequencies, which made it more difficult for the invaders to monitor our conversations. It was a plan I'd implemented for this very reason. Once we were all on the same channel, Riggs ordered, "Everyone to your posts!"

My adrenaline was pumping at max speed as I rushed towards the house. Once I'd gotten inside, I met Gunner at the living room closet, and we started collecting the M249s and the extra ammo. We were both busy pulling everything out when Riggs had come up behind us. "Do you think it's them?"

"Got no idea," I answered.

His voice was filled with panic as he asked, "How in the hell did they find us?"

"No way of knowing." I tried to remain calm as I continued, "You gotta remember who we're dealing with here, brother. If Navarro hired someone to take us out, he'd hire the best. Someone who knows how to watch for our mistakes. One fuck up is all it would take."

"We were careful! We played everything by the book!"

Knowing we were wasting time, I ordered, "Keep one of these for yourself and give the other to T-bone. He may need something with a little more punch. He's out on the front porch."

Before he walked out, Riggs asked, "Where's Rider?"

"Out back."

"Reece and Tate are upstairs in the closet."

"Good." With a stern voice I told him, "I know you're worried and I get that, but brother, we've prepared for this. We've got to stick to the plan. It's the only way we're going to get out of this alive."

He nodded and headed out the front door. From there, things had gotten interesting. Riggs had only been gone for several seconds when there was a commotion outside and shots were fired. It was clear to see that whoever was out there was getting closer. I didn't realize *how close* until Riggs came busting through the front door and announced that T-Bone had been shot. As things started to escalate, we all knew time wasn't on our side, which made each of us a little rattled. Once we'd tended to T-Bone's wounds, I sent Riggs upstairs to guard Reece and Tate. After he was gone and in position, I grabbed two rifles and headed for the roof. One way or another, I was going to find the asshole who'd just put a bullet in my brother. He had to be dealt with before another one of us was taken out.

I crawled out of one of the upstairs' windows and carefully stepped out onto the snow- and ice-covered roof. After taking several treacherous steps, I spotted Crow's body sprawled out in the snow. He was planted face down with blood pooling around his neck and chest, leaving no doubt that he was dead. Anger surged through me as I scanned the woods, searching for the man who'd killed one of our most promising prospects, but my view was obstructed by the low-lying branches that were weighted down with snow. I eased forward and adjusted my footing in the snow and then lifted my rifle. As soon as I looked through the scope, I saw a slight movement coming from the west side of the creek. I zoned in on the area, and just as I noticed a branch start to quiver, the gunman stepped out into the open and started shooting several rounds towards the rear of the house. He was aiming for Gunner and hadn't noticed that I was on the roof. Taking the opportunity, I aimed for his head and quickly took the shot.

FOR MORE, be sure to check out Murphy: Satan's Fury MC- Memphis on Amazon.

Made in the USA
Monee, IL
19 February 2020